ONE BULLET
AT A TIME

ЛЮБОВ И ОМРАЗА

Assassin Publishing

ONE BULLET
AT A TIME

MICHAEL JOHN BARNES

Michael John Barnes

www.michaeljohnbarnes.com.au

This edition published 2017
by Assassin Publishing

First published in Australia 2015
by Assassin Publishing

ISBN 9 780994 323804

Dedicated to Blue and those who believed in me

CONTENTS

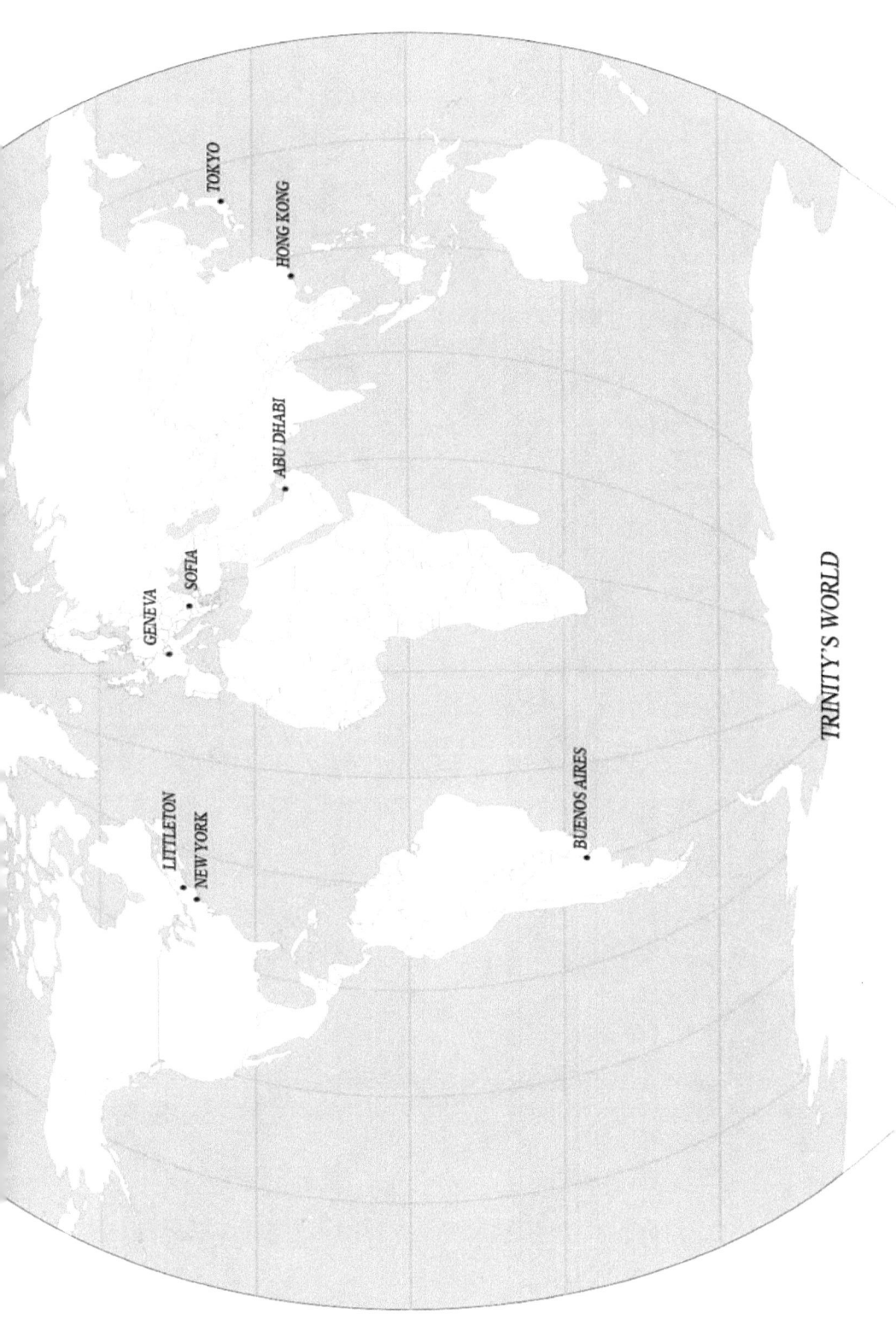

TRINITY'S WORLD

FOREWORD

I feel honoured to have been asked to write the foreword to *One Bullet at a Time*. The author and I have known each other, professionally and socially, for more than twenty years, mostly through our love of combat/ballistic sports and work.

You may be wondering who I am and what qualifications I have to write a foreword. Well, I am not a writer that's for sure, although I know a good book when I read one. So that just leaves me with experience. Having served with the Australian Special Air Services Regiment (SASR) for more than twenty-three years, I am currently the senior instructor for all combat training within the unit. For a two-year period I was seconded to Britain's Special Boat Service (SBS) and participated in numerous training and operational tours alongside other international black Special Operations Forces (SOF) units. I have had fourteen operational tours of duty, from Timor to Iraq and Afghanistan as well as many smaller but no less important tasks across the world. Even with this vast experience, I have learnt a lot from Mick and hopefully will continue to do so for a long time.

I saw Mick's professional, dedicated yet relaxed approach in action during national shooting matches and invited him to conduct his exceptional brand of weapons training for members of the SASR. Word spread quickly through the secretive and close-knit Australian military special forces community and Mick was soon invited to conduct his weapons-based training for 2 Commando (2CDO).

Mick's shooting techniques and training methodologies were the start of a paradigm shift in the way we (SASR) conducted combat shooting training for the next decade, both physically and cognitively, and a major factor in shaping the way we continue to develop and conduct our training to this day.

It's his brand of enthusiasm, dedication and professionalism, and an eye for all things different, that Mick brings to this sequel to his exciting, racy and action-packed debut *Shot through the Heart*. As with many good authors, his books get better with experience and age.

In *One Bullet at a Time*, he takes us on a wild, breathtaking and erotic ride with the protagonist Trinity, a gorgeous assassin, trained from a young age in all the required arts that make her the best. After many years of killing without retribution, she has finally ticked-off the wrong man. The Russian has her in his sights for elimination and the only way she can prevail is with the aid of some of her closest friends – an explosive collection of individuals, each with their own extraordinary skills. Trinity's adventures take her to some of the world's most exotic, exciting and dangerous places.

Mick has travelled the globe more than once over the past ten years and has gained marvellous perspectives on the locations used in this book. He has captured the atmospheres of the cities and the vibes of their people, rewarding readers with involvement and emotional attachment. His ability to highlight settings gives the book a sense of poignancy and reality all too often lost in action stories.

For those of us who crave action and adventure, this sequel is a delight. Mick has enviable access to professionals in the firearms fraternity, high-end security, special forces military and tactical police. His narratives testify to his wealth of knowledge across varied fields and in-depth experience of conducting high-level protection details – not to mention a keen eye for minutiae on the complexities of planning and conducting dangerous missions. This is evident in his authentic, fast-paced and action-packed storyline. Mick's attention to detail and realistic urban battlefields seamlessly meld into an underworld seldom seen. The combat scenes guarantee enjoyment for even the most pedantic aficionado as fight sequences are well thought out, credible and tactically sound.

Once again, Mick has produced a gripping story by applying the professional and dedicated mindset with which he trains elite soldiers, and with the commitment and passion that has made him successful in life.

I found it difficult to put the book down, even when the demands of my own work were calling. If you have a penchant for action, guns and excitement, and appreciate the unexpected, I recommend *One Bullet at a Time*.

Regimental Sergeant Major
Warrant Officer First Class – *WW*
SASR

ABOUT THE AUTHOR

Born and currently residing in Perth, Western Australia, Mick is happily married to his beautiful wife Blue. They have two children – son Jesse and daughter Brittany, now both in their mid-twenties.

A highly acclaimed and sought-after weapons specialist, Mick has provided training for Australia's elite military special forces and law enforcement tactical units.

For many years, Mick and his good friend, former SAS Trooper Tex, provided personal security in some of the world's most glamorous and exciting cities – Hong Kong, Tokyo, New York, Dubai, London and Geneva.

AUTHOR'S NOTE

Writing my first novel, *Shot through the Heart,* gave me much-needed solace during dark times. It was therapeutic and allowed me to release dangerous emotions that smouldered deep within.

With a heavy weight cast from my shoulders, the comfort and joy I had discovered whilst writing thankfully remained.

I continue to draw on my own experiences and overseas adventures, and the urge to express myself through writing is stronger than ever. Long days at work are now all too often followed by even longer nights at home, basking in the glow of a computer screen, quality sleep all but a dwindling memory.

ACKNOWLEDGEMENTS

I am blessed to have good friends who, in busy times, were prepared to suspend their lives to read and critique my work.

Holding their breath, they willingly immersed themselves into a dark world, treading carefully, ever-mindful of losing their own sanity while traversing the myriad pathways of Trinity's tragic mind.

My deepest, warmest gratitude goes to fearless travellers Mickey G, Amie, Wayne, Nicky D, Buzz and Estelle, and of course, my muse Anita.

Thanks go to my Bulgarian friends on the other side of the world: the beautiful Stella, with her mesmerizing smile and infectious spirit, for providing me with inspiration and direction, Mitko and Georgi for sharing with me the wounded, yet captivating city of Sofia, and Buba, a real-life Bulgarian gun-wielding beauty, whose patient translation of my words during many late-night online conversations is something I sorely miss.

Once again Gavin and Dusty provided important snippets of information and technical data.

To my editor Jo, you will never truly know how happy you made me when you came to my rescue, agreeing to work on my manuscript. Your professionalism and ability to look deep inside my words—without turning around and running for the hills—all the validation I needed, that you were the right person to help lift my story from the constraints of a 6x9 inch piece of paper and into the reader's mindscape.

BUENOS AIRES

The Obelisk

Trinity occupies the cramped, rear passenger seat of the speeding yellow and black taxi, taking care to steady her outstretched hand as she points the barrel of a Glock 17 beyond the driver's head. She does however fail to notice a black cat dash through the white light of the taxi's luminous headlamps.

The driver slams on the brakes.

The wheels lock and the tyres screech.

Trinity instinctively pushes her boot into the floor; her fingers grip the armrest tight. The other fingers follow suit and reflexively snatch at the gun's trigger, the snappy recoil weakening her grip, the spent case deflecting off the windshield.

The muzzle flash causes her pupils to contract.

The unintended gunshot creates minimal mess inside the cab's interior, yet maximum damage throughout the driver's head, the bullet having entered his ear and exited his eye socket.

Without warning, Trinity lurches to one side and then the other. Momentarily steadying herself with the arm rest, she leans across the driver and reaches for the out-of-control steering wheel.

Relieved to be outside of the airport and breathing in fresh air, Trinity throws her sheathed sword onto the taxi's back seat and squeezes in through the rear passenger door.

'The Obelisk,' she mutters, her voice sounding raspy, dry from the long-haul flight's air-conditioning.

'El Obelisco?'

She draws on her limited Spanish.

'Si señor. Gracias.'

The driver's eyes flash in the rear view mirror.

'Perfecto!'

He switches off the 'Libre' sign, and without first bothering to check, pulls out and away from Ezeiza International Airport, luckily not another car in sight.

The top of Trinity's head brushes the cab's caved-in roof, her bent knees uncomfortably pressing against the front seat's ripped cloth.

Looks like a body fell on the cab from a great height.

Not that unusual in Buenos Aires.

Her eyes struggle to keep up with a dozen dangling toys spread across the top of the windshield, bobbing, spinning and smiling. And with good vision of the driver from the backseat, she allows herself two points of exit should the need arise.

Her eyes seesaw between his face and the photo ID on the dash, alongside an old digital clock: 02:00 a.m.

Alberto Vázquez.

Bald … late fifties … fat … yep that's him.

Watching him sing to himself, reclined in his seat — the chair pushed as far back as it will allow — Trinity enjoys not having to make small talk. Not being hit on is a bonus.

The drive from the airport is uneventful. About thirty-minutes in, Trinity angles her head to stare at the Buenos Aires skyline as the taxi skirts the western side of the autonomous city, heading north before turning east and eventually south onto the broadest avenue in the world — the Champs - Élysée-inspired Avenida 9 de Julio.

She peers through rolling reflections of white and gray colonial and Art Deco buildings. The modest European-influenced architecture of Buenos Aires clashes with all the monstrous, uninspiring rooftop billboards advertising Mercedes-Benz and Samsung.

There was a time, not long ago, when I killed for money. Now I do it because I have to … to survive. My life as an assassin wasn't always good … void of friends … void of relationships, but it wasn't all bad either. Money … loads of it … a place to live in New York.

I had purpose, a reason to get out of bed every morning, even if it was to kill. For a while I meant something to someone … Yamada, father figure, teacher—master executioner —

beheaded by Tanaka's men, leaving my life lonelier and emptier than ever.

Christ almighty, it should have been easy; put a bullet in Fujisawa's head, like Tanaka paid me to do, collect all the money, reset. But life had to throw me another curve ball … Gabriel.

Of all the FBI agents to protect Fujisawa, they had to send him; caring, honest … pure … big and strong with dead blue eyes and a broken heart.

Shooting him and leaving him to die was the biggest mistake I ever made.

If only he'd killed that fucking Russian butcher, Gabriel would be alive and I wouldn't be sitting here in this fucked-up cab.

Beyond the silhouettes of tall, lush trees that line both sides of the avenue, the large and rectangular-shaped Teatro Colón slowly reveals itself to Trinity, the exterior lights of the city's premier opera venue radiating far and wide into the surrounding darkness.

Alberto glances at the mirror.

'Obelisco!' he announces, as they now approach the 219-foot high Córdoba white-stone monument.

Trinity leans forward and looks up at Plaza de la República situated in the middle of the avenue.

'Gracias.'

A white light suddenly floods the cab's interior.

Trinity spots Alberto's bulbous eyes in the rear-view mirror. She shifts about in her seat to look over her shoulder.

A motorcycle closes fast.

Trinity shields her eyes with her hand and turns back around. Forming a grip on the Glock, tucked into her faded blue jeans, the harsh steel of the slide digs into her hip.

Alberto looks at the black trail bike speeding alongside them. A chrome-tinted visor conceals the identity of the leather-clad rider.

Trinity draws her Glock and points it beyond Alberto's head.

'Keep your eyes on the fucking road!' she cries.

A refraction of red light beams through the glass and onto her chest.

A black cat dashes through the white light of the taxi's luminous headlamps.

The driver slams on the brakes.

The wheels lock and the tyres screech.

Trinity instinctively pushes her boot into the floor; her fingers grip the armrest tight.

Trickles of blood warm Trinity's temple. Her eyelids stutter before opening. Repeatedly blinking, everything appears blurry at first but quickly comes into focus.

The taxi's crumpled bonnet is wrapped around a tall, steel post. At the top is a green, circular Seiko clock, its glass face shattered.

Smoke hisses and billows from the engine.

She turns to Alberto slumped in his seat, his bleeding head to one side, eyes cold and eerie. In the background, beyond a patch of green grass and purple flowers, is the four-sided Obelisk.

Trinity tugs the handle and shoulder slams the door.

'Come on,' she mutters, striking the window with her elbow. Her sweat now mixes with blood.

Fuck me!

Wiping her forehead with the back of her hand, her eyes dart around the cab. She shuffles across to try the other handle.

'Are you fucking serious?' she murmurs, turning and leaning her back against the door. Raising one leg, Trinity kicks across at the window with her boot heel; fragments of glass shower the backseat. She sits up and stares into the smoke outside and to the dark shape shifting within.

Fuck!

Scratching through the darkness for her gun, Trinity's burning eyes witness the ghostly figure come to a standstill and remove a matte-black helmet. Revealing blond curls, blue eyes catch the light even though the face is in shadow.

Carla!

You Nazi bitch!

Trinity recognizes the assailant at the exact moment her fingers recognize the coarse texture of the Generation-4 Glock's plastic grip. Violently twisting her torso, she thrusts the gun through the broken window.

The blond exterminator lunges forward and presses the weapon against the glass, bending Trinity's wrist at an impossible angle.

Trinity groans and throws back her head as Carla easily disarms her, throwing the pistol on the ground. Dragged by the scruff through the jagged hole, her defiant hand is forced to relinquish its grip on the seat belt.

Shards of glass tear through her white T-shirt and lacerate her skin.

Carla unceremoniously dumps her prey on the bitumen.

'The once great Trinity kneels before me,' she sneers, her voice husky and deliberate.

'Fuck you,' Trinity growls, down on her hands and knees, looking up through the corner of her eye, sweaty strands of hair partially covering her face. 'The Russian put you up to this, didn't he?'

'You know he did. Just about every professional killer in the world is looking for you.'

'I know. I've killed five in the past two years. You'll be number six, cunt!'

Carla's reinforced motorbike boot swings through and jolts Trinity's chin. Rolling onto her back, she licks at a tinge of red blood smeared across her teeth.

'I don't remember you being this tall?' Trinity says, making small talk, needing to buy time.

Carla stands with hands on hips.

'Cute. How does my boot taste?'

'How did you find me so fast?'

Carla raises her eyebrows.

'Your colleague Federico was extremely helpful.'

I should have known not to trust him.

'How much did you pay him?'

'Pay him? I simply fucked him … that was more than enough.' Carla sits astride Trinity. 'Maybe you should have tried that approach too, instead of keeping your pretty little lips all to yourself.' She lightly runs her finger around her captive's nipple. 'Your tits truly are magnificent.'

Trinity slaps her hand away and arches her back, but Carla's position of dominance is too strong. She grapples with her long arms, but Carla muscles her on to her stomach, her weight bearing down, compressing Trinity's ribs so that a sharp breath of air escapes her mouth.

Carla's strong thighs pin Trinity's arms to her sides.

She grimaces, forced to look up, her ponytail yanked from behind.

Carla gently brushes aside a lock of hair, leans in close and smiles, 'You smell nice.'

'I'm gonna fucking kill you,' Trinity mutters, her spine abnormally arched.

Carla looks over both shoulders and seeing no sign of people or passing traffic continues to toy with Trinity.

'Don't take it personally,' she says. 'You and I are the same.'

Trinity clenches her teeth.

'We may breathe the same filthy air, but we are nothing alike! I don't get off on my kills like you do.'

'Whatever. Anyway, I'm going to kill *you*, but not before I see what all the fuss is about.'

Trinity tries to pull away, but a sharp pain fills her eyes with tears and causes her mouth to open wide.

Carla leans forward and pulls hard, her forceful grip threatening to tear hair from the scalp. With her moist tongue she teases Trinity's charcoal-colored lips.

They tingle and her heart quickens.

Two can play at this game, bitch.

Trinity's lips respond in kind as she feels Carla's other hand weasel underneath her chest to grab at her breast.

What the fuck!

Is she for real?

Changing tack, Carla releases Trinity's ponytail and grips her by the neck.

'So, how do you like being strangled?'

Her windpipe steadily crushed one corner of Trinity's dry mouth curls upwards. Panting like a dog, she struggles to fill her lungs with oxygen.

'You like this shit, don't you?' Carla whispers in her ear.

More than you think.

Responding to her attacker's twisted sense of fun, Trinity's nipples burgeon, brought to life by Carla's playful fingers. Trinity's lips, soft, inviting — vulnerable — once again attract Carla's fleshy mouth only this time forcibly parted by her tongue.

Game over.

Trinity clamps her teeth and locks her jaw.

Carla shrieks and lurches backward, her mouth flowing red. Rocked off balance, her leg lifts, allowing Trinity to free one arm, reach up and grab a handful of hair, yanking her to one side.

Trinity rolls away and moves to her hands and knees. Desperate to locate her gun, she spots it lying behind the detached and twisted wreck of the front bumper.

Carla sits up and wipes blood from her mouth.

'You fucking whore!'

Trinity scrambles toward her and launches herself at Carla's throat, wrapping both hands around her neck.

She pulls down on Trinity's hands. Her teeth grind, 'Get off me, you heartless slut!'

Trinity repositions herself and slips in behind. Gaining the upper hand she curls an arm around Carla's neck and wraps both legs around her waist.

She tightens her stranglehold.

Carla panics. Fighting to get to her feet, she stumbles backwards, slamming Trinity against the taxi's front tire; rusted wheel nuts dig into her back.

She rides the bump with a groan.

Realizing she has no choice but to deal with the current situation, sweat falls from Trinity's face. She can hear Carla's boots scrape the asphalt, the desperate murderer more concerned with breathing than bringing her thigh-holstered pistol into play. Trinity reaches deep, employing all of her physical strength to restrain her.

Unlike the indigenous Criollo of Buenos Aires with their pure Spanish ancestry, Carla's vigor is a derivative of her mixed-European heritage.

Trinity's fingertips fall short of Carla's pistol.

Fuck!

She swipes her brow and blinks her eyes, ridding them of sweat. Her outreached boot slips off the Glock.

Fuck me!

In an effort to consolidate her position, Trinity uses her free arm to intensify the choke-hold, cutting the flow of Aryan blood and oxygen to Carla's brain. Deep inside her bulging eyes, Gabriel's blood-red eyes stare back.

Trinity blinks, Carla's eyes close and her body falls limp. Resting her head upon Carla's temple, waves of vanilla and musk notes prickle the back of her nose. Hiding in the background is a warm, resinous scent of amber.

Trinity stares into the distance, her mind somewhat blurred. Interrupting the unnerving silence surrounding the two female assassins, the all-too-familiar wailing police sirens penetrate deep into her mind.

Trinity's eyes close as she twists Carla's neck, fracturing her vertebrae and severing the spinal cord, the innocuous click sending goose bumps across her skin. Reopening them, she stares at her face and gently places Carla's head onto the road, her bloodied fingers caressing her colleague's smooth complexion.

Loud sirens redirect her focus.

Trinity wipes her eyes. Sliding herself up the side of the taxi and to her feet, she looks down at her shredded T-shirt, removing it entirely with one rip. Standing exposed in jeans and black bra, small cuts and bruises cover her torso.

Squatting alongside Carla, she relieves the beautiful

dead assassin of her leather Dianese motorbike jacket. Zipping it up tight the soft Italian leather presses against her bulging breasts and sensitive skin, causing her to wince. She recovers her Glock and draws Carla's Brazilian-forged pistol by its black, checkered, polymer grip, awkwardly releasing it from the level III retention holster.

Taurus G2 semi-auto ... adjustable rear sight ... double-action trigger for the first shot ... 4.2-inch barrel ... manual safety ... seventeen-round 9-mill magazine.

In an automatic, subconscious motion, drilled into her mind by thousands of repetitions, she releases the magazine and visually inspects it.

Bombed ...

She reinserts the mag with her palm and tugs at it with her fingers. Retracting the slide ever so slightly, she cants the gun upwards to look inside the chamber.

... Actioned.

Trinity fist-bumps the slide forward, ensuring it's locked into place. Reaching underneath, she detaches and discards the laser from the Picatinny rail. Shoving both guns down the back of her jeans, the cold steel cools her skin. She notices a small crowd of early-morning McDonald's patrons emerging from the store located on the nearby corner of Avenida Corrientes and 9 de Julio.

Trinity straightens and scans the area, her stare fixing on the spectators lingering behind the curtain of darkness surrounding the Obelisk. Considering them to be of no threat to her she turns her back on them and retrieves Yamamoto's sword from the taxi. Slinging it over her shoulder she rushes to Carla's trail bike.

Once there, she glances to the lifeless form on the road alongside the trashed taxi. Following a pause, she takes up the bike and attempts to start it.

Come on you piece of shit!

She twists the throttle and rests her boot on the kick starter, her entire body weight pushing down - nothing. In a last-ditch effort she leans the bike over.

The sound of gasoline sloshes to one side.

Bouncing her boot on the kick starter, the leather jacket sticks to her clammy skin. She eventually pushes all the way through, but the engine doesn't respond.

Trinity pushes the bike away, her eyes sneaking a look up and out. Two flashing vehicles from the Policia Metropolitana de Buenos Aires skid to a stop at the edge of darkness; half-shaded, half-lit.

She whips out the Taurus and fires a dozen well-placed bullets in quick time, the pistol rocking in her hands, gun smoke smudging her view.

Half the dispatched military-spec FMJ projectiles swamp the cars, breaking glass, puncturing the soft outer skin - the other half don't. It matters not to Trinity; the effective fire forces the pair of cops to stay low.

Hiding behind their bullet-riddled cars, they radio in for assistance.

She spins to the clips of boot heels running, her long hair whipping across her shoulder and around her neck. Adopting a combat crouch—knees bent, arms straight—the presentation of her threatening gun and itchy trigger finger halts several men breaking from the crowd of onlookers. Her narrow gaze shifts to empty hands thrown high into the air, then pockets and finally their faces.

Trinity's eyes follow their stares.

What the fuck?

Her pistol's front sight tracks a lone man's wary steps. She lowers the weapon as he stops to pick up the bike and motions with his head for the others to assist him. She watches his amigos rush to the rear of the bike.

They look to Trinity and gesture with their waving arms for her to join them.

Sirens herald the arrival of two more cars - Policia Federal Argentina.

Trinity doesn't know why the men would put their lives at risk for her, but she's running out of time and options, so she decides to take a dangerous chance on the locals. Running over to the bike, she jumps onto the seat, pulls in the clutch and clicks down to second gear.

The police open fire.

In retaliation, she shoots back, dropping the hammer another six times before the slide locks open. A quick peek inside and she tosses the empty gun aside.

'Rápido!' Trinity shouts.

The men all grin.

Bending their backs and locking straight their arms, their feet slap against the asphalt as they pick up speed.

Wind tousles Trinity's hair.

Bullets crack above her head.

She hunches over the fuel tank and looks across her shoulder, watching as Feds spill from their vehicles and fire their M4 carbines.

One of the amigos stumbles; blood soils the back of his white singlet. The other men all lift their heads and shout in unison, 'Ahora! Ahora!'

Trinity lets out the clutch and the bike splutters to life. Rolling on the throttle, she pulls away, her eyes drawn to the side mirror and to the sight of the men left behind jumping up and down cheering as she vanishes into the darkness.

True Colors

In the south-east corner of Buenos Aires, close to the old port, lies the small, working-class neighborhood of La Boca, one of forty-eight barrios that make up the *Paris of South America*.

On her stolen motor bike, Trinity approaches the colorful Caminito, a cobblestone walkway at the heart of La Boca filled with street-side performers during the day, vibrant bars and cafés at night. A former dried-up stream and long-time eyesore, its buildings were built using recycled timber and corrugated iron from the old shipyard.

Trinity kicks down the bike stand and swings her leg over the fuel tank. Standing next to a blue wall, she glances up and down the walkway. It's mid-week, early in the morning and no one else is around.

The lingering smell of milanesa, fainá and polenta, traditional cuisine introduced to the city by early Genovese immigrants, causes Trinity's hungry stomach to rumble. Shrouded in dark silence, she makes her way along the cobblestones.

A barking dog spoils the tranquillity.

One block down, she walks by a tall, gothic street lamp and passes through its white light cast against a bright yellow wall. She runs her finger along the top of a red, hand-painted bench.

Reaching the end of the block, she slows to peer down a dark side-street. She glances over her shoulder before making her way to the far end and a café with flashing lights.

Soft and alluring music greets Trinity as she steps on to the cafe's wooden patio. Off to one side, a large dog stands sentinel. He refuses to blink, his dark eyes set wide apart in his over-sized head.

Trinity freezes.

Walking home from school by an open patch of recently cut grass bordered by a small clump of bushes, a young Trinity and her friend Mizuki laugh, leaping into the air like ballerinas. Halo plays football with school friends nearby.

Caught up in their fantasy the girls miss the approach of a large, tan and black Rottweiler. He growls as they encroach on his territory.

Trinity stands still, her youthful eyes growing in size, drawn to his bared white fangs.

Mizuki screams and runs. The hound instinctively chases, mowing her down within seconds. Trinity wants to scream, to move, to help Mizuki. But she stands frozen, squeezing her eyes shut to the sounds of the dog savaging her friend's face.

The owner yells, his anguish adding to the nightmarish scene. Taking hold of the studded collar, at last he pulls the beast clear.

16

On hearing Mizuki's cries, Halo and his friends rush to her aid. She continues to scream as they comfort her, and Halo wraps his arms around Trinity, his hands across her ears.

Trinity's heart races; she feels hot and flushed. She can hear the Dogo Argentino breathing through his blackened, moist nostrils, her eyes drawn to the pure-white glossy coat of his massive chest rising and falling.

She gingerly slides her boot forward.

His cropped ears twitch.

Sneaking another step, Trinity's eyes make contact with those of the dog who follows her every move.

She steps through the doorway.

Thank fuck for that!

Still trembling, Trinity scans the intimate café filled with a dozen small wooden tables, two of which are occupied by young couples. Gloomy lighting conceals their faces, preventing Trinity from reading them. Up at the bar, another patron sitting on a stool slumps face down on the thick wooden bench; his only companions an empty beer glass and overflowing ashtray.

The barkeep, holding a cloth in one hand and a sparkling-clean wine glass in the other, watches a couple dancing on the parquet floor.

Trinity approaches him.

'Malbec,' she says, craving her favourite red.

The barkeep's handlebar mustache flutters as he heartily responds, 'Argentina!'

Trinity smiles at the drinking game reference.

Holding up a bottle of wine, he raises an eyebrow.

'Luigi Bosca?'

She shakes her head.

'Ahhh, Catena Zapata!'

'Si!' she smiles.

Trinity sits at a table and sips her plum-colored wine, savoring the fruity flavor of dark berries and oak as it slides down the back of her throat. The strong aromas of tobacco and rich spices tickle her flared nostrils.

The wooden chair creaks as she leans back, her eyes mesmerized by the candle light flickering on the glass in her hand. Straightening her posture, she massages her neck and stretches her back, her interest focusing on the couple dancing.

The dancers, entwined, glide around the floor in a counter-clockwise direction, neither ankles nor knees brushing against one another, their spines perfectly erect. Clasped hands held high, bodies pressed in an interminable embrace, their faces rest together, each looking across the other's shoulder. Sweat glistens down the man's bared chest and across his well-defined arms. The woman's ample breasts strain at a sweat-soaked white singlet.

Valentina.

She hasn't changed since I last saw her … years ago … so beautiful … so dangerous.

In a public display of showmanship, Valentina's partner lunges forward, pushing her backwards, dipping her body close to the ground. She extends an arm parallel to the floor and he nestles his cheek against her chest, one hand clutching her breast.

Valentina closes her eyes and hangs her head back, her ponytail touching the floor.

Trinity admires Valentina's exposed flesh, stretched from ankle to buttock. A warm flush engulfs her face, as she watches the man's hand explore his partner's breast—every curve, every bump. His little finger pulls aside her singlet; she lets slip a smile as his lips envelop her nipple.

Trinity's pounding heart fills her throat.

Pulling away sharply, he lifts Valentina by the hand and raises the elbow above his shoulder; his other hand moves from her breast to around the waist.

She straightens and hooks one leg around his knee.

He breathes deeply, sweat running from his cheeks to his square jaw. His eyes, fixed on her full red lips gaze downward and along her stretched neck to her heaving breasts.

Trinity's eyes follow the same course.

Stepping back he spins Valentina around.

She stamps her black stiletto and arches her back, head tilted, chin raised, eyes barely open. Releasing his hand, she throws her outstretched arms by her sides, fingers spread wide.

Trinity cannot look away.

He moves up from behind and rests his flushed cheek against hers, his finger tracing one of many facial scars.

She opens her eyes and draws her leg behind his hip, the slit in her tight red dress revealing white panties.

His palm slides across Valentina's breasts; her eyes close, her fire-engine-red lips part.

Trinity's thighs press together, her eyes focused on the outline of Valentina's nipples stretching through the thin, wet material. She watches as the young man brushes his thumb against them several times before sliding his hand to her waist.

Trinity's eyes widen, watching his hand disappear into Valentina's skirt. Captivated by the scene unfolding in front of her, she grinds her thighs. The old wooden chair creaks and her breathing accelerates.

It seems her brush with death by Carla's hands has only heightened her arousal.

The dancer's buried hand rhythmically moves about.

Valentina leans back, her black ponytail draped across

her shoulder. Placing her hand on his face, she draws it closer.

His experienced fingers press deep.

Valentina's honey-tinted eyes burst open and lock with Trinity's.

She gasps.

Valentina shudders.

Regret

Valentina sits across from Trinity.

'Did you enjoy the show?'

'It's been far too long,' Trinity replies, smiling, happy to hear Valentina's melodic accent again.

Valentina leans on her elbows.

'Three? No. Four years?'

Trinity nods, 'Three.' Her eyes flick over the young man from the dance floor walking toward them - hands, pockets, then his face.

He carries a glass of water and another wine for Trinity. Lowering the drinks to the table, he kisses Valentina's neck and makes for the door.

Trinity's eyes follow him outside.

'He doesn't say much,' she says.

'He doesn't need to. His actions speak for themselves.'

'Where'd you find him?'

'He's a local. He used to play for the football team up the road. Not that I care – stupid game.'

'I need your help.'

'I was wondering when you would approach me. I heard you'd recruited that fool Federico to help you.'

'And I heard you were out of the game. I was desperate.'

'We are never truly out of the game, Trinity. You of all people should know that.' Valentina runs loose hair behind her ear. 'Speaking of which, I'm sorry for your loss. I once owed Yamada my life. He was there for me when I needed him.'

'And now I need you, Valentina.'

'How much is The Russian offering for your head?'

Trinity looks around the café and then stares into her friend's eyes.

'Ten million.'

Valentina leans in close.

'American?'

Trinity nods.

Valentina sits back in her chair.

'That is a lot of money. But then again, you did kill a lot of his men. More importantly, you killed Tanaka.'

'Tanaka? I didn't kill Tanaka.'

'Well if you didn't kill him … who did?'

'I don't know. I assumed it was The Russian.'

'Word on the street is *he* blames you.'

Trinity sits up.

'Well, I didn't do it, though I would have if I'd had the chance. He's the one who had Yamada killed.'

Valentina looks smug.

'What makes you think I won't kill you for that sort of money?'

'Because of our history together.'

Although Valentina frowns, her pitch playfully elevates.
'We shared a bed for one night …'
'What about the fact you don't kill for money anymore, the fact that you owe Yamada?'
'Yamada is dead …'
'The fact you enjoyed that one night as much as I did?'
Valentina responds with a cheeky 'so-so' gesture across her face.
Trinity smiles, looks down and then up.
'Have you seen Federico lately?' she asks. 'Do you know where I can find him?'
'I have not seen him for more than a week. I heard he was involved with Carla.'
Trinity narrows her eyes.
'Carla?'
'Yes. That crazy German bitch, you should speak to her.'
Trinity looks away.
'What's wrong?' Valentina asks.
Trinity sighs and looks back.
'I can't speak to her, to Carla.'
'Why not?'

Because I fucking killed her!

I snapped her fucking neck.

I didn't need to do it. I could have left her there for the police to deal with, but I did it anyway.

It's what I do … it's who I am … a monster.

Trinity speaks softly, 'Carla's dead.'
Valentina's eyes shift from side to side. Leaning forward, she lifts her brow.
'Dead?'
Trinity nods.

'She tried to kill me earlier tonight,' she says. 'And now I think she may have killed Federico.'

Valentina screws up her face and flicks her hand in the air.

'I never liked her anyway. And Federico was nothing but a fool.'

'I'm over it, Val.' Trinity says, watching her hands, 'I'm truly over it. I don't want to do it anymore.'

'Do what?'

Trinity stares at the table and fiddles with the salt shaker and mumbles, 'Kill.'

'Kill? Trinity Blue doesn't want to kill anymore? I don't believe that, honey. It's in your blood. It's who you are. It's who we are.'

'I know, I know,' she says, looking up. 'But I want out. Help me get out.'

'I could be killed just for talking to you.'

Trinity reaches across the table and takes hold of her hand.

Valentina smiles then rolls her eyes.

'You can stay with me and Hector for as long as you like,' she says, stroking Trinity's thumb with her own.

'Who is Hector?' Trinity asks.

Valentina whistles loudly.

'He is the love of my life!'

Trinity turns to the sound of pitter-patter across the timber floor as Hector strolls in from the patio and sits beside Valentina.

His eyes close as she runs her hand down his back.

'Trinity Blue, meet Hector. Hector … Trinity Blue.'

'We've already met, on my way in. How long have you had him?'

'Not long. His previous owner, Máximo, who no longer breathes air, much to everyone's relief, enjoyed throwing him into the pits against Córdoban Fighting Dogs.'

'I thought the Córdoban breed was extinct.'

'Not quite. Very few breeders continued the original bloodlines, those that did now sell the dogs for extraordinary amounts of cash on the black market.

'Fortunately, Hector was a good fighter. He survived an encounter with two Córdobans, long enough for me to arrive and even the playing field with the help of my pistol.' Valentina grins, her eyes and hands becoming animated. 'That was the first time I ever shot a dog and the only time I enjoyed killing someone. I shoved the barrel so far down Máximo's throat the bullet blew his spine out of his back. And now Hector looks after me. Don't you, big boy?'

The first rays of daylight inch their way over the tiny, white-tiled balcony, through the tall arched window and across Trinity's twitching eyelids. She can feel their warmth. Opening her eyes, she sees the outline of Hector, keeping watch.

Valentina sits across from her house guest at a small wooden table in the middle of the living room in her one bedroom flat. A strong aroma of freshly brewed coffee from the kitchenette drifts from one side of the room to the other.

'He must like you.'

Trinity rubs her eyes.

'What makes you say that?'

'Every night, without fail he silently sits by my bed staring at me. But last night, he stayed with you.'

'I seem to have an effect on animals. I'm able to relate to them, certainly much better than I can relate to humans ... especially men.'

'Speaking of men ...'

Trinity sits up on the couch, her makeshift bed and rolls her eyes.

'Do we have to?'

'Who is Gabriel?'

How the fuck does she know Gabriel's name?

Trinity shrugs her shoulders.

'What do you mean?'

'You mentioned his name while you slept, along with some other things.'

'Like what?'

'It sounded like he was forcing you to do something and you didn't want to do it ... but you did it anyway. Does that make any sense?'

Trinity again shakes her head.

Barely anything I do makes sense ... well, not to anyone else.

What else do I say aloud in my sleep?

I know I dream ...'

'How long was I asleep?'

'Two hours.'

'No wonder I still feel like shit.'

Valentina sips her coffee.

'Well, we have much to talk about and plan. You will only be safe here for a short time, then more assassins will come for you, of that I am certain.'

'I'm sorry to have dragged you into my mess. I thought I could handle things on my own. I just needed someone to help access my cache.'

Valentina nods.

'And what of Halo?'

'The last I saw of Halo was in Tokyo, three years ago when I stole his motorbike.'

'I heard he was in the UAE looking after some Arab,' Valentina says. 'But what happened between you two?'

'We parted ways ...'

'I'm sorry ... *we?* It was mutual?'

Trinity throws the blanket off her legs.

'It's too early for this shit!'

'If you require my help, I need to know where both your life and your head are at.'

'Okay. Okay. I ... decided to leave ... *him*. Satisfied?'

'Why?'

'I don't know why, really. Life was great. Halo was incredible. He looked after me, loved me. I loved him back I guess, but just not in the way he wanted me to. I wanted to ... but I couldn't. I know it sounds strange but I just couldn't.'

'Because of the way your father brought you up to hate all men?'

'I'm sure that had something to do with it, perhaps quite a bit, but ... there's something else going on inside my head. It's always bothered me, but now it scares me.'

'Your mother?'

Trinity goes cold. Her eyes feel heavy and she drops her head forward

'Fuck this shit!' she says, standing up. 'I'm taking a shower and then I'm going to get my guns. Are you coming with me or not?'

Valentina quietly sits and nods.

City of the Dead

T rinity leans over a heavily-folded tourist map flat-
tened out across Valentina's small round kitchen
table. White salt and pepper shakers, along with a
steak knife and fork, hold the map in place. She examines an
area in the northern barrios of the city, where a twelve-foot
high brick wall, spanning four city blocks, surrounds a tree-
lined labyrinth of paved streets and lanes.

Behind the 190-year-old walls is the Cementerio de la
Recoleta, a sprawling necropolis home to former presidents,
military leaders, poets and laureates. Separated by time,
hopes and dreams, they all have one thing in common -
death.

'Whereabouts in the cemetery is it?' Valentina asks.

'It's inside an empty crypt. No one has been buried in
there for several decades.'

'But the cemetery contains more than 40,000 tombs ...'

'Precisely,' Trinity says, pointing to the cemetery entrance. 'There's only one easy way in and out of this place, and that's through the main gate.'

Valentina shifts the knife and fork closer to the edge of the map.

'The entrance is guarded 24/7.'

'I know.'

'I think we should risk scaling the walls.'

'The walls are too high to climb, especially carrying guns and all my other shit,' Trinity points out. 'We'll be seen for sure. It's one thing dealing with the local police. Add some of The Russian's goons into the mix, and all the would-be hit men in the world, and things could quickly escalate.'

'Are you sure they will be watching the cemetery?'

'I can't be positive they are. But given that Federico is missing and that he was most likely involved with Carla, I now have to assume they know the whereabouts of my cache, and my need to access it.'

'What is hidden away?'

'The usual … passports, money, guns, cell phones.'

'I could chase up some old leads and organise most of those items for you.'

Trinity places her hand on Valentina's shoulder.

'That would take too long. I burned my last passport coming here and I'm real low on cash. Now they know where I am, I have to move on again, sooner rather than later.'

Biting down on the inside of her cheek, staring at the table, Valentina shakes her head.

'When will this all end?'

'I don't know. Most likely when I'm dead.'

'You can't keep running.'

Trinity smiles to herself.

'What's so funny?' Valentina asks.

'Someone I once knew said the exact same thing to me.'

'You should have listened to their advice.'

'I did … but it was too late.'

'It's never too late.'

'Yeah, it kind of is.'

'What was his name?'

Trinity pauses before answering, 'Never mind.'

Valentina rolls her eyes.

'And even if you were able to get your weapons, then what? It's not like you can just jump on the next available flight with an M4 slung over your shoulder. Wherever you go, you'll have to start again … another fight to survive, another cache to plunder, another battle to win. No wonder you're over it, Trinity. I'm amazed you can sleep at night.'

'Well, what the fuck do you expect me to do?' she says, shrugging her shoulders. 'I'm living conversation to conversation, let alone day to fucking day! Without weapons I'm fucked. I need more than a Glock loaded with a handful of bullets and a damn sword.'

Valentina raises an eyebrow.

'It's a cool sword, by the way.'

'They're coming for me, Valentina. I need to get my gear a.s.a.p. Then I can at least fight and buy my way through this shit and work out what to do next.'

'I know exactly what you should do.'

'And what's that?'

'Stop. Fucking. Running! Slow down. You're going to crash.'

Trinity straightens her spine and opens her mouth to disprove Valentina's simplistic solution to all her problems, but the words elude her.

'Stop running from your demons, Trinity. Man the fuck up! Do what you do best …'

You mean destroy everyone who ever loved or cared for me?

Run from everything I can't deal with?

'Fucking kill that Russian abomination! Cut off his fucking head!'

'It's not that easy.'

'How do you know? You haven't even tried.'

Trinity lowers her head.

'If only Gabriel had killed him in Tokyo, I wouldn't be in this predicament.'

'Gabriel! Tell me, who the fuck is this Gabriel? What are you hiding from?'

Trinity looks away.

Valentina leans across the table.

'He's the one you missed out on, the one who offered the same advice as I have?'

'He had the chance, but he let The Russian escape.'

'Stop blaming others, Trinity. You at least once had a perfect upbringing. I never did, but I don't go around blaming everyone else for all the shit that's happened in my life.' Valentina's hand subconsciously touches the scars on her face. She looks down, then up again. 'I've made mistakes, but I've tried to learn from them. But before you can even do that, you have to admit to yourself you've made them.'

'My fucking mother left me!'

'Yes, but your father stayed by your side, raised you and loved you more than anything else. Even Yamada, a cold-hearted killer, loved you. You know what it's like to be loved, Trinity. You've just forgotten.'

'But if she hadn't left …'

'Remember, *you* chose to listen to Yamada. *You* chose to kill. *You* chose to leave Halo. *You* chose not to listen to others. You alone are responsible for where you are ... right here, right now ... you and no one else. You've made mistakes, but don't let them define who you are. You are exceptionally beautiful, Trinity.'

'That's half my problem. Men just want me for my tits.'

'That's not what I meant,' Valentina says, casting her eyes over them. 'Although, I must admit they are exquisite.'

Trinity folds her arms across her chest.

'What happened to him, to Gabriel?' Valentina asks.

Trinity's head pounds; her eyes fixate on the steak knife in front of her. She blinks once then switches her gaze to her arm.

Valentina reaches out.

'Don't even think about it.'

Trinity covers her eyes with her hands.

'I fucking shot him. I killed him.'

'You shot Gabriel? Why?'

'I don't know why. He told me to. So I did it. And then ... and then I ran away.'

'Are you sure he's dead?'

Trinity lowers her hands, narrows her eyes.

'I blew a fucking hole through his chest!'

'I once shot a man in the head at close range. He survived. I did hunt him down a year later, but he didn't die from those head wounds.'

Trinity's voice is cold, 'Gabriel's dead.'

'Have you checked? Records? Death notices?'

'I've had more important things to do. You know, like survive. Of course I checked.'

'And ... what did you find?'

'Nothing. There's no sign, no mention of him any-where.'

'That doesn't mean he's dead. Someone must know what happened to him.'

Trinity sighs and wipes tears from her eyes.

'Anyway,' she says, pointing to the map moving on. 'The vault containing my gear is here.'

Valentina looks at the map and shakes her head, frustrated with Trinity's unwillingness to confide in her.

'That's not far from Evita's tomb.'

'Correct, and it has a skull-and-crossbones attached to the door with an iron cross on the roof.'

'So how do you plan on accessing it?'

Trinity stares at the map.

'First of all I need to visit the cemetery and look for any sign left around the crypt. I need to establish whether or not it's being watched.'

'Is this wise?' Valentina queries, 'You are increasing your chances of being spotted.'

'It's been more than five years since I last visited Recoletta. Things could have changed.'

'Time is not on your side.'

'True. But recently I have made too many mistakes by rushing and not thinking clearly. The recon mission will be time well spent.'

'How do you expect to get in there unnoticed?'

She pauses before answering, 'Like I said, via the front door.'

Valentina nods.

'You'll need a disguise.'

Shaded by the reaching spread of a centuries-old rubber tree, Trinity follows the square tiles snaking across Plaza Francia. To avoid spying eyes and a triggerman's cold-blooded bullet, she wears a black veil and shawl, within her grasp a guide dog harness, fitted snugly to Hector's chest.

Flanked by lush grass and park benches, the path leads to a pair of black Gothic lamp-posts and the grand white-stoned entrance to the Recoleta cemetery. Carved above its towering Doric columns is the hopeful declaration:

EXPECTAMUS DOMINUM

Trinity hides beneath her veil, her observant eyes free to roam without consequence. Off to one side, she notes three armed metropolitan police officers keeping watch, each partnered with a vicious-looking black-and-tan Doberman.

The guard dogs stand to attention, barrel chests high and wide. On picking up Hector's scent, their hairline shoots up. Dipping their heads, peering through battle-bred eyes, frightening snarls reveal razor-sharp teeth.

Hector holds his head aloft and looks straight ahead.

Trinity and her companion merge with a coach-load of tourists shuffling across white tiles to join an orderly line moving through a black, neo-classical iron gate.

Once inside, eerily beautiful Art Nouveau and Neo-Gothic mausoleums and crypts line both sides of the main thoroughfare, each adorned with elaborate and finely-crafted statues of cherubs and angels. The city of the dead is home to more than 350,000 resting souls.

A little further along, they arrive at Cristo Central a small roundabout surrounded by tall pine trees and even grander tombs. Situated in the heart of the cemetery, the grassy circle takes the place of what was once an old drinking well, but is now occupied by a somber statue - Cristo El Redentor; narrow streets radiate in all directions.

Trinity and Hector dawdle past more endless rows of concrete tombs, most well kept with small touches of life: fresh flowers and photographs. Many others are derelict, with broken-down doors, shattered stained-glass windows or upturned and dusty above-ground caskets.

Trinity looks down at a well-fed tabby cat, sprawled across the half-open entrance to a run-down crypt, preening its mottled tawny coat.

He's not alone.

Across the way, she spots a curious clowder of feral cats sitting atop a domed mausoleum. They're everywhere, and well cared for, because the locals view them as guardians of the cemetery. Most believe they possess the eyes of the dead, allowing them to see from the Underworld.

Nearing the end of the street, Trinity and Hector pause outside the entrance to the tomb of Rufina Cambaceres, a young woman rumoured to have been buried alive, unconscious, in the early 1900s. For several days, screams from within were ignored by nearby groundskeepers.

Once investigated and the coffin prised open, the underside of the lid bore signs of desperate scratch marks. So too did her face.

I know what it's like to cry out for help, and have no one hear you or care about you.

I wonder what Carla's final thoughts were as I choked the life from her?

Turning left then right, moving past Eva Perón's final resting place, Trinity wanders down a small lane, coming to rest in front of a small, shunned crypt.

Hector sits at her feet.

She looks past the baroque gravesite in front of her and to the dark marble chamber next door, where a skull-and-crossbones plaque is bolted to the solid iron door. Above the entrance on the roof, leaning to one side, is an iron cross. A hastily prepared arrangement of carmen-red Ceibo flowers rests across the chipped marble doorstep.

Moist sap from the stem glistens in the sunlight; ants feast on the flower's nectar.

That means the flowers were picked no more than four hours ago ... placed here in less than two.

Trinity goes down on her knees as if to pray, discreetly looking for more sign.

Three cigarette butts nearby, all smoked down to the same size ... disturbed dust on the doorknob.

Amateurs ... a goon perhaps, maybe even local.

Trinity rises to her feet, her cloaked eyes searching for anyone sitting, watching. To her left, offering zero conceal-ment, there is nothing but similar crypts and a façade of bronze plaques extending another twenty meters to the wall surrounding the cemetery.

Making her way out onto a larger road lined with many more mausoleums, her initial snapshot reveals nothing out of the ordinary, just the soft voices of random visitors and the whispered prayers of grieving families.

Her pupils refocus to take in more detail, ready to proc-ess any unusual shapes or unnatural shadows in relation to the predictable square edges of the concrete and marble tombs. Scanning for movement where there should be none at all, a glint in the distance catches her eye.

Trinity's breathing stops and her heart pounds. At first she doesn't move. Then, calmly leaning to one side, she watches the flash of light disappear, revealing a bronze cross nailed to a crypt's weathered door.

'Come on Hector, let's go home. I've seen enough.'

Full Moon

Back at Valentina's apartment, Trinity studies the cemetery map.

'We'll enter the main gate separately,' she says, 'at least one half hour apart. You take the Glock and I'll take Hector again.'

'What time do you want to arrive?'

'Two hours before closing.' She taps the map with her finger. 'There's a crypt here where we can hide until after the cemetery shuts. But make sure you're not being followed. Casually walk around for a little while before you go in.'

Valentina places a folded newspaper on to the table.

'I checked the weather guide and the hours of darkness are from 18:00 until 06:00.'

Trinity lifts her head.

'What about the moon?'

'Unfortunately it will be full.'

'Any cloud cover?'

'No.'

'Not ideal, but we'll have to work around it. We'll stand down until two hours after dark to make sure everyone else has gone.'

'At least the moon should still be low in the sky.'

Trinity nods.

'Dressed in black we should blend into the shadows quite easily.'

Valentina motions with her head to the corner of the room.

'What about Hector? His white coat will stand out in the dark.'

'Will he stay where he's told?'

'Yes, you do not have to worry about him.'

'Good. He can wait there in the crypt for our return. Once we've got what I need we'll return to him and wait until the cemetery opens in the morning. It won't be comfortable, but we should try to get some rest during the night.'

'Trust me,' Valentina grins. 'I have slept in worse places.'

'Haven't we all,' Trinity says, smiling, before returning to the map. 'Mid-morning, shortly after the tour buses arrive and the cemetery is at its busiest, we'll walk out the front gate.'

She brushes a lock of hair behind her ear and points to the road outside the exit.

'If it all goes off without a hitch, take the third taxi waiting in the queue and have the driver take you to Plaza de Mayo. Once there, hail the second taxi that drives past, not from the queue, and head to Galerías Pacífico. As soon as you get out of that taxi, immediately get into the very next one you see and have them bring you here. I'll be waiting for you.'

'Controlled random matrix - three, two and one,' Valentina says, remembering her training, having served two terms in the Argentine defence force.

Trinity smiles, nods and scrawls a large red circle on the map.

'Okay. In case we get compromised and separated from each other, this will be our immediate fall-back position.' She marks the map with a small cross near the roundabout in Cristo Central. 'Not only does it have clear vision and good angles of fire in all directions, it has multiple escape routes. With the layout of the streets and lanes inside the circled area, it's easily divided into four quadrants.'

Valentina reorientates the map and draws an arrow pointing north.

Trinity runs the red marker down and across the circle dividing it into four.

'I figure the immediate meeting point *here* will be defendable for no more than ... two minutes ... maximum.' Her eyes shift to Valentina and then back again. 'Whoever makes it there second, only enter from the northwest quadrant.' She runs her finger along the map to avoid any confusion. 'Anyone approaching from the other quadrants is going to be shot in the face.'

'How do we ID ourselves?'

'Raise the non-master hand into the air.'

Valentina raises her right arm.

'And left hand for me.'

Valentina smiles.

'If either of us doesn't make it to Cristo Central in time,' Trinity says, 'then push on and wait here at the rubber tree.' She draws another circle. 'Come in from the corner of Quintana and Ortiz near the café. Let's make the window open for, say, ten minutes from the initial compromise at that location?'

'Sounds good.'

Trinity straightens and looks to Valentina.

'From there, head over to Floralis Genérica and wait until the hour's end before meeting up at Harrods through the old service entrance on San Martín near the corner of Córdoba.

'It's imperative to get in there before the sun rises, and stay out of sight until darkness that night. Under no circumstance come directly back here. I don't want anyone tracking us to your home.'

'Once you have all the money and bullets you need, what will you do then?' Valentina asks.

Trinity sits down.

'Like I said, I'm flying by the seat of my pants. Let's get my shit first then worry about what to do afterwards.'

'If you wish, I will come with you to kill The Russian.'

'No. You've done enough for me already. You don't even have to come to the cemetery. Hector and I will be fine.'

'I want to come. It's been a while since I had this much excitement.'

Trinity leans back into the chair and runs her hand through her hair.

'We should get a good night's rest.'

Valentina nods and smiles, then says, 'By the way, Jorge is visiting tonight. You are welcome to join us if you wish.'

Trinity fidgets with her fingers.

Valentina looks good. Her dreamy eyes just draw me in.

Not to mention her hair. Those dangly bits in front of her face drive me fucking wild.

And it has been three years since I've been with anyone.

She sighs.

'As tempting as it is, I should get some sleep.'

'I shall leave my door open should you change your mind.'

Trinity smiles, her eyes following Valentina down the hall.

Trinity knows he's there, hiding amongst the shadows. He's always there, no matter where she goes, no matter what she does.

She can feel his presence, his eyes watching her every movement, his mind probing her thoughts. It doesn't affect her. She's neither frightened nor concerned, rather, per-plexed as to why he doesn't step from the shadows and re-veal himself to her.

She moves toward him.

He backs away, deeper into the darkness.

Trinity wakens to find Hector watching over her. She places her hand on his head and glances at the clock on the wall illuminated by beams of moonlight cutting through the slats of an overhead window: 02:40 a.m.

Her attention switches to a dull light at the end of the hall. Pulling back the sheets, she slides out of bed, her hand gently stroking the top of her protector's head.

'Stay,' she murmurs.

The timber floorboards creak under her feet.

Valentina's bedroom door is ajar.

Trinity's heart races as she peers through the gap at Valentina lying on her side, Jorge holding her from behind. A lamp shines soft light on their naked forms.

Valentina reaches behind and runs her hand across Jorge's face. Her mouth barely opens as her other hand cups her breast.

Trinity steps closer to the door, her wide eyes drawn to the gentle rocking of Jorge's hips. She stares at the two lovers. Reaching in through the sleeve of her white singlet she mauls her fulsome breasts, her fingers digging into the flesh bringing her nipples to life.

Trinity's throat is dry. The inside of her thighs is wet.

Jorge removes Valentina's hand from his face and guides it between her legs, his thumb returning to tease her nipple.

Valentina moans.

Trinity swallows, hard, and pulls down the front of her singlet, exposing one breast. Her fingertips caress the skin; the sensitive flesh prickles with excitement.

I can tell he loves her.

The way he looks at her … the way he touches her … even the way he smells her. He breathes in her essence.

What they have is real.

I could have had that.

Valentina massages her inner thighs, her breathing becoming loud and fast. Jorge fucks like a man on death row. Sweat streams from his skin; he shines.

Trinity clamps her thighs and bites her lip.

Jorge gradually slows the tempo and leans in close, softly kissing his lover's trembling lips.

Valentina relaxes into his slippery arms, her hair soaked through. She whispers into his ear, gasps as he nods and withdraws his cock. Standing, she slowly moves toward the door.

Trinity quickly covers up and turns to walk away.

Valentina reaches through the door and takes her by the wrist, guiding her inside and toward the ruffled bed.

Trinity lifts her arms as Valentina pulls her singlet over her head.

Jorge climbs out of bed and moves in from behind, his stiffness pressing against her skin.

Trinity reaches behind and strokes at it, her eyes fixed to Valentina's, the Latin beauty approaching to kiss her.

Trinity's skin tingles at Valentina's touch, her probing fingers more than she can handle.

She turns and pushes Jorge to the bed, straddling then grinding his cock, her breath short and sharp.

He pins her arms and holds her still.

'Let me go,' she mutters.

Valentina touches her shoulder.

'Relax, Trinity,' she whispers, 'slow down and enjoy.'

'I don't want to enjoy it. Just let me fuck him!'

Jorge rolls Trinity on to her back.

She resists at first, but then allows him to ease inside.

'Fuck me hard you dumb cunt,' Trinity moans. 'Hard … make it hurt!'

Gently sliding his cock in and out of Trinity, Jorge's dark eyes look over to Valentina watching from the corner of the room, her strong scent still clinging to his diamond-cut torso.

Trinity slaps his face.

'Fuck me, not her, damn you!'

Trinity grabs his hands and places his fingers around her neck, Jorge easily breaking her hold and lifting her toward him, her breasts pressing against his chest. She pulls back, but he again draws her close, and she lets him.

His lips on her skin, she fights in vain against a tidal wave of rapturous sensations, Gabriel's face the night he approached her at the bar in New York flashing through her mind, a look of hope in his sad eyes, the inch-long scar on his cheek catching the light.

Trinity's muscles tighten and her eyes roll back into her head. She presses her forehead deep into the side of Jorge's temple; her fingernails draw blood from his back.

Relaxing her legs from around his waist, she rests her head forward, hair falling about her face.

Jorge just did to me what Gabriel tried to do, what I would never let him do. If I had, maybe things would have turned out differently.

He once told me he wanted to see the world through the color of my eyes.

Am I now the one looking through his?

Trinity untangles her legs, looks at Jorge's hard cock and reaches for it, Valentina's hand gently intervening.

Trinity manages a small *thank you* smile.

Resting her back against the wall, she draws both knees to her chest and through tired eyes watches Valentina take control.

Ten Million Reasons to Die

T rinity peeks at her watch through the silk veil: 16:00. Perspiration tickles her temple, her black mourning dress allowing little respite from the late afternoon heat. She notices only one police officer and his dog stationed near the entrance and with so many tourists arriving they don't look up as she and Hector enter the cemetery.

Strolling through the mishmash of streets and lanes, Trinity and Hector drift in and out of guided tours and groups of the bereaved. Taking a seat on a bench beneath a towering pine, a cooling breeze from the Rio de la Plata flutters her veil.

Having wandered the cemetery to ensure no one has been following her Trinity arrives at the entrance to the crypt containing her cache and goes through the same motions as the day before. She kneels on a pebble, grimaces and flicks it away, her eyes more interested in the new clues to her left.

Fresh flowers … but not the same type as yesterday.

And no cigarette butts.

Someone else has been here.

She stands and pauses, tugs on Hector's lead.

It's time to make like a ghost.

Inside the run-down crypt being used as a staging area, Trinity closes the door as far as the rusty hinges will allow. Stale air and the smell of cat piss sting her face.

Hector sneezes more than once.

Trinity lifts her veil and scans the dust-covered crypt; cat footprints the only sign of recent activity. A wrought-iron chair lies on its side near the door and some unused shelving is askew on one wall. Thick cobwebs hang from the ornate plaster ceiling. In one corner, a black hole devours small marble steps.

Trinity negotiates the stairs one careful sideways step at a time, her skull-crusher flashlight showing the way.

She feels a clumsy Hector brush against her heels.

Reaching the bottom, her circle of white light illuminates marble walls and a dusty wooden casket sitting atop a concrete base in the center of the room.

She swipes a spider's handiwork from a silver candelabrum before lighting its three well-used candles, the gentle glow from its flames filling the pitch-black crypt. Trinity reaches inside her mourning dress and removes her sword, placing it on top of the casket.

Hector's ears prick up.

Trinity squats and strokes his head, her eyes following his stare to the top of the staircase and to the soft tread of heavy boots. Rising, she snatches her blade and blows out the candles. As the sound of steady footsteps grow louder, she backs into the wall, her heart jackhammering against her ribcage in anticipation of a fight.

Fuck this!

Deciding to take the initiative in case the approaching boots belong to someone other than Valentina, and with Yamamoto's sword at the high-ready, Trinity steps from the wall and blips her flashlight in the hope of temporarily blinding the intruder should the need to run her sword through their chest arise.

Even in the dark, Trinity's eyes gleam.

'And you're certain no one followed you?'

'I'm positive,' Valentina whispers. 'I wandered around for almost an hour.'

Trinity is not afraid of the dark. She loves it. It's where she feels most comfortable and at home.

Hector's meaty-breath swamps her face.

She fumbles for his head and rubs behind his ears, hoping she hasn't dragged Valentina into something that will impact her new life with Jorge.

I'm glad Val's here; she's been a good friend for a long time.

It's nice to talk to someone who understands me ... well, somewhat anyway.

And at least she's been in the game.

Although I have to admit, I don't agree with everything she says.

Even though it is late in the afternoon, several hours must pass before it is dark enough for the two assassins to venture back outside and raid the weapons cache before returning here until the gates open in the morning. Until then, they must sit tight and battle to stay awake, waiting silently in the darkness below the crypt.

The fact she knows he's here makes her happy although she wishes he would come to her.

She knows he's watching.

She also knows what he likes ... what he wants ... what he needs.

One at a time, slowly, Trinity unbuttons her blouse exposing more and more of her ample flesh. Naked, her breasts hang in full view.

A patchwork of colored light from a nearby stained-glass window washes over her body.

She waits.

She knows he will come.

She knows he has no choice.

Before long, Trinity feels his comforting and healing warmth fill the room.

He no longer runs from her.

She watches his shadow move nearer: cautiously, but still … nearer.

She feels her heart pounding.

Her mouth opens.

She can hear her shallow breath.

His hand reaches from the shadow.

He whispers her name … 'Trinity' …

'Trinity … Trinity, wake up, it's time to go.'

Trinity opens her eyes.

Valentina gently tugs at her arm.

'You were asleep,' she whispers. 'It's a little after eight, it's time to get ready.'

Trinity sits up straight, her wide eyes staring across the room, her startled heart racing. The light from the candelabrum illuminates one side of her face.

'It's okay,' Valentina says, reassuring her, sensing Trinity's anxiety. 'You needed the rest more than I did.'

'Fuck. Okay. Let's do it.'

Valentina slips from her dowdy disguise, revealing her black figure-hugging, one-piece outfit. She closes her eyes and breathes deeply.

'I love the smell of leather.'

Trinity smiles, zips her catsuit tight and slings her sword over her shoulder.

'I'm good to go,' she says.

Valentina crouches beside Hector.

'Stay.'

Hector doesn't move.

The two assassins make their way up the staircase, Trinity the first to creep over to the entrance. She pauses and tilts her head - the drone of a light aircraft interrupts the eerie silence. She pulls the handle and the door creaks ajar. Trinity stops and listens some more before opening it wide and sticking her head outside.

A bluish hue bathes the cemetery, allowing her to see uninterrupted for quite some way. She looks both ways before darting to the shadows across the street and waits a moment before raising her hand.

Valentina keeps her head low and joins her in the dark.

Trinity points to her own eyes and then a tree, signalling to Valentina the location of her next bound. On Valentina's nod Trinity sets off, staying close to the neighboring mausoleum façades.

Valentina holds firm and checks over her shoulder.

Trinity takes a knee but as soon as she signals for Valentina to move, something makes her skin crawl. She swivels and raises her fist level with her head a warning for Valentina to halt and go low.

A black cat jumps from the roof of a mausoleum.

Trinity's head flops forward and her eyes briefly close. Looking up, she nods at Valentina to move. Returning her gaze to the front, Trinity reacts to Valentina's comforting tap on the shoulder.

She takes off, pushing forward to a T-section at the end of the street. Hugging the corner of a fading burial chamber, she looks left and right before again nodding.

Cloaked within the shadows, Trinity watches over the crypt containing her cache. This time she senses Valentina squat behind her and cover the rear. Looking down, she smiles as her playful friend reaches behind and fondles her breast.

Trinity slaps away the roving hand.

Valentina smiles to herself.

Making her move, Trinity skulks toward the crypt.

Valentina shuffles up to the corner and takes her place, covering her movements.

Other than the iron cross on the roof, lit by the moon's radiance, the front of the crypt is black. It's not until Trinity steps close to the door that she can make out the telltale skull and crossbones.

Twisting the doorknob, the stiff door creaks open.

She pauses before disappearing inside knowing Valentina is behind her providing security, scanning the shadows and both ends of the street.

Trinity's eyes adjust to the dark, and with the aid of moonlight flowing through the doorway, filling the crypt, she sees more marble, more cobwebs and not much else, not even a staircase to another level. Drawing her focus is a hexagonal mahogany coffin on an old wooden frame.

Like everything else inside the cemetery's many crypts and mausoleums, it has a generous coating of dust.

The quicker I get my shit and get out of here, the better.

Trinity leans outside and taps her watch signaling Valentina into the crypt, Valentina executing one final scan before moving.

Drawing her sword, Trinity prises open the coffin lid; the six-inch nails groan against the wood and the hinges lock into place, holding the lid up.

Merry Christmas!

Inside, where she left them five years ago, are her plastic bags filled with passports and cash, alongside boxes of ammunition, loaded magazines, shotguns, pistols and cell phones. Packed to one side are two grab-bags with easy-to-access outside pockets and rows of Velcro for attaching tactical pouches.

She slips one across her shoulder and passes the other to Valentina. Fossicking through the coffin, she smiles, hauls out a SPAS-12, glad to be reunited with the innovative and dual-mode shotgun.

If looks could kill then this beast is the Reaper.

Trinity throws the heavy, futuristic and evil-looking shotgun to Valentina, who catches it with both hands in front of her face.

She folds the stock onto the top of the receiver and smiles as two boxes of ammo also come her way. Ripping them open, she dumps the loose rounds into her grab-bag.

Trinity pulls out her Mossberg 590 pump-action shotgun. With a small bead for a front sight and a heat shield covering the 20-inch matte-black barrel, it contains nine rounds of 00 buck. Not quite reaching the rock star status of the SPAS-12 and second only in popularity to the Remington 870, the 590 is considerably lighter than both and comes with an ambidextrous safety, something the highly-skilled Trinity appreciates.

Breaking open a box of rounds, Trinity shoves two more shells into each side of the black, speed-feed synthetic stock and empties the remaining rounds along with a few more boxes of ammo into her grab-bag.

Valentina forms the shape of a pistol with her fingers.

Trinity slings the Mossberg over her shoulder and retrieves a Glock 21 from the coffin, along with three spare magazines.

Her fussy friend folds her arms and shakes her head.

Rolling her eyes, Trinity digs around some more inside the coffin before eventually passing Valentina a Smith and Wesson M&P 9-millimeter pistol.

This time Valentina smiles.

Trinity keeps the Glock and checks to see if it's loaded.

It is.

She shoves it into her belt and for good measure drops three bombed-up 14-round .45 mags into her grab-bag.

Reaching back into the coffin, she pulls out an old flip phone and the plastic bags containing cash and passports. She opens a side pocket of her grab-bag and secures them away inside. Before closing the coffin's lid, she looks inside one more time.

'Fuck it,' she whispers, snatching out an M-16.

Trinity removes the magazine and pulls back the bolt. Digging around inside the breach with her little finger, she feels the flat base of a bullet. The rifle has a round in the chamber and its curved mag a further 30-rounds of fifty-five grain full metal jacket .223 bullets.

More than halfway back to the staging area, where Hector patiently waits, Trinity and Valentina caterpillar across another street. Trinity goes first and blends into a shadow; beads of perspiration run down her cheek.

A black cat silently sprints up the middle of the road, as though the devil himself were chasing it. As quickly as it appears, it vanishes into the darkness. Trinity cautiously remains still. Seconds later, a Doberman runs past in hot pursuit. Trinity's eyes snap to Valentina, her attention focused toward the rear.

Trinity looks back to the dog.

Unable to catch the street-smart feline, the Doberman slows and stops just meters from Trinity. Picking up on her scent, the four-legged killer inches his way toward her; drool hangs from his fangs.

The hair on the back of his neck sticks up.

Still fearful of vicious dogs ever since her terrifying childhood encounter, Trinity is forced to steel her mind.

Again, her eyes turn to Valentina, who now watches, her shotgun poised, ready to fire. Trinity holds up her hand, hopeful of a far quieter outcome. She slowly reaches over her shoulder and draws her sword, the keen edge of the blade catching the full moon's soft blue light.

The devil-dog's snout enters the shadow in which Trinity hides; his red eyes burn with anger.

She stops breathing and doesn't blink as she readies herself to strike first. Without warning, her hand snatches at his black studded-collar.

The predator reacts, snapping at her wrist.

Drawing him close, her sword runs through his chest.

The Doberman pulls back his ears and yelps.

Trinity clamps his mouth shut, the powerful jaw trying to force itself open; drool runs through her fingers, down her forearm.

She waits a moment before removing her sword.

With little more than a whimper, his legs give way and he slumps to the ground in a rich, warm pool of blood.

Leaning her back against a small wall, she rests her forearms across her bent knees. Trinity takes in a mouthful of air. Beyond the rush of adrenalin, her gaze turns to the breathless hound lying on its side at her feet. She leans forward and strokes its flank. Trinity blinks, looks to Valentina and signals for her to move.

Valentina lowers her shotgun, and no sooner does she step onto the moonlit street, she turns her head.

Trinity watches in horror as two more Dobermans suddenly appear. Baring their teeth they lunge toward

Valentina and take hold. She desperately tries to stay on her feet because she knows if she goes to ground it could mean certain death.

But the dogs are too strong and they drag her down.

Concerned for her friend's safety, Trinity yells, 'No!'

Struggling to free herself, Valentina unintentionally lets off a round. The shotgun boom shatters the still night.

Well-trained and conditioned to fight under fire, the security dogs ignore the loud noise and plunge their canine teeth into her leg and arm.

They hold firm; Trinity fears they could tear her apart.

Valentina strikes their skulls with the shotgun's butt.

They barely flinch as the skin above their eyes split.

On the ground fighting for her life, this time she pulls the trigger but misses.

Trinity decides to break cover and moves to help her friend when something flashes by.

Bred to serve and to protect, to fight and to kill, and capable of great bursts of speed over short distances, 120 pounds of loyal Dogo Argentino hammers past Trinity. Lowering his head, Hector slams into the Dobermans like an out-of-control juggernaut. All three dogs helplessly roll across the paving, their rigid legs pointing in all directions.

'Valentina!' Trinity cries, desperate for feedback on her condition.

'I'm okay!' she yells back, looking down at her bleeding limbs.

Trinity makes it to the center of the street, but gunfire forces her to crouch with one palm flat to the pavement.

Valentina rolls to the gutter, her focus directed toward the shooting.

'Twenty meters,' she yells. 'Cops, near the corner!'

Trinity raises her M-16 and cracks off two rounds in their direction.

While scattering for cover, the police officers again fire their nine-millimeter semi-automatic pistols.

Hector is the first to regain his feet. Lunging at the closest Doberman's throat, he locks his giant jaw around its neck. The dog yelps and attempts to shake itself free, all four feet slipping across the pavement. Hector swings his head side to side, his teeth cutting deep, and with great strength he pins down the helpless dog with one of his paws.

The other Doberman attacks Hector, gnashing at his head before latching on with razor-sharp teeth. Hector refuses to let go and continues to thrash about.

Trinity looks over at Valentina sitting, leaning against a tree.

'Are you okay?'

'I'm good, I'm good. What now?'

'Can you get to me?'

'I'll try.'

Valentina rises to one knee and prepares to dash across the street, while Trinity shuffles into a firing position, tilting her head, her sideways glance awaiting the go-ahead.

Valentina nods.

Trinity's eyes shift to the front. She fires, the recoiling rifle jolting her shoulder three times.

Hector tears the throat from the Doberman, leaving it to bleed to death on the cobblestones. Flexing his shoulders, he shrugs off the other beast. Both Titans steady themselves before rising on their hind legs and snapping their jaws at each other. Entangled, both fall hard, fighting for supremacy, rolling, biting and clawing.

Unsteadily, Valentina steps out into the street, her arm and leg savaged. Bullets rip past and smash into the shrine behind her; marble and concrete chips spit everywhere.

She goes to ground.

Trinity spins around.

What the fuck!

Where the hell did that come from?

More marble explodes, small pieces striking Trinity's cheek, instantly drawing blood.

'Where the hell are they?' she cries, seeking guidance.

'Big tree ... thirty meters ... two, maybe three muzzle flashes,' Valentina yells, her SPAS-12 expelling two rounds, their powerful report adding to the confusion.

Trinity identifies the tree and joins in firing.

Taking advantage of the distraction, the police again fire their weapons trapping the two women in a partial cross fire.

Knowing they have to move quickly or face being over-run by superior numbers and firepower, Trinity fires multiple rounds in both directions and hollers, 'Valentina, go!'

Valentina picks herself up and hustles ten meters to a half-shaded mausoleum, slamming her shoulder against the door.

It's rusted shut.

She crouches down and brings the SPAS-12 up to eye level. Unfolding the stock, she digs it into her shoulder and pushes the fore-grip forward, her finger pressing the selector switch to semi-automatic.

'Trinity, go!'

Trinity heads for a large tombstone leaning to one side. Once there, she hits the ground hard and rolls onto her back. The M-16 rests across her chest and the shotgun digs into her kidneys. She breathes hard and fast, her face awash with sweat and dirt. The comforting sound of the SPAS-12 unleashing hell in the background buys her time to catch her breath.

Several rounds later, Valentina's shotgun runs out of ammo.

Trinity's ears ring loud in the unexpected quiet. She moves to one knee and provides covering fire for Valentina, two and three-round bursts in both directions. The bright flash from the muzzle lights up her contorted face and bared teeth.

Valentina sits with her back against the door. On both her flanks are tall statues of angels, providing cover from her adversaries. She pulls a handful of shotgun rounds from her grab-bag and quickly loads them.

Trinity's M-16 stops firing; she can feel the impulse of the bolt locking back against her cheek. Having trained extensively with the weapon and after using it so often over the years, she's confident it's empty, and with no spare mags, she doesn't bother to check.

She throws the rifle on the ground.

Rather than slinging the big shotgun around into action, she draws the Glock .45 from her belt and continues to provide suppressive fire, keeping the cops at bay.

Valentina actions her shotgun and re-enters the fight, sending a twelve-gauge round toward the police. The booming noise echoes across the cemetery and beyond its protective walls.

'We have to fall back, Trinity!'

'Say again!'

'I said we have to fall back! We have to move!'

'I know!'

'I'll delay their movements,' Valentina yells. 'You make it back to the rendezvous.'

'Okay,' Trinity shouts over the sound of gunfire. 'Two minutes! Two minutes only!'

'I'll be there. Go now!'

The SPAS-12 erupts.

Trinity springs to her feet and runs toward the street corner.

This is so fucked-up!

She rounds the corner at full pace, her body leaning to one side, Cristo El Redentor within view. She sprints past the mausoleums and the curious cats, her hand reaching around to prevent the slung shotgun from swinging about.

A large male, dressed in black, steps from the shadows of a small lane, his cut-down double-barrel shotgun levelled at Trinity.

Killers!

She recognises him as one of the men locals call *Killers*. Desperate men, ugly men—mentally unstable men—some forced and some choosing to live on the often unclean, volatile streets of Buenos Aires. They cheat, they lie … they steal and they kill, with whatever means are available to them, for whatever small gains they may make: food, clothes, money … especially money. Money buys them paco, a cheap cocaine paste for a violent, two-minute high.

Having ten million reasons to kill makes a Killer very dangerous.

Trinity doesn't stop running, but does ask a lot of her Glock and rattles off half a dozen 230-grain full metal jackets. Four of them miss wildly but two don't; one nicks the Killer's right shoulder, the other hits just below his left eye. Like a marionette with its strings cut, the Killer collapses. Trinity checks over her shoulder.

Come on Valentina.

Entering the roundabout, Trinity slides into position. She looks to her G-SHOCK and starts the countdown.

Two minutes.

Before switching out the Glock for her Mossberg shotgun, she tactically reloads her pistol with a full magazine. Two slow-moving shadows slice across her peripheral vision.

KA-BOOM, roars the Mossberg, punching into her shoulder, jarring her fingers on the trigger … KA-BOOM!

Two figures slump from the shadows; their spilled blood flows across the moonlit paving.

Trinity has good fields of fire. She can see in all directions the streets and lanes that lead to the roundabout. Her weapon remains shouldered with her uncompromising stare fixed across the top of the front sight. Seeing nothing, she takes the opportunity to replace the rounds fired, inserting them from underneath, never once shifting her gaze.

Incoming rounds hit the statues behind her, sending chunks of marble in all directions. Instinctively hunching her shoulders, she struggles to make out the shooter's exact location through the dust and low light, but her experience tells her where that might be.

She fires a deliberate burst of two rounds.

The first strikes the paving some thirty meters in front while the trajectory of the second remains no more than twelve inches above the ground.

Prone, in a shallow gutter to one side of the street, a police officer catches a face full of rubble and some shrapnel kicked up from the first round. Confused, he sits up, only to be struck in the groin by several pellets from the second.

Bullets from another direction strike the ground close to Trinity. Swinging the shotgun around, she returns fire. The flash from her muzzle makes it difficult for her to locate where the shots are coming from.

This is fucked!

She checks her watch.

One minute.

As fast as she loads more rounds, the Mossberg eats them up. Trinity holds her ground but knows that without Valentina's help, it won't be for long.

Her watch alarm sounds.

Trinity rapid-fires rounds in each direction. Hauling in the shotgun, she jumps up and runs toward the entrance.

Bullets chase, but fall short every time.

Another shirtless, grubby-looking Killer runs from the shadows, his hands filled with knives.

Trinity point-shoots the shotgun from her hip.

He doubles over, his stomach torn apart, entrails spilling in a bloody, twisted mess.

Trinity rushes past him and detects movement atop a marble tomb: another dark figure stands and raises his rifle. She extends one arm and fires a desperate shot, the heavily recoiling shotgun straining her wrist.

Lead pellets wreck his leg; he drops his rifle and clutches at his bleeding knee.

Trinity looks ahead - two more Killers stand between her and the gate. She brings her weapon to bear and pulls the trigger, the hammer falling on an empty chamber to the terrifying sound of *the dead man's click.*

Fuck!

She decides against transitioning to the Glock: the shotgun will be more effective at this longer range and whilst moving. Her hand reaches into the grab-bag for more ammo; some rounds fall from her grasp.

Trinity closes ground on the Killers fast as they aim their beaten-up, bolt-action hunting rifles at her and fire. She flinches to passing bullets, her sweaty fingers fumbling to get a round into the magazine tube.

'Come on!'

Out of the corner of her eye, she unexpectedly sees Hector running alongside her, his tongue flopping from his mouth. He turns his head to look at her before powering onward.

Reacting to the additional threat of the charging dog, the Killers drag their barrels down toward him. Bullets ricochet off the paving next to his paws.

Trinity, her eyes focused ahead, eventually loads and works the slide back and forth.

Hector launches himself and knocks one of the Killers to the ground, gnashing at his face and neck. The other one looks at his rifle and works the bolt to the rear, but it sticks and won't go forward.

Trinity raises her weapon.

The Killer bashes the bolt forward with his palm, forcing an old military surplus bullet into the chamber, and points his rifle at the dog's head.

Trinity howls, 'No!'

Hector looks up and bares his bloody fangs, the pure-white skin around his muzzle stained red.

Trinity pulls the trigger sending nine copper-coated lead pellets hurtling through the air. She watches the Killer's rifle lift. The sound of its blast takes away her breath.

Blood and bone fragments explode outwards from the Killer's head.

He and his piece-of-shit rifle hit the deck.

Hector yelps.

Trinity storms up to the two Killers, draws her sword and with no concern for her own safety stands over them, screaming, and stabbing at their torsos. Both men are dead, but her frenzy continues, blood covering the paving, the blade and her hands. Leaning on her sword firmly wedged between two ribs, she gasps for air.

Hector whimpers.

Trinity stomps her boot on the dead man's chest and reefs the sword free.

She turns to Hector. Crouching down beside him she lifts his heavy head onto her lap.

'I'm sorry, so sorry, Hector.'

His tail wags a little.

She strokes the short hair on his head.

'It's okay, big boy, just rest.'

Blood leaks from a hole beneath the fur on his rising chest.

Everything good in my life either dies or disappears.

What's the point?

Hector releases one final breath through his nostrils. His eyes close and his tongue slides from his mouth.

Trinity tenses every muscle in her body. Leaning forward she presses her head against Hector's and squeezes his limp body.

Living on the run for three years, and now this brave dog across her knees, Trinity's blood pressure elevates; her heart and head pound madly. The buildup behind her eyes is immense; closing them relieves some of the stress.

Sitting up with Hector's head across her lap, Trinity's breathing becomes more rapid and her chest tightens.

Her face and neck heat up; the skin across her back flushed as her core body temperature rises. Unzipping the tight leather sleeve covering her forearm, she peels it back, revealing many scars.

Reaching for her sword, the fine edge slices her skin; blood surges down her arm. Trinity sits back on her heels and lowers her head, black hair falling about her face. Her blood pressure drops and a sense of relief overcomes her.

For Trinity, pain is more than just her friend and

companion; it's more like a big brother … a guardian.

It does not judge her.

Trinity relaxes her breathing and the pounding inside her head subsides. She opens her eyes and stares through a mess of hair.

I don't know how much more I can take … or lose.

The sound of a gunshot shifts her mind back into gear. Grabbing her sword and shotgun, she runs toward the front gate.

Screaming bullets fill the air.

Police sirens wail.

Trinity thumbs a round into the shotgun and blows apart the lock, kicking the gate open with her boot. Turning to take one last look at Hector, she dissolves into the darkness beyond.

Killing Time

The full moon sits high in the late-night sky. As per their plan, Trinity sits off not far from the gigantic rubber tree; the acrid scent from its milky, white sap irritates her eyes. She observes the area around the tree's base from the safety of the shadows at the nearby closed café, situated at the corner of Quintana and Ortiz.

There is a colorful park bench and large garbage bin, but no sign of Valentina, or anyone else for that matter.

Content the area is secure, Trinity creeps up to the wrought-iron fence that surrounds the thick tree trunk. Dropping to one knee and from a slightly elevated position, she looks down over the plaza.

Several matte-black four-wheel-drive vehicles arrive, rooftop lights flickering, headlamps beaming. Emblazoned in large blue letters across their rear doors are the letters GEOF: Grupo Especial de Operaciones Federales -

(Federal Police Special Operations Group).

Tagged '4T' (todo tiempo ... todo terreno: all time ... all land) GEOF was formed in 1998 to deal with counterterrorism and hostage situations far beyond the scope of daily policing within the city.

In a country plagued with a long history of corruption coupled with a burgeoning list of diverse police and security agencies, GEOF stands tall, beyond reproach in its endeavours to fight the deathless battle against extremists, dishonest politicians and increasing crime.

Bullets emerge from within the cemetery causing GEOF assaulters to take cover and return fire. Quick off the mark, one of them, clad in black and wearing a helmet and a skull-face mask, mans the vehicle-mounted .50 caliber machine gun. Embroidered across his shoulder is a condor grasping within its talons an M-16 and trident.

A twitch of his finger ends the fight, the brief cadence of loud bullets resonating beyond the plaza.

Trinity glances at her watch: 21:10.

Where in the fuck are you Val?

Hurry up.

Trinity sits beneath the tree and removes a boot. Peeling off her sock, she tightly wraps it around her bleeding forearm; a pang causes her to clamp her teeth together. Zipping up the leather sleeve holds the sock in place, compressing the wound, stemming the flow of blood.

Fuck!

Now that these guys are here ...

... shit is going to hit the fan.

I've heard the GEOF are ruthless.

Loud voices draw her attention back to the GEOF.

The federal police heavy-hitters stream through the gates and into the cemetery.

Trinity hears random bursts of small-arms fire and the unshackled thunder of a shotgun. The ensuing silence is painful as she sits waiting, not knowing if Valentina is alive or not.

Minutes later, she watches as GEOF assaulters casually return to their vehicles, satisfied weapons resting calmly by their sides or across their broad shoulders.

The men laugh and smile.

Trinity again checks her watch. Rubbing her face, the reality that Valentina may not have made it out of the cemetery, sinks its claws into her chest.

More loud voices carry across the plaza.

Looking up and over the open space, Trinity watches as an assaulter escorts a Killer out through the gates and into the glare of a 4WD's headlamps.

The Killer doesn't struggle.

Thrown to his knees, he pleads for mercy. Holding up two fingers he first points inside the cemetery and then back outside into the darkness.

The assaulters look in Trinity's direction. A spirited discussion erupts before several scramble inside their vehicles.

Fuck!

I have to get out of here. Now!

Trinity pulls on her boot.

A gunshot rings out.

She looks up and sees the Killer lying face down.

From within the shadows cast by the tall, white marble columns atop the steps of Universidad de Buenos Aires Abogacía, Trinity looks across the empty parking lot at a resplendent monument: Floralis Genérica. Glimmering in the moonlight, the giant stainless-steel flower with its six petals rises an angular seventy-five feet toward the sky, high above the surrounding four acres of manicured grass and trees and the protective reflection pool at its base.

Waiting out the hour in case Valentina makes the rendezvous window, Trinity slinks even further into the darkness, her eyes following two GEOF vehicles patroling nearby Avenida Figueroa Alcorta.

A lifetime of killing: it's all I've ever been good at.

I've missed out on so much. A real family, my childhood, true love. Halo ... Gabriel.

I want it to stop. I want it to stop now.

If I get through this ... when I get through this ... I want to leave it all behind, start afresh, never kill again.

Be normal.

Huh! Normal.

Trinity rummages through her grab-bag and swaps out the partially depleted mag from her Glock pistol with a fresh one full of bullets, then tops up the half-empty mag. Scooping a handful of shotgun rounds, she stuffs them into the magazine tube of the Mossberg until no more will fit.

She rips open the remaining two boxes and dumps them into the bag. After checking her watch, she again looks across at the sculpture.

Sirens wail through the city streets.

I swear, if anything has happened to Valentina, I'll fucking kill everyone.

I should never have involved her.

She has her own life now, outside of this fucked-up world I still live in.

And I knew she did, yet I still let her come along.

I want to fucking scream!

Sitting with her knees in front of her face, the shotgun held vertically between them, Trinity rocks back and forth, her eyes shut tight. She bottles her emotions perilously deep inside. And although her frustration levels may be danger-ously high, her senses are electric.

The hair on the back of her neck stands up.

She opens her eyes.

A dark shadow moves from behind a column.

Trinity rolls onto her back as a crowbar swings past her head, flicking her hair. Using her foot, she sweeps the Kil-ler's leg out from underneath him, sending him crashing on to his back. Springing to her feet, she muscles her shotgun by the barrel and wields it like an axe, splitting his skull in two.

More Killers rush from the dark.

Trinity tees off on the closest one's chin, the impact of the synthetic stock making a strange cracking noise. She watches him spin around and keel over, knocked out cold. Jumped from behind by his companion, she stumbles and together they fall entwined to the ground, rolling down sev-eral marble steps.

Trinity throws out her arms and they come to a stop.

Looking up at him sitting over her, she gasps as his un-clean, jagged fingernails slash her cheek. Trinity's fist splits his top lip, squirting dirty blood into her eyes. Temporarily blinded, she frantically wipes them clear.

The Killer takes advantage of the distraction and at-tempts to strangle her.

Through murky eyes, she sees the wild animal lean in close, baring what few black and broken teeth he has.

If I catch a disease you piece-of-shit, I'm gonna be really fucking pissed!

Trinity strikes his throat with the heel of her palm and he yelps like a wounded dog. She takes in a gulp of air and bucks him off. Drawing her Glock, she uses it to hammer the bridge of his nose into his brain, blood pooling around his eye sockets, splashing across her face.

Although arduous and messy attempting to crack the rigid bone, she'd rather beat him to death than fire her gun and alert the police and other Killers to her whereabouts.

Having been separated from her shotgun during the struggle, Trinity makes her way back to the top of the steps to retrieve it, scooping up rounds that fell from her grab-bag along the way. Trinity nears the top when she notices a shadow move from one column to another.

She stops; many more shadows catch her eye.

Fuck!

Leaping several steps at a time, she attempts to get to the shotgun before anyone else.

A Killer scrambles from the shadows and reaches for the weapon, but Trinity stamps her boot on the barrel, pinning it to the ground. He looks up at her and hisses.

She looks down at him through the sights of her gun.

Fuck this shit!

The gun recoils in her hand as the forty-five loads another round into the chamber; blood sprays her legs, chunks of brain exit the back of his head.

During the commotion, Trinity lost track of all the Killers, but it matters not now, as they rush at her from all sides. Pivoting back and forth, her foot never steps off the shotgun.

The Model 21 Glock spits out bullets until the magazine is empty and all the Killers are dead.

Hot, empty cases spin and bounce along the ground.

Trinity reloads and scans with her gun from side to side. Unable to see any more attackers through the smoke and the dark, she picks up the shotgun and slings it over her shoulder.

Even if Valentina was coming here, after that little shit-fight, she'd turn right around and head straight for Harrods.

I know I would.

Trinity hugs the bushes and the safety of their shadows, following the chain-link fence that separates her from the railway lines leading in and out of Retiro Railway Station. The looming giant overpass makes her nervous. With no option but to pass underneath, she approaches with caution and monitors a lone cartonero, the only other person in sight.

He pushes his rickety yellow carro overloaded with neatly flattened-out cardboard boxes, like so many others forced by the country's steady economic decline to make a living by scavenging and recycling the waste of others. His gray mustache matches the color of his baseball cap and — not by design — complements his black-and-white checked shirt.

Trinity makes her way from the bushes and saunters past the old man, and despite his obvious sore back and weathered knees, he manages a smile, caring not who the pretty girl in blood-soaked leather is or why she carries a shotgun and sword.

His plight is his own, and so is hers.

Trinity awkwardly smiles back. Looking ahead, she slowly runs from the glare of the overpass toward the octagonal copper roof of Torre de los Ingleses: Tower of the English.

Two hundred and fifty feet high, built from imported white Portland stone and red brick, the enormous clock tower—a gift from English expatriates—has kept correct time for the trains of Buenos Aires for the better part of ten decades.

Trinity looks across the plaza in front of the railway station to the clock tower: 21:55. She turns to look back toward the overpass, where the ever-optimistic cartonero places one foot in front of the other.

A car's headlamps come into view.

Trinity melts into a small shadow near the station's wall. As the car approaches, heading in the opposite direction, a black GEOF 4WD patrols the avenue.

Once the vehicles have passed, Trinity emerges from her concealment and makes a break for it, sprinting across a dozen deserted lanes and entering the grounds of Plaza San Martín.

Unfurled above the nearby trees, a triband flag flaps in the strong wind: two strips of light blue and one of white, with the yellow Sun of May in the center.

Fuck!

Idiot!

She'd forgotten. That when arranging the final meeting place at Harrods, the Plaza San Martín overlooks the Monumento a los caídos en Malvinas, a curved, walled memorial dedicated to the Argentine soldiers who died in the Falklands War. Ironically, perhaps deliberately, it faces across the avenue and toward the English tower, and is guarded around the clock every day of the year by the proud nation's armed forces.

Trinity keeps to the sidewalk surrounding the plaza and bounds from tree to tree up its steep slope. Nearing the top, beyond notice of the memorial's heavily-armed sentinels, she steps over a small wire fence to enter an open space. Cutting across the grass, she negotiates a veritable minefield of dog shit.

To her right, the bronze figure of General José de San Martín sits astride his reared mount.

Trinity makes for the shadows of the nearby giant ombú. One of three hundred and fifty trees within the plaza, this one offers by far the most protection with its long-reaching branches and substantial girth. To her surprise, numerous homeless persons sleep beneath its leafy shelter, stretched out along park benches and curled up on the grass with nothing more than memories, hopes and dreams to help keep them warm.

She rests upon a small, stone wall that surrounds the base of the tree. Leaning back against the wrought-iron fence with her shotgun across her lap, she stares across the road at Edificio Kavanagh, a slender, tapering, Art Deco residential skyscraper. Beside it is the Plaza Hotel. Trinity admires the decorative façade of the elegant, boutique hotel.

Interrupting Trinity's view, an old man wearing mis-matched shoes, torn, loose pants and a ragged coat, steps from the darkness and moves toward her. She flicks off the safety on her shotgun and glances at his hands grasping a plastic bottle.

She then studies his craggy face.

For Trinity, it's like reading a book – a tragic tale.

His deep-set eyes, with heavy bags underneath them, clutch to a dwindling spark within.

He once cared for others.

Chiselled wrinkles down his cheeks and across his forehead.

Not the scars of battle, but the result of reminiscing for too long about a life now long past.

Gray messy hair sprouts beneath his cap.

This is a man who needs nothing more than that which will get him through the night.

She makes her gun safe and stands.

The man with few possessions extends his battered, bear-like hand and crinkled, half-full plastic water bottle.

Trinity looks at the half-empty container.

'Gracias,' she says, taking a sip before handing it back.

Again, he pushes it toward her.

This time she drinks it all, and he smiles. Returning the bottle, she squeezes his hand with her fingers and reaches into her bag. She pulls out a hundred dollar bill and offers it to him.

He clenches the bottle.

She again offers, but the old man simply smiles, turns and walks away.

The ombús' mighty branches extend over the uneven sidewalk that runs parallel with Calle Florida. Trinity takes advantage of the tree's protection and moves to the edge of the shadows. Yellow ambient light from the four large decorative globes of a nearby lamp-post softens the darkness.

She waits a moment before crossing to the other side of the street. Once there, she stays close to the buildings' ornate façades, passing several gigantic doors of intricate steel and impenetrable timber. Turning a corner, Trinity opts for the smaller, darker backstreets.

A little further on, she approaches an intersection. On

one side of the road, is a taxi with its hood propped open. The driver tinkers with the engine.

Nearer to a crosswalk, a man too poor to own a mule drags his own carro laden with garbage-filled plastic bags. Rotten refuse lines the streets, most of it bagged, but piled so high Trinity cannot see over or around it.

A homeless man is asleep on the cluttered sidewalk, cardboard his bed, a white plastic bag filled with paper, his pillow.

Trinity maneuvers around the rubbish and then back to within the shadows, moving along another wall, down another street.

Like the old man in the park, Trinity thinks, the aged walls of the backstreets of Buenos Aires tell a story … a story of two cities: one, a beautiful city rich in its colonial and artistic past, the other, a city suffering from economic and political uncertainty.

The towering wall next to Trinity is awash in legalised graffiti: political slogans, anti-commercialism ideals and anti-American messages. Across the street, an epic, elaborate black-and-white stencil of a post-apocalyptic Buenos Aires.

I love the way this city not only permits but encourages its citizens to freely express their thoughts on any subject, on any wall.

She passes by a public telephone plastered with stickers of a voluptuous blond woman, blatantly advertising a gentlemen's club. Beyond the phone box, a corrugated iron roller door is pasted over with dozens of posters featuring local bands and musicians.

Trinity looks up at the grimy shell of a building, unoccupied since closing its doors fifteen years ago. Occupying the adjacent block, is the seven story high, Belle Époque department store: Harrods.

Trinity remembers the first time Yamada brought her to the distant and muddy shores of Buenos Aires for her 16th birthday, her Oya-kata introducing her to the fine tastes and opulence of the popular London namesake: cream tea in the grand salon, ice cream in the parlor ... shopping for a new hunting rifle.

Crossing the street to a small loading dock where overflowing dumpsters conceal her from view, Trinity squeezes past them to stand before a dented and locked roller door. Drawing her sword, she runs it through the lock before pulling up the heavy door. Once inside, she lowers it back down.

It's dark inside the abandoned store, but gentle lunar light filters through the graffiti-covered, unwashed glass of numerous giant arched windows. Lengthy white drapes make it difficult to see inside, offering a medium level of privacy for Trinity.

With little fear of detection, Trinity freely wanders the vast empty areas of this forgotten place, touching some of the square, timber-clad pillars that support the decorative ceilings with their dusty chandeliers.

She makes her way across the cedar flooring to one end of a hall and stands in front of an ornate, bevelled mirror. Brushing away a layer of dust reveals detailed cut-glass underneath. Trinity's long hair is messy, and splashes of dried blood cover her face. She picks off the blood, wipes her face clean with her hand and fixes her hair the best she can.

Everywhere I look I see nothing but death, blood, misery.

My life.

I should have let Valentina kill me and collect the reward money.

Nobody would miss me.

What the fuck have I got to look forward to?

More death?

More misery?

And not just for me, but for everybody I come into contact with.

Unable to stand her reflection any longer, she turns from the mirror and approaches the grand marble staircase in the middle of the room. She runs her hand along the timber balustrade as she ascends, then, standing at the top, brushes the dust from her fingers.

More vastness and more emptiness greet her.

Walking over to the window, she leans her forehead against the glass, her tired eyes staring at the sidewalk below.

Hopefully I can remain here, as planned, until dark tomorrow night.

If Valentina isn't here by then, I'll have to leave.

Where to? ... I don't know.

I'm slowly running out of places to hide and people to trust.

Maybe Valentina was right. Maybe I need to stop running. Maybe I don't even have a choice.

Finding and killing The Russian won't be easy ... maybe even impossible, probably suicidal ...

Yeah.

Suicidal.

Trinity turns around and slides her back down the window. Sitting on the floor, cradling her shotgun across her chest, she rests her head against its barrel. Before long, she falls into a deep sleep.

She smells him.

He's nearby.

She stands, closes her eyes and listens carefully.

He steps softly and moves up behind her; he's never been this close before.

She wants to turn around, but doesn't. She wants him to feel comfortable, to come even closer.

And he does.

The hair on the back of her neck stands; her tender skin prickles.

His breath warms her neck.

He reaches around and places his hands gently over her breasts.

She was right.

She knew exactly what he wanted.

They all want it.

They can't help but want it.

He unbuttons her blouse and pushes the sheer fabric aside.

Her legs weaken and begin to buckle. She desperately wants to turn and face him. She wants to know who he is; it kills her not to know.

Taking hold of her naked breasts, his fingers lightly press into the flesh.

She leans her head back, keeps her eyes closed.

He runs his fingers around her nipples and then down her stomach.

Shuffling her feet spreads her legs apart. She wants him inside … she needs him inside.

His finger enters her.

A lone tear rolls from Trinity's eye down her cheek and on to her lips.

She can taste it.

More follow.

She can't help it.

He slides his finger in and out.

She gently breathes.

He wraps his hand around her neck.

Her legs quiver with pleasure and she slumps into his arms.

Slowly he pulls back.

She hears his footsteps move further and further away.

She desperately wants to turn and follow, but she can't move her legs.

Trinity sits up in a cold sweat, her heart beating out of control, her throat dry. She looks down at her chest; her breasts are exposed and the skin between her legs feels wet and sticky.

What the fuck?

What just happened?

She stands and zips up her catsuit, tugging at the leather between her thighs.

What is wrong with me?

Trinity turns to the sounds of footsteps.

She stops what she's doing and listens, quietly.

Going prone, her shotgun at the ready, she lies motionless, her racing heart pressing against the unforgiving wooden floorboards.

The window casts a dull light across the room, and all the way to the marble staircase. Shadows from the huge window frame criss-cross the floor.

Trinity spots a dark figure slowly shifting from the top of the staircase and into the open area.

She blinks more than once.

Peering across the room, squinting in the low light, a lock of hair falls across her face; she gently blows it aside and presses her finger against the trigger, taking up the slack, ready to fire.

The wraithlike shadow turns and slowly approaches her.

Trinity levels her shotgun, the outline of the small bead at the end of the barrel blotting out half the intended target. Her heart rate increases and her elbows threaten to slide apart on the wooden floor, shifting her point of aim.

The shadow stops.

Trinity makes out the dark outline of a hand raising a gun in the air.

'Valentina?'

'Trinity?'

'I was worried you hadn't made it out alive,' Trinity breathes, jumping to her feet. 'I feared the worst. I thought you were dead.'

'For a moment back there I didn't think I was going to make it either!'

The two friends embrace, soaking up the peace and quiet. Valentina slowly releases her hold.

'What of Hector?' she says, her brow raised, her stare digging deep into Trinity's eyes.

Trinity stares back and pauses.

'He's dead. He died protecting me. There was nothing I could do.'

Valentina lowers her eyes and sighs, then looks up, clenching her teeth to hold back her anger.

'I would expect nothing less from Hector,' she says.

Trinity strokes Valentina's hair.

Another footstep from the staircase travels quickly across the open floor.

Trinity steps around Valentina and swings her shotgun into play.

'It's okay,' Valentina says, pushing the barrel toward the floor. 'It is only Jorge.'

'What the fuck is he doing here?'

'After I escaped the cemetery I had no choice but to call him. I could not follow you, it was too dangerous.'

'That wasn't the plan!'

'Is okay, Trinity, I trust Jorge as much as you trust me.'

Trinity keeps her finger on the trigger as Jorge slowly steps toward them, his hands in the air.

Valentina touches his cheek.

A little nervous, and still unsure off his intentions, Trinity's hands squeeze her shotgun.

'Show her,' Valentina says.

Jorge carefully lifts his shirt and slowly turns.

'See,' Valentina says with a smile, 'there are no concealed weapons, only his tight stomach and muscles.'

Trinity removes her finger from the trigger.

Valentina glances at Jorge, smiles and sighs. She turns to Trinity and asks, 'What now?'

Trinity hoists the shotgun over one shoulder. With her other hand, she rubs her brow.

'I need to move on,' she says quietly. 'I have everything I need now to keep traveling for a little while.'

'Where will you go?'

'I've decided to take your advice.'

Valentina smiles.

'I'm going to find The Russian and end all this shit.'

'I will come with you.'

'No!'

'And why not?'

'No, Valentina. You have a life here with Jorge. I should never have gotten you involved. You have what I want, and I'm not going to let anyone take that away from you.'

'Let me help you!'

Jorge steps up alongside Valentina and nods.

'It's not happening,' Trinity says firmly.

'How will you find him?'

'You said Halo was working in the Middle East?'

'Yes, mostly in Dubai and Abu Dhabi.'

'Then that's where I'm heading. I guess I have to start somewhere. Hopefully his contacts can help me uncover news as to Gabriel's fate and The Russian's whereabouts. Do you know exactly where he is working?'

'I do not. But I should be able to find out. I will keep you updated. Are you certain Halo will assist? You have broken his heart many times … maybe once too often?'

Trinity thinks carefully before answering.

'Halo will do anything for me,' she says with a wry smile.

'For your sake I hope so. When will you leave?'

'Sooner, rather than later.'

'The police will be watching the airport.'

'You're right. I need something to distract them.'

'Then let Jorge and I do that for you.'

'Are you sure?'

Valentina's eyes light up.

'Yes! We will make much noise near La Casa Rosada. I hear the president is currently in residence. We will attract attention very quickly.'

'Please be careful.'

'Do not concern yourself. There's a freight train that departs Retiro Station twice a week for Guayaquil, Ecuador. I've used it before to smuggle certain items in and out of Argentina. You should be able to fly out from there with no difficulties. Money talks loudly up that way.'

Trinity smiles, 'So when is the next train departing?'

DUBAI

City in the Sky

Trinity breaks away from the late-afternoon rush to rest in the shade beneath the rustling fronds of a tall palm tree, one of many that line the busy Mohammed Bin Rashid Boulevard.

It's from there she observes locals, ex-pats and tourists all bustle their way across salmon-colored marble pavement, up and over eight lanes of traffic to the futuristic Burj Dubai Metro railway station.

Peering through a small slit in the fabric of her niqab, its soft silky cloth shields her head and face from a gritty haze. A lengthy black traditional abaya, like that of the other women nearby, hides Trinity's voluptuous body. No one pays her any attention.

A developing low pressure area, hundreds of miles across the border in Saudi Arabia, has sent strong southwesterly winds sweeping through the desert, stirring-up the sand and dust that now envelopes Downtown Dubai.

Trinity strains her neck and looks up at the Burj Khalifa. The veritable city in the sky is both the world's tallest building and its tallest man-made structure, a record previously held for almost four millennia by the Great Pyramid of Giza. Coating the building's façade in bright orange, dying rays from the retiring sun—tinted caramel from the desert's haze—bounce off the 830 meter high tower's reflective glazing and stainless-steel panels.

The unique, throaty sound of a twin turbo-charged 6.7-liter 500-horsepower engine catches Trinity's attention. A midnight-black Bentley Mulsanne, similar to one once owned by her deceased master, Yamada, enters a huge traffic circle.

Trinity spears her stare toward the number plate.

Less than three digits.

He must be important ... rich ... most likely related to one of the royal families.

Her eyes track the mammoth yet elegant car as it slowly loops around the circle and its dancing water jets. Squinting, she studies the smokey-colored bullet-resistant windows. Rated to stop three closely-placed high-caliber .308 Winchester rounds, the two-and-a-half-inch-thick laminated glass also prevents Trinity's angel-blue eyes from prying.

The street-legal tank exits the circle, rumbling up a curved driveway lined with hedges on one side and a wall of oil-soaked timber slats on the other.

Trinity strolls up a concrete pathway that cuts its way through a maze of manicured hedges and a light spread of trees. At a distance safe enough to make out what is happening up ahead, but far enough away so as to not draw attention to herself, she stops to enjoy a carpet of honey-sweet alyssum. Her eyes lift as a hulking North African security guard exits his security booth.

Standing beside the boom gate, he takes one look at the number plate and motions for the barrier to rise.

The Bentley rolls through and around to the right, pulling up outside the entrance to the Armani Hotel and alongside a black Audi and gray convertible Maserati.

While enjoying the fragrant garden, Trinity's eyes look to the stoney-faced, solid-framed man dressed in a black suit exiting the vehicle, grinding his teeth.

He wears his war face well.

He closes the door and for a moment remains by the car. Swivelling his head from side to side his trained eyes look for something, anything out of place. He drifts from the vehicle to meet the approach of his modern-day Nubian-warrior counterpart, one of three security guards posted outside the hotel.

They shake hands and exchange words.

He nods, walks away and enters the hotel doors located beneath a small, curved over-hanging roof, the orange glow from its flushed lights complementing the dusk ambience.

A short time later, he emerges and stands off to one side of the door, his back against a wall of glass blocks, his gaze projected outwards.

Trinity recognizes the significance behind the gentle nod of his head, her eyes darting to the Bentley's rear passenger-side door.

Halo, dressed in a shiny, fitted, black suit, emerges from the back seat, taller and wider than his colleague.

His presence detonates the air around him.

All three of the Nubians widen their eyes.

A stylishly dressed female guest distracted by Halo, trips over the curb.

Exiting the hotel, a group of Emirati men clothed in traditional long white kandura's and sandals, cut short their conversation and stare at him standing firm by the car as he soaks up the atmosphere of his surroundings.

Halo pushes the car door closed; his fingers prevent it from shutting. He waits for the men to move on, tracking one in particular: the only one not wearing traditional headwear. Instead, the man sports a John Deere trucker's hat.

Halo knows this is not unusual - he's seen anomalies like this in Muslim countries before, especially in the mega-wealthy UAE. But he does question the man's mind-set and wants to be sure he poses no threat before allowing his Principal out of the car.

He watches the Emiratis say their goodbyes.

John Deere jumps into the Maserati and speeds off; the others wander down the driveway.

Halo's inquisitive eyes question everything, even the guards' style of dress, from the quality of their shoes to the cut of their suits. He studies the buttons on their jackets, citing in his mind a simple mantra he learned to help with the complexities of etiquette as part of his personal protection training … *sometimes, always, never.*

For confirmation on the guards' level of training and a simple cross-check of their authenticity, his focus shifts to the tie and the Four in Hand dimple knot correctly looped through the top, left then right … just as he was taught.

Nodding with approval, he scans within his bubble and turns to face the car door. He motions with his hand, directing his Principal to exit.

The Principal's kandura is noticeably longer than the other Emiratis, a sign of eminence. He does not wear a trucker's hat.

Halo shuts the door and escorts his VIP toward the hotel entrance.

His partner times it perfectly and peels away from his post to enter mere seconds ahead of the Principal with Halo following diagonally behind.

Trinity has seen enough and heads back down the pathway.

It's always good to see Halo.

He looks great.

But if I know Halo … and I do … what he shows on the outside doesn't always reflect what's on the inside.

A fine spray of water from the nearby dancing water jets sprinkles across her eyes.

I hope he's not still pissed off over Tokyo.

I guess I'll find out later tonight.

Stairway to the Stars

Trinity drops 400 dirham on the counter to receive her immediate-entry pass. She overtakes a lengthy line brimming with tourists. A female attendant punches the golden ticket and escorts her directly to the elevator. Once inside, she shares the lift with a group of Asian tourists. The men look at the ground and the women pull their children in tight.

They're scared of what I'm wearing.

It's the fear of the unknown. It's natural … I guess.

They probably think I'm carrying a bomb.

Trinity smiles beneath her head to toe garb.

The Armani Dubai Suite occupies the entire thirty-ninth floor of the Burj Khalifa. Designed by Giorgio Armani, the exclusive suite's windows not only overlook Downtown Dubai, but the Arabian Desert as well, and out across the warm waters of the Persian Gulf.

Halo's blank stare reaches beyond his reflection in the glass and into the darkness beyond. Lowering his eyes, he moves away from the window and toward the circular entrance hall.

'It's all quiet, mate.'

Carlos sits reading the newspaper.

'That's how I like it these days,' he says, looking up.

'How's he going?'

'I checked on him a moment ago. He's in the office, fuckin' around on his laptop. He seems fine.'

'Cool. I'm not feeling so well.'

Carlos lowers the newspaper.

'What's wrong?' he asks.

'I'm not sure. I think I just need some fresh air. I'm going to head up top for a bit.'

'Now that you mention it, you've seemed a little flat ever since we arrived.'

'I'm sure it's nothing to worry about. Call my cell if you need me.'

'Take your time buddy, I got it covered.'

'Thanks mate.'

Trinity looks up at the screen: 120 … 121 … 122 … 123 … 124. Seventy-three seconds and 1,483 feet later, the elevator comes to a smooth stop. Its doors silently slide apart.

She opens her mouth to pop her ears.

Standing to one side, she allows the others to exit first before stepping onto the softly lit observation deck. A handful of people enjoy the view, most choosing to congregate inside behind the powerful telescopes.

Trinity moves across the open-air terrace to the chrome railing. A light breeze flows through the thin fabric of her abaya. She hangs her head back and closes her eyes, re-opening them onto a huge, yellow half-moon and brilliant white stars littered forever through the black emptiness.

Free from the earthly distractions below, Trinity's mind flickers with flashes of Gabriel and Tokyo past.

'What do you want from me?' Gabriel pleads. 'What is it you want? Look at me … I'm all messed up!'

'Don't give up on me, Gabriel.'

'Give up on you! I'm prepared to die for you!'

Something solid strikes the timber decking behind her. Everyone else turns their heads, but Trinity spins entirely around and braces for a fight. The surrounding darkness accentuates her ghostly, light blue eyes.

Halo stands next to a wooden chair on its side. Bending down, he picks it up, then walks over and positions himself next to her, his forearms resting on the rail, gaze straight ahead.

Trinity pauses, her heart pounding. Slowly turning back around, she fixes her own stare in the same neutral direction, a nervous tremble rolling through her legs.

'Well, that was quite an entrance,' she remarks.

'I had to make sure it was you.'

'Was it my eyes?' she asks.

Halo nods.

'I noticed them when we drove past the water jets this afternoon, while you were standing by the side of the road. They stood out like dog's balls.'

'I figured you would ... well, I hoped.'

'I've stared into them a million times or more, Trinity. Even in my dreams. I could pick them out a mile away. I still remember the first time I saw them, when we were just kids. I had nightmares for a week ... I thought you were some kind of vampire.'

'I remember.'

Both Halo and Trinity smile to themselves. Breaking the awkward silence, he turns his head and comments on her unusual choice of dress.

'You look like a ninja.'

She smiles some more.

'So what's it like wearing one of those things?'

'I kind of like it. I could get used to it. I can hide under here and people leave me alone. They can't stare at my tits anymore.'

'Well, that's just not on!' he playfully frowns, then smiles. 'What *do* you wear under there?'

'Wouldn't you like to know?'

Halo straightens and smiles.

'Actually, yes I would.'

Trinity pauses, slides her hand along the railing and takes hold of his wrist, gently guiding it through her sleeve, placing his palm against her bra.

His fingers caress its patterned embroidery.

From there, she slides his hand down the bare skin of her stomach and around onto her buttock. A tingling sensation replaces the nervous tremble in her legs.

His fingers carefully explore, finding more bare skin and a G-string running between her toned cheeks.

'Bloody hell!'

'You wanted to know,' she smiles, slowly returning his hand to the railing.

'I bet you have that bloody sword under there as well?' He flinches at a sharp pain in his ribs.

'I fucking knew it!' he whispers, shaking his head. 'You'd better not be here to kill my guy.'

'Don't worry. I'm not in Dubai to assassinate anyone.'

'Good! Because he's the prince's cousin and they pay bloody well … plus, he's not a bad bloke.'

'Who's your partner?'

'Carlos?'

'The guy built like a Greek statue.'

'Carlos,' Halo says, nodding. 'Ex-SF … we work well together.'

'Do you trust him?'

'Do I trust him?' he quietly repeats to himself.

Halo looks back out over the blackened desert, casting his mind back to the first time he worked with Carlos.

What was supposed to be a routine pick-up and drop-off for Halo and his small team of four men went to shit one day, real quick, twelve months ago.

Security work in Algeria was regarded as low-key compared to most of Africa, but that day, driving from Algiers through the Médéa Province and into the barren shithole of Adrar Province, Halo's convoy of two soft-skinned Land Rovers came under fire.

From the sound of the first shot fired to the last round took a few seconds, tops. Afterwards, Halo's car resembled Swiss cheese.

His driver was dead. A giant .50 caliber bullet had made sure of that, removing the top of his head from the bridge of his nose upwards, brain included.

So too was Halo's Principal. His bloodied body was slumped forward in the rear seat, a .50-cal exit wound soiling a hole torn through the back of his white business shirt.

Halo's car had careened off a lone stretch of highway and into a roadside ditch, out in the desert at high noon. He managed to scramble to safety outside the vehicle and huddle up close to the passenger-side rear wheel for protection.

The big 5.0 liter V8 petrol engine, shot to pieces and no longer running, billowed steam from beneath the hood.

One side of Halo's face and all down his left arm glittered in the sunlight, painted crimson with the blood of his two companions.

Shouldering his weapon, he pointed the M4 in all directions, having no real sense of where the incoming fire had originated. Sweat formed across his forehead; his heart pounded. Swallowing was a struggle at best, a luxury, given all that concerned him.

Silence filled his ears.

He lowered his rifle and tried to make radio contact with the lead vehicle. Nothing but static noise came across the airwaves.

Breaking the fragile silence, a .50 caliber machine gun released another stream of black-tipped armor-piercing rounds.

The monstrous bullets, spearing through the air at almost 3,000 feet per second, penetrated the soft-armored vehicle with ease; nearby rocks disintegrated into puffs of smoke and clouds of dust.

Showered in glass and debris, Halo hunkered down, expecting the worst.

The rear tyre blew and went flat.

Halo's bulky frame, laden with webbing, its pouches filled with bullets, made it impossible for him to squeeze himself beneath the car to take cover from the ambush.

More silence followed.

Then, seemingly from out of nowhere, the shredded, bullet-riddled, lead vehicle pulled up alongside Halo's wreck of a car, sliding its front tyres in the dry gravel. Behind the wheel was Carlos, a recently retired Navy Seal, new to the team.

Leaning across, he flung open the passenger door.

Halo jumped to his feet and, with his chin pressed into his chest, sprinted through the dust toward the car.

The snipers again opened up with black tips as Halo closed the ten-meter gap.

Despite the incoming rounds, despite his own safety concerns, Carlos steeled his nerve. After waiting for what seemed an eternity, he floored the gas pedal the moment Halo launched himself safely inside.

Halo stirs and then turns to Trinity.
'Fuck yeah,' he says. 'He's solid as fuck.'
'Why'd he get out of the special forces?'
'He reckons he's had enough.'

I know the feeling.

'Why are you here?' he asks.
'I'm here to see you.'
'I heard you were in trouble.'
'I've been in a world of shit.'
'After all that drama in Tokyo, I'm not surprised. They say you killed Tanaka.'
'Well … *they* are wrong. I had nothing to do with it.'
'Who blew his brains out then?'
'I don't know. Did you …?'

'Whoah there!' Halo jumps in, his pitch rising.

'Keep it down,' whispers Trinity, a little agitated.

'You think I did it?' he murmurs.

Trinity doesn't blink.

Halo shakes his head.

'Fuck me.'

'Look,' Trinity says. 'It doesn't matter who killed Tanaka. I want out.'

Halo ponders for a moment.

'I've had enough,' she adds.

'Getting out won't be easy. Not with a ten-million-dollar bounty on your head.'

'My eyes.'

'Huh?'

'The bounty is actually for my eyes. The head is optional.'

Halo sighs.

'How do you know that *I* won't throw you over the edge?'

How come everyone asks me that fucking question?

'Do I really have to answer that?'

'Yes.'

Trinity swallows. Her eyes look off to one side and then back again.

'Because you love me more than anyone else on this planet and you'd do anything I asked you to do.'

'Anything?'

'Anything.'

Halo lowers his eyes.

'Let me ask you something, Halo.' Trinity pauses. 'Would you die for me?'

Halo clenches his jaw and narrows his eyes.

Trinity can almost hear his heart beating. She leans in close and grabs his arm.

'Would you, Halo? Seriously, would you die for me?'

He grinds his teeth, locks his eyes on hers and lifts her niqab to expose her face.

'You know the answer. You fucking know I would.'

'Would you kill for me?'

He furrows his brow.

'If I wanted you to, would you kill for me?'

'Where is this all leading, Trinity?'

'Nowhere,' she says softly, 'nowhere.'

'You didn't come all this way to play games with me.'

'I just wanted to know where we stand. I'm sorry if I've upset you. Can I get a hug?'

Halo pulls her close, holds her tight.

She rests her head upon his chest and wraps her arms around his waist. Feeling the Tomodachi beneath his shirt press against her cheek makes her smile.

'I need your help,' she asks.

'What do you want from me?'

'I need information.'

'What kind?'

'An address, I want The Russian's address.'

'The Russian!' Halo holds her at arm's length. 'What do you want with him?'

She looks up.

'I'm going to cut off his head. I want it all to end. It's the only way.'

Halo looks around the deck.

'How do you plan on doing it?'

'I haven't got that far. It's a work in progress.'

Halo shakes his head. He knows Trinity well. He knows nothing he says will change her mind once it's made up.

'What makes you think I can help?'

'You must know someone?'

He scrunches his face and looks away.

'You do, don't you?'

Halo doesn't answer.

Trinity grabs his arm.

'Tell me Halo.'

'Zubair,' he says softly.

'Zubair?'

He turns to face her.

'Zubair can find what you seek.'

She smiles.

Halo replaces her niqab.

'It's nothing to smile about, Trinity. You think The Russian is evil?' He shakes his head.

'But will he help me?'

'He owes me a favor. But he cannot be trusted. He likes to play games. Give him an inch, he'll take a mile ... fuck, he'll take your life.'

Trinity is silent.

Halo squeezes her shoulders.

'Are you sure you want to do this?' he asks.

'Yes!'

He pauses.

'Promise me you'll get what you want, nothing more, and then get the fuck out of there.'

'I promise.'

'I'm not fucking around Trinity, this guy is dangerous. He's a sick bastard. Do not listen to his bullshit. Ask only for what you need. I can guarantee you that much, nothing else. Get in and get out.'

'Come with me.'

'I can't. If I could, I would,' he says. 'I shouldn't even be here with you now. Fuck, we could be arrested just for showing affection in public. Anyway, Carlos is downstairs on his own.'

'I'll be fine.'

'If you find The Russian and you kill him, then what?'

Trinity shrugs her shoulders.

Halo looks deep into her eyes.

'Do you think that … I mean, maybe you and I …'

Trinity presses her finger against his lips and gently moves her head from side to side.

Halo lowers his eyes.

His chest rises, holds and then falls.

She can feel his warm breath on her face. Turning to walk away, her finger slides down to his chest and across the Tomodachi she once gave him to remember her by.

Can You Keep a Secret

A cream-colored taxi with a red roof exits the highway linking Dubai to Abu Dhabi, the political capital and spiritual heart of the United Arab Emirates. Sitting in the backseat, Trinity's interest is focused on the distant shimmering towers rising from the desert's scalding hot, yellow sands.

Funded from the region's many oil reserves, the richest city in the world is home to major financial institutions and international corporate headquarters.

But with all this money comes power ... often more money and greed.

Leaving the city behind for the suburbs, the taxi turns a corner and slowly drives down a wide street lined with palm trees. As if the surreal sight of this modern oasis wasn't enough, a young domesticated cheetah with a collar stretches its legs, wandering around a large vacant lot.

Trinity smiles as the big cat casually makes its way through an open gate and back into its compound.

The taxi pulls into the driveway of a mansion and stops; its engine continues to run. The driver turns to Trinity, clicking his fingers and rudely snapping at her.

'Three-hundred dirhams. You give me money now ... quickly.'

Trinity gives him a handful of crumpled, smelly notes. Stepping from the air-conditioned comfort of the cab, she is confronted by a harsh noon sun and a warm easterly breeze. She squints at a huge steel gate with white columns on either side. High, rendered brick walls extend for thirty meters in both directions.

Trinity walks to the security system positioned next to the gate and presses the button as the departing taxi squeals its wheels and speeds away.

Inside the mansion, Halo's contact, Zubair, studies the video monitor from his swivel chair, his fat stomach pressed against the edge of his desk. He zooms in on Trinity's covered face as she looks up at the fish-eye lens; her pupils flicker on his screen. A small window pops open on another monitor.

NAME: TRINITY BLUE
BIRTH DATE: 25 MAY 1983
SSN: 321-00-6969
BIRTH PLACE: LITTLETON, NEW HAMPSHIRE, USA
NATIONALITY: AMERICAN
FATHER: MICHAEL JOHN BLUE
MOTHER: ANNA BLUE
SIBLINGS: NONE
RESIDENCE: NO KNOWN ADDRESS

Zubair squeezes his cock through his kandura while his other hand pans the camera to take in the substantial bumps beneath Trinity's abaya. He starts rubbing his groin.

Living in Kuwait, a relatively small Arab country where literacy rates are high, Zubair knew he had to broaden his education and specialize, be different from everyone else, in order to stand out from the pack.

Most university students his age followed a predictable though still competitive path into the finance sector.

Not naturally gifted at anything, Zubair studied political science and worked hard to better himself.

His father, Salim, had been a Cabinet Minister in the National Assembly of Kuwait for many years. Resultant cronyism saw Zubair offered a full scholarship to study abroad in the United Kingdom.

Returning home to Kuwait several years later, Zubair joined the Air Force, like his father had once done, long before entering the government. With an English education under his belt and a degree in his fat, sweaty palm, Zubair was promptly placed in Air Force HQ at Al Mubarak Air Base.

It was here he found the calling that would one day set him apart from everyone else: Information.

The short-lived Gulf War in the early nineties - the result of the annexation of Kuwait City by neighboring Iraq - allowed Zubair to further his knowledge and skills in information-gathering by working closely with the coalition force, most notably the Americans, the world's best in this particular field.

Long after the war had finished, low on money and with an ever growing debt owing to his blond whore addiction, Zubair recognised his services were grossly under-valued by the Kuwaiti Armed Forces. At the earliest opportunity, he re-tired.

Through a network mostly formed via his Russian whore contacts, Zubair, utilising his skills, began to accumulate and pass on sensitive information to the highest bidders, regardless of country, religion or political persuasion.

If you spent the money you would receive the information. No one was safe from his tentacles; rumour had it, not even Bin Laden.

Zubair's network and list of clients grew exponentially, along with his bank account, his power, his stomach and his in-satiable taste for women.

Leaving his cock alone long enough to activate a but-ton, Zubair allows Trinity access through the gate.

Clunk!

She hears the solenoids unlock and pushes the heavy metal gate open just enough to press herself through to the other side where two armed guards fast approach.

Arabs dressed in suits … never a good sign.

Using her limited time wisely, she quickly studies their weapons, right down to the materials they're constructed from, hoping to gather as much information about them as she can.

Old school AK-47 … 30-round steel curved mag, and the other one looks like a variant.

I'd guess the three cooling slots on the lighter-colored teak fore-grip make it a Serbian Zastava M70.

Both 7.62x39 millimeter and both nasty.

Shoulder holstered handguns.

The guard carrying the M70 slings it over his shoulder and directs her with his stare along a path toward some steps leading up to the front entrance of the house.

The other keeps his distance, his AK in a low-ready position; barrel slightly lowered but the muzzle and his eyes always on target.

Back in his room, Zubair monitors Trinity's movements from every angle.

She makes her way past two metallic granite-crystal Dodge SUVs and a phantom-black Charger. Greeted at the top of the steps by a third member of the security detail, she notices a deep scar runs the length of one side of his face.

He gestures for her to step inside a full-body scanner.

Impressed with the high level of security Trinity nods as she enters. Following a whirring noise, two antennae simultaneously rotate 360 degrees, reflecting electromagnetic radiation off her body.

The active millimeter waves make her clothing appear translucent on Zubair's monitor screen. Observing a 3D inverse image of Trinity, his fat finger presses a button and converts it to color, so that a clear, naked, frontal picture of Trinity begins to morph.

He sits up straight and again grabs at his cock, switching the camera to a rear view. Stirring in his seat at the sight of a katana strapped to her back, he activates a red flashing light attached to the outside of the scanner.

Scarface motions for Trinity to step forward.

She cautiously exits the X-ray machine, her eyes following the armed guards as they creep closer to the bottom of the steps in front of her. Her heart-rate slowly increases in anticipation of a fight.

Holding both arms out as Scarface sweeps a hand-held detector down her back, her eyes remain focused on the other two guards, despite the warning sensor's rapidly increasing tone.

They raise their rifles.

Trinity takes a small step back, hands in the air.

'I'm going to reach inside and remove my sword,' she says, hoping to not spook the guards. 'Okay?'

Scarface nods.

Trinity slowly reaches in and unties the sling. She exaggerates her movements and removes the sheathed sword, placing it at her feet.

He kicks it aside.

Trinity assumes the position once more and feels his sweaty palms on the skin of her hands.

He drops the detector and steps closer.

She looks him in the eyes.

He looks away as his hands ruffle the outside of her abaya, along her outstretched arms and under her arm pits. From there they slide down her ribs and then back up via her stomach, stopping just below her breasts.

His eyes lock with Trinity's.

She tightens her stare.

Scarface swallows hard and smiles. His hands sneak across her breasts.

Trinity coughs.

Yeah cunt, you keep smiling.

Zubair watches from inside his mansion, his cock filling his hand through the robe.

Trinity's eyes follow Scarface's movements as he circles around behind her. She cringes at his pungent desert breath. She feels his hands run across her shoulders and around her neck, giving it a playful squeeze.

You're fucking with the wrong chick.

Her eyes watch his hands massaging her breasts.

You're playing with fire, you smelly fucker.

Trinity shrugs her shoulders, feels his hands move on and slide down to her hips.

He squats and drags his hands to her ankles.

Her eyes strain to look behind and in anticipation of his next move she growls, 'No!'

He looks at his colleagues and smiles as they hustle up the steps.

Trinity looks down the barrel of their guns.

Oh you guys are so fucking dead.

The adventurous Scarface slides his hand underneath the soft fabric and gently runs it up the inside of her legs. As he stands, his fingers brush between her thighs.

Trinity's heart accelerates and she clenches her teeth. Spinning around she raises her elbow high. There is a loud crack as bone meets bone and blood spurts from his nose.

Zubair releases his cock, his eyes glued to the screen.

Scarface jumps back, screaming and holding his face; tears stream from his eyes.

Trinity drops to the ground and sweeps the armed guards' legs out from under them, one of the guards falling on his back and spraying the roof with bullets. She jumps to her feet and wrestles control of his rifle.

'Stop!' booms Zubair's voice from a speaker near the front door. 'Stop, do not kill them!'

Shoving the rifle toward the guard's face, Trinity threatens to pull the trigger, her eyes wide and crazed, mouth open and panting.

Clunk!

Her eyes shift to the front door as it automatically unlatches and pops open.

'Please, come inside,' Zubair says, in a calming tone.

Trinity blinks twice, drops the rifle and picks up her sword.

Zubair's lair is at the end of a long dark corridor.

Entering the spacious room, Trinity's senses are caught up in a maelstrom of body odour, spicy food, cigarettes and a cocktail of stale farts.

What the fuck?

I can literally taste someone's shit in my mouth.

Trinity's eyes turn to the mess: strewn food wrappers, left-over food and miles and miles of multi-colored cables hanging from the roof and running across the cluttered floor, all connected to video monitors large and small, new and old. If it has a screen and it works, it is plugged in and stacked off to the side, on a crate, on a box, on top of another one just like it.

A mélange of images flashes across them, news reports both local and international, all telecast at once in snowy black-and-white, funky, faded technicolor, and ultra-high-definition video.

The hair on her neck stands up as a fat pig of a man wearing a stained kandura, swivels in his chair and smiles. The image scrambles her eyes; they don't know where to look, darting from his bald head to his cracked bare feet to his dyed-black mustache.

He labors to his feet and extends his arms.

'Miss Blue,' he announces in a strange English-Arabic accent, with perfect pronunciation. 'Please accept my most sincere apologies for the way my men conducted them-selves. It is truly out of character and something I would never condone or foster.'

Lying cunt.

Trinity turns to Scarface with the broken nose.

His bruised and blackened eyes shoot straight down to the ground.

The other two guards suddenly appear sheepish.

'Shut the door,' Zubair orders.

After Scarface closes the door, he and the other guards stand silently in the background as their boss turns his attention back to Trinity.

'Feel free to remove your head-dress.'

Trinity hesitates. Then, in a show of force to confirm she is their equal, she removes not only her niqab, but her flowing cloak.

Zubair recoils at Trinity's presence.

Standing tall in eight-inch high, desert-tan army boots, she tightens the zipper on her catsuit.

Staring at her chest, his hand instinctively moves toward his groin. Zubair checks himself at the last moment and asks, 'May I call you Trinity?'

She nods.

'Please, relax. Put down your sword, you will not need it here.'

Trinity places it within arm's reach on the table next to her.

'Is there anything I can get you? Perhaps you would like something to eat or to drink?'

Some fucking fresh air, you filthy fat pig.

'Air, some fresh air would be nice.'

Zubair glances sideways and addresses the guards, 'Open the windows!' He returns to his chair and motions for Trinity to sit. 'You are a friend of Halo's?'

Trinity remains standing.

'Yes, I have known Halo a very long time. Look, I don't want to take up any more of your time. Halo said you can get me an address.'

'Yes. He called. Halo once did me a huge favor and I would be more than pleased to help you. Any friend of Halo's is a friend of mine. Are you sure you won't sit?'

'Yes. I really must go. Can we get on with it?'

'Of course, a young lady such as you must surely have better places to be than here with someone like myself.'

Trinity remains mindful of the three thugs standing behind her.

Zubair gets comfortable in his chair, swivels and faces the screen.

'And what is the lucky person's name?'

'The Russian. I only know of him as The Russian.'

Zubair stares at the screen. Puffing his cheeks before blowing the air out he slowly turns to face his guest and leans back.

'Is this some kind of joke?'

'No. Why?'

'The Russian? You want Sergei Vasilenko's address?'

Trinity's heart beats faster.

'Yes. You know his name! You know of him?'

'Of course,' Zubair answers with pride. 'He is one of my best customers. Sergei, or The Russian if you prefer, is always trying to locate someone and in need of my services.'

'Halo mentioned you have a price for finding anyone, anything. That's the address I want. I want to know where The Russian lives.'

Zubair leans forward in his chair.

'And Halo is correct. But the price you wish to pay, well, it does not cover Sergei Vasilenko. If you like, I could give you President Putin's whereabouts instead?'

'This is bullshit! You owe Halo. Give me the address.'

'Let us not get too carried away. As mentioned, the price you wish to pay is too small. Halo's ... *credit* ... does not cover this item. Perhaps for a little more we can come to an agreement.'

Trinity stares at Zubair's smug face.

Halo was right, this cunt can't be trusted.

But I need that address.

I'd be a fool to come all this way and walk away empty handed.

She clenches her fists.

'How much money do you want?'

'Money,' Zubair repeats, with more than a hint of contempt in his voice, a smirk across his face. 'I have more money than I can count, and I suspect you do not.'

'Then what is it you want?'

He stirs in his chair.

'I want you to reveal your breasts to me.'

Silence.

'Seriously!' Trinity blurts. 'Are you for fucking real? You want to see my tits?'

'Yes, my lovely. For that I will give you his address.'

'You will give up one of the most dangerous men in the world … for my tits?'

'In addition to the favor I owe Halo of course, let us not forget that.'

Fuck me … this is bullshit!

I should kill everyone in this stinking shithole.

Trinity shakes her head and lowers her eyes. She breathes loudly through her nostrils and looks up.

'Give it to me first.'

Zubair shrugs his shoulders.

'Of course.'

He turns to tap away at the keyboard.

Trinity lowers her head and peers sideways, taking note of the positions of the guards.

One covering the door and the other two spread wide, out-flanking me.

The printer next to Zubair fires up and within seconds a piece of paper emerges.

He removes it and spins to face her.

'As promised.'

She snatches it from his hand.

'Bulgaria!'

Zubair swivels back and forth.

'I hear Sofia is lovely this time of year.'

'There is no address!' she cries. 'I want his house address. You said you would give it to me.'

'Unfortunately this is all my computer can find.'

'You fucking lied!'

'A moment ago you had no idea of his real name or where to look for Sergei. But now … now you have a country and a city. You cannot complain. Someone of Sergei's … shall we say, *character* … is never easy to find.

'Of course, if you would like to be my guest and wait perhaps a few days, then I am certain I can tell you where he lives, what he had for breakfast and what he is wearing.'

Trinity's face turns bright red. Her eyes look as though they could cut steel.

'If this is bullshit, I'll come back here and cut off your fucking head!'

'Such spirit … I like that.'

Fuck you!

'Now,' Zubair continues, 'I believe we had a deal.'

You didn't get exactly what you want Trinity, but the fat cunt is right, it's better than nothing. Now show him your tits and get the fuck out of here.

Or … kill them all, right now.

It's tempting.

But what if the information is bogus?

I'll have no recourse to come back and torture the info from his fat head.

Fuck.

Trinity sighs, slides her zipper down and peels back the soft leather over her shoulders, removing both arms from the sleeves.

Zubair grabs at his cock.

'Oh ... my...'

She stares at his groin.

'Stop doing that shit.'

'Remove your underwear.'

'I'm only showing my tits, nothing else!'

'Yes, yes,' Zubair spits, 'quickly!'

Mechanically and without emotion, Trinity snaps her bra undone and drops it to the floor.

Even though his mouth is wide open, Zubair is speechless. His beady little eyes don't blink; his lecherous stare burns a hole in Trinity's skin.

Sweat forms across his brow.

Trinity lowers her head.

I can't believe I'm doing this.

This fat cunt makes me sick.

Is this where my life is ... is this all I'm going to be remembered for ... my tits?

Zubair comes to life.

'They are perfect,' he says, 'absolutely perfect. I must touch them.'

Trinity raises her head.

'Fuck you. You've seen them, I'm putting them away.'

'No! Please, I beg of you. Let me touch them ... just the once.'

Trinity takes hold of the zipper.

'I will give you another address if you do … give me a name!'

Trinity stops what she's doing.

Her mind spins its wheels.

This is fucking absurd. The pathetic fat pig is begging to touch my tits.

Is he just playing games with me? One word from his smelly mouth and his goons could try and take me by force.

Or is he worried if he pushes too far, he will have to answer to Halo?

I know Halo said to get the fuck out of here … but maybe I'll play along a little longer and see what happens.

'I want two! Two more addresses … and not just the fucking city.'

Zubair's twitching fingers hover above the keyboard.

'Yes, yes. Give me their names.'

Trinity pauses and then sighs before selling what little self-worth she has left.

'Gabriel Hart and my mother, Anna.'

Zubair spells out loud, 'H.E.A.R.T?'

'No, H.A.R.T.'

'I remember that name.'

'Bullshit!'

Zubair faces Trinity.

'No, I do. It appears our other mutual friend, The Russian, also once sought the whereabouts of your Mister H.A.R.T.'

'How long ago was he asking?'

'According to my records it has been almost three years. How time flies.'

Trinity appears anxious.

'Did you find him? Did you give The Russian his address?'

ONE BULLET AT A TIME

'No.'

'And why not?'

'Gabriel Hart is listed as dead.'

Trinity's heart stops beating.

She can feel it sink deep within her stomach; she wants to vomit.

'The report I have indicates he died from a gunshot wound to the chest, in Tokyo ...'

She's held on to a thin thread of hope for the past three years that he may somehow have survived the shooting. Now, hearing it in person from Zubair's dry lips feels like a metal stake driven through her chest.

Standing topless in the middle of a foreign room full of strangers, stripped of clothing, stripped of dignity, Trinity tunes out, her sad eyes staring straight ahead, focusing on nothing at all.

Still, years of stress-inoculation training and life experience ensure that her subconscious mind, void of emotion, remains active, filtering Zubair's words, picking and choosing those which to pay attention to.

'... killed in the line of duty ... Hong Kong ... Yoshimura ... Mako ...'

Trinity blinks.

It takes a moment, but she pulls herself from the shadows and back into the fringe of the here and now.

'Mako,' she says softly.

'Pardon? Speak louder.'

'Mako. Give me his interpreter Mako's address instead.'

'As you wish.'

A moment later, the printer spits out two more addresses. Zubair spins around with a smile on his face, one hand firmly planted in his lap, the other offering two sheets of paper to Trinity.

She closes her eyes. Then, opening them, she rolls her catsuit down to around her waist and draws the paper from his grasp; her hands fall by her side.

With an evil smile, Zubair rises from his chair.

Trinity stares at crusty food wedged between his camel teeth. Her skin crawls as she looks away. She can feel his plump, clumsy fingers grab at her breasts before they begin to stray down her stomach toward her thighs. She brushes them away and stares him in the eyes; a cold flash overcomes her as his gaze shifts to one side.

Trinity groans as one of the guards restrains her arms and another bangs the muzzle of his AK-47 against the back of her skull. Zubair's perverse desires and greed get the better of him. He now wants to take by force what he cannot legitimately have.

She attempts to break free.

'Let me go!'

'Bring her to the table!'

'I'll fucking kill you, you cunts!'

The brute straightens her arms.

Trinity screams in pain and her legs buckle as her face slams against the table and both her legs are kicked apart. Struggling to move her outstretched arms, they are pinned down with force.

The muzzle presses her skull to the wooden table top.

Trinity looks up through the corner of one eye.

'Don't you fucking dare, don't you fucking dare, I'll fucking kill you all!'

'You will do nothing of the sort.'

Zubair saunters up behind her and shucks her catsuit to her ankles.

'Halo will tear you apart!'

'First I will deal with you, and then I shall deal with our friend Halo.'

Trinity's muscles bulge and her veins engorge with blood as she musters all her strength. She screams as the guards apply more pressure.

Tears fill her eyes.

Heat from Zubair's sweaty fat stomach with its matted hair radiates against her legs.

Her buttocks clamp tight.

Ripped from her body, the G-string burns her skin. Trinity continues to struggle as the rifle's muzzle pushes hard. Her arms feel as though they are going to snap at the elbows. She tenses her muscles to prevent Zubair's fat fingers from prising apart her butt cheeks.

KA-BOOM! Chit-chit! KA-BOOM!

Trinity's ears ring. Splinters of wood pierce her skin.

Halo has breached the door, blowing off the hinges with his shotgun, kicking it in with his boots.

Zubair and his cronies turn toward the carnage.

With grace, Carlos drifts through the gun smoke and enters the room firing three rounds from his M4.

Life, mostly measured in years, is now measured in milliseconds as all three cronies' heads pop blood, the look of shock etched into their faces.

Assisting Trinity to wriggle free from beneath the slumped bodies of her lifeless captors, Carlos helps pull up her catsuit.

Zubair's hands shoot up in the air.

'This is not what it seems!'

Halo materializes through the gun smoke and approaches Zubair, his all-black customised Remington 870 shotgun down by his side.

'Halo! You know who I am, Halo,' Zubair whimpers. 'Think this through. Too many people, important people, rely on me... even your bosses, the royal family. If you kill me, someone will kill you! You'll be hunted down like a rabid dog.'

Trinity looks up at Halo, her eyes growing in size. His towering presence fills her with instant joy, a feeling she hasn't experienced since they were young children living in Tokyo. He was always there for her back then - protected her, loved her more than anything else.

Trinity, exhausted, falls to her knees.

'Money!' Zubair says. 'Money, more than you can spend. I give it to you.'

Halo levels his shotgun at Zubair's trembling face.

Zubair points wildly around the room.

'I have cameras everywhere. You will not escape. You cannot hide. They will know who you are. You are a dead man!'

Halo cocks his head, his eyes fixed on Zubair, his voice directed at Trinity.

'Did you get what you want?'

She gathers her thoughts, scans the floor, scoops up three sheets of paper. Trinity looks to Halo and nods.

Halo leans in close to Zubair.

'Delete the data you accessed for Trinity and any mention of her details. Do it now!'

Zubair sits and hammers away at the keyboard.

'Is done,' he says, turning toward Halo. 'I do as you ask.'

'Trinity,' Halo says, his stare still fixed on Zubair, 'you asked would I die for you … kill for you.'

Her head barely moves up and down; her chest pounds.

Zubair turns his face away, his hands high in front of the menacing barrel.

'I do as you ask.'

'Put them down.'

Zubair doesn't comply.

Halo pokes him in the forehead with the shotgun's barrel.

Urine pools around Zubair's feet. His chest muscles constrict and his breathing becomes short and sharp.

'Halo,' he whispers, 'please, don't do it!'

'Hands, Zubair,' Halo says, calmly. 'Put them down.'

Halo kneels beside Trinity, one arm around her shoulder.

'I've never seen you this vulnerable before.'

'Me neither.'

'You're getting old and weak,' he jokes, trying to lift her spirit.

Resting her head against his chest, she confides, 'I've never felt like that, Halo. I wanted to kill them all, but I couldn't. I was unable to break free from their hold. They were so strong. I felt helpless.'

Halo strokes her arm.

Trinity lifts her head.

'The people I've killed all these years,' she says. 'Did they experience the same emotions in the final moments before they died? A sickening sense of helplessness?'

'Never try to analyse it,' Halo responds. 'It only does more damage than good. We do what we do.'

'Even toward the end with Zubair … I've never wanted to kill someone so bad. I dug deep and there was nothing. I couldn't move. In the end I wanted you to do it, I was happy for you to do it for me.'

'Where do you think your head was at?'

Now's not the time to tell him about Gabriel.

'I don't know. I let my guard down. Maybe I was too worried about The Russian, maybe all this running and hiding and killing has caught up with me. Seeing you walk through that doorway, it was the most amazing experience.'

'Glad to be of service, ma'am.'

'No. Seriously Halo, it was ... I don't know how to describe it. It was ... spiritual.'

Halo laughs.

'Don't laugh,' she says. 'I'm serious. It was instant relief to see you there. I felt safe. It was as though all my problems had simply disappeared, as though nothing else mattered. You looked ten feet tall. I thought Jesus Christ had just entered the room.'

Halo, turns to Carlos.

'Hear that, mate? I'm ten feet tall and bullet-proof.'

Carlos stands post in the background, peering out the window, keeping watch.

'She's obviously delirious. Must have you confused with me.'

Trinity smiles, just a little.

'How did you get away from the hotel?' she asks. 'What about your Principal?'

Carlos grins.

'He's sleeping like a baby.'

'Back at the hotel, I had to tell Carlos about you,' Halo says. 'It was eating away at me, the thought of you here with this sick prick. So I ... *we* ... drugged the prince's cousin.'

'I can't believe you did that,' Trinity mutters.

'I asked Carlos to just look the other way, but he insisted on coming here.'

She glances at Carlos.

He shrugs his shoulders and smiles.

Halo takes Trinity's hand.

'What now? You have The Russian's location?'

'Bulgaria.'

'Bulgaria!'

'Yes … Bulgaria.'

'Where the fuck is Bulgaria?' Halo asks.

Carlos scratches his head.

'I think it's in Germany,' he jokes.

'No. It's the capital of Russia,' Halo quips.

Trinity shakes her head.

'You guys are pathetic.'

They all laugh.

'When are you planning on going?' Halo asks.

'Not just yet. I have some other shit to do first.'

'Does it have anything to do with the other two addresses Zubair gave you?'

Trinity remains silent, unsure how to answer.

'One of them is your mother's, isn't it?'

She nods.

'And the other one?'

Trinity wipes some of Zubair's dry blood from Halo's cheek and temple. She feels bad evading his question, but does it anyway.

'What about you Halo, what will you do now?'

The muscles in his face tense up. He shakes his head and sighs, frustrated with her lack of commitment.

'If Zubair was telling the truth—and I don't doubt the sneaky little prick was—then there's no going back for Carlos and me. Killing Zubair is as good as a death sentence.'

Trinity stares at Halo.

Halo putting everything on the line I can understand; he would do anything for me.

But Carlos, someone I've never met before, prepared to sacrifice his life … for me?

Carlos turns from the window.

'We should probably leave soon,' he says. 'We ought to rig this place to slow-burn.'

Halo nods.

'That'll take us some time to prepare.'

'Exactly, that's my point. And we'll need to go pack our shit and get a good head start on everyone.'

'Come with us, Trinity?' Halo asks.

'I can't. I need to see this thing through.'

'Then we'll come with you.'

'I need to deal with my mother alone.'

Halo reluctantly nods his head.

'The heat we've just generated is sure to burn bright,' Carlos says. 'If some intelligence agency hasn't taken us down within forty-eight hours, then some terrorist cell or assassin will. The last thing Trinity needs is to be with us.'

'You're right,' Halo says, gesturing toward Zubair's body. 'Up until I blew his face off, that dead beached whale was one of the most influential people on the planet. Some governments and intelligence groups are going to assume we killed him for his knowledge. So, if anything, our being a target is just what Trinity needs right now.'

'How so?' she asks.

'For the moment you're yesterday's news. As long as we're running, everyone will be chasing us, not you.'

Halo pauses.

'Trinity,' he says. 'Do what you gotta do, but don't fuck around doing it. Then find that Russian piece-of-shit and take off his head with that sword of yours.'

'Halo, I'm sorry. I'm sorry this has happened. I never imagined my actions would impact on others the way they have today. You know I would never wish my life of pain on anyone, especially you, my longest and dearest friend.'

Halo rubs her shoulder.

'It's okay, Trinity. It's not your fault. I should never have told you about Zubair.'

'No, Halo. My whole life has led me to this point. It is my fault.'

Carlos stands tall.

'I'll do my best to look after him for you. After all, I saved his sorry ass once already.'

'I don't know what to say Carlos.'

'Meh! It's all good. Don't sweat it.'

Trinity hugs Carlos, knowing this may be the last time she ever sees him.

Halo rises to his feet.

'Tell me which direction you're heading in and we'll steer clear.'

Trinity steps away from Carlos and looks at Halo. She pauses.

'Littleton.'

'You're going home.'

She nods.

'And then where?'

Trinity stares at Halo then lowers her eyes.

'Geneva.'

'What's in Geneva?'

Looking up, she answers, 'Honestly … I don't know.'

Carlos is anxious to leave.

'Let's wind it up.'

'What will happen to you two?'

'The so-called legit players will hit us hard immediately, believing we killed Zubair. If we can evade capture for the first seventy-two hours, their techs will go through the mess of equipment left behind here and work out that

MICHAEL JOHN BARNES

we didn't actually access anything. They'll most likely leave us alone.'

'They won't be happy, but yeah, they should let us be,' Carlos confirms.

'It'll take a while longer for all the mercs and assassins to get their contracts issued. But once word filters out, I suggest your bounty will look like chump change. Zubair had some powerful friends.'

'If the slow-burn goes to plan,' Carlos adds, 'that should buy us another twenty-four hours or more before anyone knows what went down here.'

'When will I see you again, Halo?'

'I really don't know. We will probably head toward Tokyo and take shelter with Yoshi. I'll leave news with him of our progress as often as I can. You do the same. That way we can keep tabs on each other without directly communicating.'

Trinity nods.

'Do you have money?' he asks.

'Yes. I accessed my cache in Buenos Aires so I'm good to go for cash and passports, for a while anyway.'

Halo points to a dead guard.

'Take his AK with you, find and carry all the ammunittion you can. You might need it to help you get where you're going.'

'Okay.'

He lowers his empty eyes and speaks softly, 'I guess this is it then.'

'I'll help you light the fire.'

'No, Trinity. You should get going. You have a lot to do in hopefully a short period of time. The longer you take to get to The Russian, the worse it will be for us.'

Trinity rushes Halo and throws her arms around him.

He squeezes her tight as she looks up.

130

'Do you ever think our lives will be normal?'

'Define normal,' he responds with a smirk. 'So you want the SUV or the Charger?'

'Charger!' she snaps back.

'I figured as much. Hey! That reminds me. Whatever happened to my motorbike you stole from me in Tokyo?'

'Ha!' Trinity laughs out loud. 'It's sitting at the bottom of a lake.'

Out on the wide open highway, Trinity feels as though she is no longer running from her past. Instead, she speeds head-on toward her destiny and her demons, in search of answers, and a future. With nothing but an ancient samurai sword and an iron resolve, she grits her teeth, plants her foot and follows the long road ahead, the Charger's head-lamps lighting the way.

In the middle of the room, Halo and Carlos stacked a half-dozen mattresses against one another in the shape of a tepee. Halo carefully places a candle on top, resting it on layers of scrunched-up toilet paper.

'Are you certain you found his collection of hard drives, discs and videos?'

Carlos nods.

'Everything I could find is packed within the tepee on top of those three wooden desk-tops.' He shuts the windows and draws the blinds.

Halo looks up at the air-conditioning unit positioned high on the wall. Setting the timer so that it will switch on in twelve hours' time, he directs the vents down toward the base of the tepee.

Carlos returns from the kitchen.

'I've turned the gas on and propped open the oven door.'

'Did you seal off the kitchen door?'

'Roger. A few wet, rolled-up towels placed at the bottom.'

'Are you sure this will work?'

Carlos pushes out his bottom lip and nods.

'Fuck yeah. It's foolproof. The candle slowly burns its way down to the shit paper, the paper burns into the mattresses, they smoulder, eventually melting the hard drives. The hot plastic ignites the varnish on the wooden desk-tops. After a while this fucking mess becomes nothing but a pile of glowing embers.'

Halo smiles.

'Meanwhile,' Carlos continues, 'the gas from the oven slowly works its way through the house and into this room. The touch of genius,' he adds, 'is the A/C firing up and blowing air across the embers, fanning them back to life.'

'Boom!' Halo says.

'Fucking boom!' nods Carlos.

'And you've done this before?'

'Hell no!'

LITTLETON

Redemption

Trinity knows he is waiting in the shadows; she can hear his heart beating.

He wants to come out, but he is cautious.

He is now no longer the only one.

He should have stepped from the dark when the opportunity first arose. Now he is at a loss what to do.

Someone else stirs nearby.

Trinity senses this one is different.

This one will settle for less.

A warm feeling overcomes her; she feels safe now. But she also feels confused. She does not know which way to turn, which way to look.

She doesn't want to upset one or the other but knows that this will be inevitable; she cannot have both.

The two of them wait in the shadows, looking to Trinity for some sign.

The Greyhound bus lurches as it comes to a stop. Trinity opens her eyes to the loud sound of compressed air as the front door opens. She sits up in her seat and checks herself, making sure all her clothing is in place, not wanting a repeat of her wet dream in Buenos Aires.

With Yamamoto's sword across her lap, she pulls aside the curtain and looks through the tall, tinted window.

It's just as I remember it ... a lot of green trees and white, timber-clad houses.

She reaches up for the green canvas duffle bag she took from Zubair's lair and makes her way to the front.

'Thank you,' she says to the driver.

'My pleasure,' he says. 'Enjoy your stay in Littleton.'

Trinity steps down onto the pavement and looks up at the gray sky. She inhales through her nose; the cold air stings, reminding her that she is still alive.

She checks her watch—two in the afternoon.

A few cars slowly make their way along the main street of the small New England town; a young family of four strolls along the other side of the road.

Trinity makes her way over the double yellow lines in the middle of the street and passes by the CITGO gas station, open for business but empty of patrons. She looks up at the US flag hanging limp from the pole.

Further on, she approaches the First Congregational Church, and admires its white, green-capped steeple.

I used to love coming here to church every Sunday morning, dressed all pretty.

But Dad stopped taking me here after Mom left.

She approaches the Littleton Diner, the only one in town. There are no cars parked out front, but the red neon sign in the window flashes OPEN. In a show of patriotism, red, white and blue swag buntings are draped beneath each of the diner's six window sills.

A small bell announces Trinity's arrival through the door. Her eyes dart around the room.

It hasn't changed a bit in all these years. I'm guessing not much else in town has either.

Trinity removes her wind-breaker and gloves. Wearing her favorite Jets sweater and navy-blue NY baseball cap, she takes a seat in a booth near the window and stares beyond the sheer white curtains, tied to the sides.

It feels weird being back here ... been a long time.

It's like the town is stuck in the past.

So many memories ... The time I fell and broke my arm skateboarding at the park ... school ... I loved arts and crafts.

The waitress approaches, pen and notebook in hand.

'What can I get ya, darling?'

Trinity turns away from the window to look at the mature woman staring down at her rag-wrapped sword. She slyly moves it under the table and out of sight.

'Do you sell apple pie?'

'Umm ... we sure do, baked this morning ... Oh my!'

Trinity is puzzled by the welcoming waitress's reaction and quickly adjusts her heavy-framed glasses to ensure her face is covered.

'You remind me of someone,' the waitress says, her hand sprawled high across her chest. Her nametag reads Janice. 'Are ya from around here?'

Trinity's heart rate picks up. She hesitates.

'No.'

'Well, you certainly resemble a girl I grew up with. Her name was Anna. Pretty thing she was, just like you. A model she was. She disappeared for many years, a long time ago. Nobody knew why or where to.

'Her husband, Michael—a lovely man, and hand-some—was devastated. He did a wonderful job bringing up their little girl all by himself. I don't recall her name, she had amazing blue eyes.'

'What became of this … *Anna*?'

'She returned home, here to Littleton, no more than a year ago, strangest thing … out of the blue.' The chatty waitress is momentarily lost for words. Leaning forward she whispers, 'Unfortunately, she passed away recently.'

Trinity short-circuits; her body, her face, her mind, all cease to function. A few seconds later her pounding heart jolts back to life and resets her senses.

She blinks.

No. No. No no no no!

She can't do this to me … she can't die … she owes me.

I need to know. I need to know why she left!

I want answers!

In the background, Janice continues to tell the story of Anna, ' … a month ago … found dead … old family home. '

Trinity's eyes turn glazy and her skin feels cold. Leaning to one side she vomits on the floor.

Janice's eyes open wide as she jumps out of the way.

Wiping her mouth with her sleeve, Trinity grabs her jacket and gloves and slides out from the booth.

'Are you okay?' Janice asks. 'What about that pie?'

Trinity snatches her sword before running out the door and onto the sidewalk. Sprinkles of rain cool her face. She throws on her jacket. Her muscles tense up and her chest tightens.

Get your fucking shit together.

She sucks in a big gulp of air and dashes across the road, scampering down a small lane.

Janice stands in the doorway.

'You forgot your bag.'

Trinity keeps running. The bag can wait; the need to remove herself from dealing with Janice is more important right now.

This is bullshit.

My whole life I've waited for this moment ... the chance to ask ... the chance to find out.

I cannot fucking believe it.

After all I went through, coming all this way ... Halo and Carlos's sacrifice ...

... Fuck!

Trinity eventually stops running, transitioning to a steady march up and over a grassy incline covered in trees. Passing through an old rusty gate and across a small field, she comes to a halt, alone in the rain beneath a giant maple tree. In front of a tilted, cambered tombstone overgrown with long grass, she drops to her knees, head bowed, wet mangled hair clinging to her face.

Her gloved hands grasp the top of Yamamoto's upright sword to support her weight.

I'm sorry it's been so long, Father.

I've missed you.

I miss your guidance, your help, your love ... I miss simply having you around.

I've tried to live by your wishes; it's been hard at times, but I've tried.

I lost my way ... I'm sorry.

I've done things ... evil things ... things you would not approve of ... but without you to look after me, I had to survive.

I know it's not an excuse, but … soon it will be over with and I can make you proud of me again.

She lifts her eyes; drops of rain glide down the lenses of her glasses.

I finally found Mom.

After all this time, she came back here. She came back home.

And then she fucking left us forever.

The selfish fucking bitch!

I wanted answers.

I needed to know if her leaving was the catalyst for me turning into the person I am now, or if I never stood a chance to begin with.

Is it in my genes?

Am I the person I was always going to be … this fucking monster?

I wanted to know why she left us.

I always missed her … although sometimes I secretly wished she was dead.

And now she is … and now I don't know what to think.

There was a time I loved her … when she still loved you.

I loved our little family, our life together.

When she stopped loving you she must have stopped loving me, otherwise she would never have left.

I wish I knew.

When you died, I knew you were gone and why you were gone. It somehow made it easier to deal with … but with her … it was different.

It's funny, I don't feel sad she's gone, not one bit.

Should I?

Trinity rolls to one side and curls up on the damp ground. Surrounded by red maple leaves, she hugs her sword.

Janice wipes down a table, looks up when the small bell above the door tinkles.

'Darling,' she says, 'come sit by the heater.'

Trinity's boots trudge mud across the black-and-white checkered linoleum floor. She takes off her jacket and gloves.

Janice walks over with a towel and Trinity's duffle bag.

'You must be freezing to death.'

'Thanks.'

Trinity removes her cap and glasses, wipes her face.

'Oh Lord,' Janice says. 'Are you sure you're not from these parts?'

'Can I get a hot drink?'

'Yes! Yes, of course. Sit down, I'll be right back.'

Trinity peels off her wet sweater. Unzipping her duffle bag, she pulls out a black hoodie and slips it over her head. She takes a seat on the soft red leather and towel dries her hair before warming her hands by the heater in the wall.

Janice returns with a hot chocolate.

'Here ya go, darling, get that into ya.'

Trinity wraps both hands around the mug.

'Are you okay? You left in such a hurry ... I mopped up all ya mess.'

Trinity takes a sip.

'I'm sorry,' she says. 'Thanks for looking after my bag and cleaning up after me.'

'Oh, that's alright darling, I knew you'd come back for it.'

'Can I ask you something?'

'Sure.'

Janice sits beside Trinity.

'That story you told me earlier. How did your friend Anna die?'

Janice sidles up close.

'Well, the official word is she committed suicide ...'

Trinity's legs shift uncomfortably beneath the table. Her hand takes hold of one wrist, her thumb rubbing back and forth.

'... died from a loss of blood from cutting herself ... her wrists.'

Trinity lowers her eyes.

Now I know where I get that shit from.

'But, the story I like to tell everyone ...'

Trinity's eyes lift.

'... is that she died of a broken heart.'

'What do you mean?'

'Well, George, the town doctor — a man I've known all my life, and somebody who I trust would not make anything up — told Alice from the church group — a lovely old lady who later confided in me — that alongside Anna's body was a shoebox filled with old photographs.'

Trinity stirs, her interest completely captured.

'She was clutching a family picture of herself with her husband, Michael, and their young daughter ... for the life of me I can't remember her name.'

Trinity! Her fucking name's Trinity!

I'm sitting right here.

'Alice said it was a beautiful picture, taken at the top of a snow-covered mountain ...'

Mount Washington. I remember it well. It was my eighth birthday.

'... most likely just down the way at Mount Washington.'

Sitting on the edge of her seat, Trinity's heart beats a little faster. With a tiny tremble in her voice, she asks a burning question, 'Before she died ... did she ... did she ever speak of her daughter and give a reason as to why she left her?'

Janice's mouth tightens and she looks up.

'Hmm ... I don't believe she ever did. Well, not to me anyway, and we were close, so I would find it strange if she had spoken to anyone else about her. I can't tell you why she left, but I can tell you it must have been one of the hardest things she'd ever done. It can't have been easy for her to make that decision to leave, the way she did, with no warning.'

Trinity stares past Janice at the blurry cash register on the counter behind her.

Janice places her hand on Trinity's knee.

Trinity refocuses and turns to look at her.

'We all make decisions throughout our lives that we regret later,' Janice says.

So I keep hearing.

I truly am my mother's daughter.

'It seems in the end Anna knew this and probably wished she'd made different choices. Why she decided to leave her family, I guess we'll never know. I just hope for her daughter's sake things worked out for her. I understand her uncle took her in and cared for her. I wonder what she is doing right now.'

Sitting next to you holding back the urge to scream ...

Desperately trying to resist cutting herself with that dull butter knife on the table to divert the pain ...

Wanting to be held in your arms and cry.

Janice tilts her head slightly to one side as she studies Trinity's face. At first she opens her mouth as if to say something, but then closes it and smiles.

'Ya know darling,' Janice says, 'I believe there is good in everyone. I try to not judge people but I do often think of what was going through Anna's mind the moment she decided to leave this world.'

'And what do you think that was?'

'Well, ya know, I like to see it this way: that in the most private of ways, she wanted to share the last moments of her life — her very last breath, her very last visions ... her final thoughts — with her family.'

She knows who I am.

Tears begin to well up in Trinity's eyes. She wipes them clear but her nose starts to run.

'I think that she loved them both,' Janice continues, 'more than anything else.'

Trinity bites down hard on the inside of her cheeks, tears streaming from her eyes.

Trinity uses Yamamoto's sword to cut away the tall grass from around the small tombstone beneath the maple tree. She straightens the slab of granite with her boot.

Behind the First Congregational Church in the town cemetery, Trinity kneels before a simple white cross with her mother's name carved into the wood.

She places a single red rose at its base.

Stepping back, Trinity looks up at the cold, blue early-morning sky, a welcome relief from the previous day's rain. She stands silent, a look of stone encasing her fragile interior.

GENEVA

City of Peace

Traveling down Avenue de la Paix in the free-flowing morning traffic, the Mercedes taxi makes good time. A mature Japanese woman with unblemished skin sits in the backseat staring through the windshield at the surrounding neighborhood flushed green with trees and bushes.

Her relaxed gaze follows the gentle curves of the roadside's neatly trimmed hedge and to a group of joggers maintaining a steady pace along the concrete sidewalk. In the opposite lane, for as far as she can see, road-works tarnish the otherwise beautiful scenery.

The taxi driver drifts into the bus and taxi only lane. Turning left at the Place de Nations he pulls to one side of the road just before Avenue de France.

An electric tram trundles past.

She hands him a green, 50-franc banknote.

'Merci, madame.'

He reaches for change.

She holds up her palm and smiles, 'C'est bien.'

Sliding out the door, Gabriel's former interpreter, Mako steps away from the taxi. She adjusts the fur collar of her long, red, double-breasted parka and dons her black Burberry sunglasses. The low, bright sun in the clean blue sky reflects off their gray-washed lenses.

She smiles, the distant white tip of Mont Blanc pleasing to her eye. Wandering toward the open-air mall of the nearby Place de Nations, dozens of commuters rush past her as choreographed jets of water shoot upwards.

While waiting at the crosswalk for the lights to change red, she pays respect with her eyes to a 40-foot six-ton broken chair towering above the multi-colored pavers of the mall.

Situated directly across from the Palais de Nations, the unmissable wooden monument stands as a determined symbol against the world's wanton use of landmines and cluster bombs—indiscriminate weapons, responsible for the deaths and suffering of countless innocents, even after the conflicts they were intended for had long been forgotten by the world.

The three-legged chair serves as a reminder to those who swore an oath to help make a difference to this world, lest they forget to uphold it.

Mako crosses the yellow strips to the other side of the road where she joins the end of a short queue. She smiles at a male and female security officer standing post, overseeing the morning's proceedings and verifying everyone's ID. Their black jackets and black trousers match their holstered Glock semi-auto pistols.

The young blond female officer's eyes sneak an admiring peek at Mako's black leather riding boots.

Mako attaches her pass to the outside of her coat.

'Bonjour madame,' says the young male guard, studying the details of her pass. 'Comment allez-vous?'

'Très bien, merci.'

'Il n'y à pas de quoi.'

Mako blushes a little, stops to glance over her shoulder before leaning forward and presses her pass against the scanner. Shuffling sideways through the tall steel revolving security gate she enters the grounds of the United Nations of Geneva – UNOG.

Back across the busy intersection, standing deep within an oversized bus shelter, Trinity monitors Mako's movements. Helping hide her identity, she keeps warm in a long, belted, black cashmere trench coat, stolen earlier on from a boutique in the city. Behind the brown tint of black Tom Ford sunglasses, her eyes follow Mako—her last remaining link to Gabriel—through the gate until she disappears from view.

Of the four major United Nations offices in the world, UNOG is the second largest; New York City HQ is the biggest. Geneva, the city of peace, houses various UN councils within the Art Deco Palais de Nations.

Situated within the grounds of the beautiful Arianna Park — with breath-taking views of Lake Geneva — the palace (formerly the headquarters of the UN's failed predecessor, the 'League of Nations') is as much a museum and an art gallery as it is the appointed cradle of hope and stability in a world seemingly hell-bent on destroying itself.

Mako strolls toward the palace along the Aisle of Flags — four rows of white flagpoles lining both sides of the road, all 193 UN member states' colors flaccid in the cool air. She approaches a large roundabout and turns right, cutting across the expansive and meticulously kept lawns toward century-old Cedars and giant Sequoias.

Dominating Mako's view to her left, the enormous palace stretches over six hundred meters, end to end, and boasts more than five kilometers of mind-numbing corridors inside. Most staff and delegates within its historical walls, be they time-conscious or simply lazy, utilize the more efficient but boring tunnel which now connects the northern and southern buildings.

Mako takes her time to traverse the gardens, clearing and preparing her mind before commencing her demanding and at times thankless job. Working behind the scenes, she and her colleagues often stay back late into the night, translating and deciphering transcripts from all around the globe.

She stops and turns toward the grand Assembly Hall. Looking across the Court of Honour, she enjoys the sunlight shining onto its clean, sharp, sandy-colored marble façade.

A squawk draws her attention away.

She looks across her shoulder to the elongated electric-blue neck of a male peacock rising above nearby bushes.

'There you are.'

The peacock rushes from the bushes and pulls up short of Mako, who is unfazed by the display of bravado and reaches into her coat pocket, removing a handful of unshelled sunflower seeds.

The feisty fowl turns its back on her, fanning its extensive bright-green plumage.

Mako places the seeds on the ground and then steps back.

Feeling he is the one in control, the peacock quickly turns to peck away at what has now become his daily breakfast.

'See you tomorrow, tough guy.'

Mako enters the palace through the E-Building, colloquially referred to as The New Building, a 1970s extension built to accommodate the ever-increasing number of member states.

She orders a cappuccino from the café and takes her place at a round, glass table. Leaning against the colorful, soft leather of her chrome-legged chair, she stares through one thousand square meters of one-and-a-half ton, 10-millimeter thick glass. The window was once the biggest of its kind in the world.

Beyond it is a commanding vista of nearby Lake Geneva and the snow-covered Alps. Every day, Mako enjoys the view, and the euphoria she derives from being inside the magnificent Spence Halls open spaces.

A young waitress places her cappuccino on the table.

'Merci.'

Mako checks her watch: 09:00 a.m.

She retrieves her cell phone from her pocket and, right on cue, it rings. Her finger slides across the screen.

'Bonjour … Oui, I'm positive. Non, no one followed, I'm all good … Oui, until 12 … Oui, au revoir.'

Rollercoaster

South of the city, encircled by a slew of railway tracks, is the Stade de Genève, home to Geneva's professional football team: Servette FC. Barely more than one kilometre due west from the stadium, located in the municipality of Lancy, is Parc des Fraisiers, a public open space comprising two adjoining football fields.

As the day's end draws near the field's lush pitches turn dark green. In contrast to yesterday's chilly but otherwise perfect weather, threatening clouds dominate the sky.

Trinity takes up position within the bushes and trees that line the park. The object of her attention is the picture-postcard barn-shaped house across the way. She doesn't have to wait long for the night sky to consume its gray slated roof.

A mistress of darkness, Trinity breaks from the shadows and swiftly moves across the slippery asphalt, her black leather knee-high combat boots making little noise. Aiding her cause, a nearby lamp-post sheds useless, yellow light.

Keeping her body close to the head-high hedge fencing off the front yard, Trinity steps over a small gate to enter the yard. She stays low and makes her way across the lawn to one side of the house.

Shadows from the neighbor's tall trees fall across the two-storey whitewashed exterior, making it easy for her to move about unnoticed. She approaches a window, its blinds drawn closed. Light from within the house casts silhouettes of furniture against the soft material.

Trinity places her ear to the glass. The only noise is the raucous television next door and the incessant barking of a dog down the road. She pulls away and sneaks around to the back of the house, creeping her way up a set of steps leading to a door. The wood squeaks, flexing beneath her boots. Her gloved hand tries the door knob.

It doesn't budge.

Fuck.

She cups both hands to peer through the door's clear glass panels. On the other side is a small darkened laundry with an open door leading into a long hallway. At the other end, ambient light filters through from another room.

I've watched Mako leave this house seven times; not once has she stopped to set an alarm on her way out.

Let's hope I'm right.

Taking off her glove, she places it against the glass and taps the soft leather with her sword's hilt.

Tink!

The glass quietly breaks; she removes sections of it one at a time and places them carefully on the ground, then reaches in and unlatches the door. Once inside the house, Trinity treads softly — heel ... toe ... heel ... toe — perspiring in her leather catsuit. Every now and then, the wooden floor beneath the carpet creaks.

Dozens of framed pictures adorn the walls. Trinity stops to take a closer look, but, without adequate lighting, fails to make out any details. Dull light from an open doorway cuts across the cream-colored carpet and shoots up the hall's light-blue wall, shading a photograph in half.

Trinity approaches the doorway with caution, going down on one knee to peer into the room. In one corner is a floral couch, in the other, a small timber desk with a lamp. Rising to her feet, she moves inside and toward the desk; behind it is the window she was trying to see through from outside.

She runs her fingertip along the desktop.

This place is spotless. When does she find the time to clean and tidy up?

Nothing on the desk is out of place.

She picks up a document written in Japanese.

Fukushima nuclear explosion update ... Sounds interesting, wish I had the time to read it.

She returns the paper exactly as she found it then turns around, narrowing her eyes and curling her top lip.

Her taste in furniture is ... different.

Trinity is drawn back out into the hallway by the half-lit photograph on the wall. She recognizes Mako, but not the man standing next to her, his muscular arm draped across her shoulders, his face hidden in the shadows. In the background, Jet d'Eau spurts water 140 meters straight up, a reflecting rainbow within its spray.

The floor down the dark hallway creaks.

Trinity's eyes shoot to one side; she doesn't move, she doesn't breathe.

Again it creaks.

Taking no chances, she turns and raises her sword, her glare cutting through the darkness, the katana's blade through the emerging shotgun barrel.

Grabbed by the scruff of the neck, she's swung to one side, the belt of her trench coat falling loose. Framed photographs dig into her shoulder; broken glass cuts into the back of her head.

She drops her sword.

Gabriel!

'Trinity!' Gabriel exclaims, shocked at first by the sight of her, then furious. 'What the fuck are you doing here?'

Pinned to the wall, Trinity's eyes are like saucers.

'But … you … you're dead. I thought that you were dead …'

Gabriel pauses and looks deep into her eyes, the reality of the awkward situation sinking in.

'I am,' he says quietly.

Trinity shakes her head.

'No! Why didn't you tell me?'

'I couldn't.'

Trinity's bursting heart beats out of control.

'All these years I thought you were dead! Why didn't you contact me? I tried to find out what happened to you … but there was nothing!'

Gabriel releases his hold and steps back, no words forthcoming.

Trinity pounds her fists against his chest.

'Fuck you! Fuck you!'

Gabriel doesn't defend himself, and allows her the opportunity to release her anger.

'Fuck you ... fuck you ... fuck you.'

Trinity's arms tire, her once-closed fists now open hands, her desperate fingers clutching at Gabriel's shirt. Drained, she rests her face upon his beating chest as he pulls her in tight. She lowers her arms to rest them around his waist and shuts her eyes, enjoying the healing warmth that not even Halo can give her.

Following a lengthy respite, where neither has moved, neither has uttered a single word, Trinity senses Gabriel become restless. Her eyes, long since opened, stare into the darkness down the hall.

She feels his fingers press into her shoulders as he gently pushes her away. Trinity looks up at him, her tired, beaten body somewhat renewed and recharged.

He looks down at her.

'You can't stay here.'

She doesn't respond.

'Things are different; I'm with Mako now.'

'I know,' she says softly.

'I have a life with her. She's been good for me.'

'But ... I thought ... I was hoping ...'

Gabriel sighs ... heavily.

'Trinity ... I can admit my life was fucked up long before I met you. But you ... you took it to another level, deep down inside a hole I never want to venture into again.' Gabriel gathers his thoughts for a moment. 'I force myself ... I force myself to smile every day and place one foot in front of the other. My life now with Mako is what I need. I'm healing.'

'But …'

'No. You have to leave now!' Gabriel's tone takes on a harsh edge. 'After love and hate collide, nothing … and I mean nothing at all remains. Looking back now … I wish I'd never met you.'

Trinity feels her mind being pulled into the darkness of a familiar chasm, a place from which she struggles to escape.

Without thought or warning, she turns and runs down the hall. Gabriel instinctively reaches out, his fingers latching onto her coat, peeling it from her body as she slips away. She runs toward the front of the house, away from Gabriel, leaving behind her sword, her one and only treasured possession.

Gabriel slings her coat to the floor, turns and breaks for the back door.

Trinity bursts onto the patio and sprints across the wet lawn.

Cold rain pecks at her face.

Gabriel dashes up the side of the house and across the yard in an attempt to cut her off, hurdling over the gate in one leap landing in a puddle. He looks up, frost clouding his panting mouth, in time to see Trinity disappear into the darkness across the other side of the road.

She runs without purpose or direction. All she knows is she must run. Her thighs scream and her arms pump like crazy.

Gabriel's eyes quickly adjust to the darkness and begin to make out Trinity's silhouette. After years of resting and rebuilding his broken body in the aftermath of Tokyo, Gabriel is now fitter and stronger than ever before and finds no challenge in running her down.

He lunges forward and tackles her at the waist. The unexpected impact expels the air from her lungs and causes her back to arch. They land hard and roll entwined across the wet grass.

Trinity looks up at Gabriel sitting over the top of her, pinning her wrists alongside her head. In an effort to dislodge him, she arches her back.

'Get off me! Get the fuck off me.'

Strands of wet hair stretch across her face. Beads of water slide along her bodysuit.

Gabriel exerts force.

'Stop struggling,' he says, 'and just listen to me.'

Trinity attempts to wrestle her arms free.

'Fuck you!'

'I'm sorry!' he yells. 'I'm sorry for what I said back at the house.'

Trinity continues her attempts to escape.

'Then why did you fucking say it?'

Gabriel doesn't answer. Instead, he slowly releases his grip and leans back.

Trinity ignores the opportunity to break free and lies there, wet from the rain and the grass, looking up at him, her chest rising and falling. She allows him to reach down and gently wipe the hair from her mouth.

Then she panics, her hands reaching wildly.

'Where's my sword? Where the fuck is it?'

Gabriel presses down on her chest.

'Relax. It's back at the house.' He stands and offers her his hand. 'Come back inside and let's talk.'

Trinity hesitates then reaches up.

The fire crackles and Trinity's face glows. She wraps her hands around a warm cup of coffee.

'Are you sure Mako won't mind me wearing her robe?'

Gabriel stokes the fire before sitting down across from his unexpected house guest.

'I'm hoping she'll never find out.'

'Don't worry,' Trinity says. 'I'll be long gone by the time she comes home.'

'How long have you been following her?'

She raises an eyebrow.

Gabriel pushes, 'How long?'

'Seven days.'

He shakes his head.

'Was it difficult?'

'No.'

'Fuck me.'

Trinity shifts the cup in her hands.

'She needs to switch up her daily routine a little ... well, a lot actually. She's too predictable. FYI, I think the young guard at the entrance to the UN has a crush on her.'

'Does she even look over her shoulder?'

Gabriel is desperate for a win.

Trinity holds up her finger.

'Only once.'

He rolls his eyes.

A log falls to one side; tiny embers spit everywhere.

'I'm sorry,' Gabriel says. 'I'm sorry for saying I wish I'd never met you.'

Trinity stares at her cup, but doesn't respond.

'It was out of line. I didn't mean it.'

'Then why say it?'

Gabriel lowers his eyes.

'I don't know. I wasn't expecting you to be creeping around inside my house.'

'Trust me, Gabriel … you were the last person I expected to see.'

He looks up.

'How did you find me?'

'I didn't.'

Gabriel looks puzzled.

'I found Mako.'

'Mako? Why? How did you find her?'

'You don't want to know.' The deep tone of her drawl sends a chill running down Gabriel's spine.

'No, I do,' he says. 'If you found me … what's to say someone else won't?'

'Trust me,' Trinity says. 'Your secret — and the secrets of many others, for that matter — go with me to the grave. No one else *alive* knows about Mako.'

Gabriel sinks into his soft leather chair.

'Why are you here? What do you want with her?'

'Don't worry, she's safe. She was the last remaining connection between the two of us. Believe it or not, I searched everywhere for any information at all on you … but I found nothing.'

'It was designed that way. Because Fujisawa died under US control, on Japanese soil, deals were cut at seriously high levels to keep it out of the media.'

'I figured it was worth a shot to find out if Mako knew anything. I didn't think I'd be sitting here next to you, drinking coffee.'

They share a rare smile.

'So what happened to you?' she enquires.

'Well, after you shot me …'

Trinity sits forward in her chair.

'You made me shoot you.'

Gabriel pauses.

'After *I* made you shoot me, I spent the next six months in hospital, in Tokyo. Mako quit her interpreting job and because of everything we'd been through together, she felt compelled to be by my side every day. I have to say … there wasn't a day I didn't think of you. Some days I fucking hated you, on others I missed you … regardless … I couldn't get you out of my head.'

'And now?'

'It's all the same,' Gabriel drones, a void growing behind his eyes. 'Some things have changed, but … it's all the same.'

Trinity lowers her eyes then lifts them.

'And then what?'

'Mako took me to the home of her ancestors. A small, relatively unknown village referred to as Aita …'

'Empty,' Trinity translates. 'It means empty.'

'Kind of makes sense; there didn't seem to be a lot of people around.'

'Where is it located?'

'It's at the base of Mount Fuji … not far from the city of Gotemba.'

'Yes. I know the area well … Shizuoka Prefecture. Their local folklore tells of ancient samurai training on the nearby mountainside. Ironically, the military train there now.'

'How come you know so much about the place?'

'When I was a teenager, my guardian Yoshimura sent me to Gotemba to learn yabusame.'

'Yabusame! So … not only do you know how to sword fight, you know how to shoot an arrow from a galloping horse?'

Trinity nods, 'Three.'

'Three what?'

'Shoot three arrows, in quick succession. But my main purpose for attending was to learn the concentration and discipline required to master the training, two principles Yoshimura believed invaluable in conquering one's own fears.'

'This Yoshi guy sounds like he knows his shit.'

Trinity stares at the ground.

'Yeah, he's pretty special.' She looks up. 'Anyway, you were saying …'

'It was in Aita,' Gabriel continues, 'I truly recovered. Life there was simple; it made me appreciate the little things and taught me to be strong, stronger than I ever thought possible. I toiled every day, cutting down trees, digging holes and trenches … swinging hammers.

'If I wanted water, I had to go onto the mountain to get it. At first, I carried back only what I needed, but soon I realised I could carry enough for the entire village. This made my legs and back strong.

'Everything I ate came from the land … from the mountain. Chickens roamed free and were abundant. The protein helped me build new muscle. I ate berries I'd never even heard of. Almost a year to the day after you … after I was shot, I finally felt ready to leave.'

'And then you and your girlfriend Mako ran off into the sunset … blah, blah, blah.'

'No. And then my girlfriend and I went and found Tanaka and put a .40-cal bullet right between his fucking eyes.'

Trinity is speechless. She sinks into her chair.

'You seem surprised?'

'You? You killed Tanaka?'

Gabriel nods.

'You have no idea do you?' she asks.

'What?'

'That psycho Russian cunt thinks I did it. I've been on the run ever since, thanks to you.'

'And now you're going to kill The Russian?'

'I have no choice,' Trinity answers, having brought Gabriel up to speed on the past few years of her life. 'If you'd shot him in Tokyo like I told you to, things would be different.'

'Don't blame me for the shitty situation you're in.'

Trinity bites her tongue. She's been down this road too many times and changes tack.

'Come with me, Gabriel. I don't think I can do this on my own.'

He stands and paces back and forth.

'No. No. Don't ask me to do this. I have a life here now with Mako. I have to consider her needs. I never asked for any of this.'

'You sit home all day,' Trinity points out. 'Doing what? Watching Oprah in fucking subtitles and doing the housework? Jerking off?'

Gabriel stands still. He turns to face Trinity.

'Do you really want to know what I do all day long?'

'Yeah … yeah I do.'

'I try not to think of you.'

Trinity's mouth opens in preparation for words to follow.

Tell him. Tell him you also think of him all the time.

You searched the world … and you fucking found him … tell him.

Second chances like this rarely come around.

Don't let another day go by on your own.

For once in your life … say what you really want to say, what's in your heart, not what's in your fucked up head.

Get over your hatred of men. Gabriel is different. He's real.

Tell him …

Fucking tell him …

Trinity's mouth closes, the sound of her gentle breath lost in the background noise of the crackling fire.

'I won't lie to you, Trinity. My life now is fucking mundane in comparison to chasing you around the world. And as fucked as that was, with everyone around me dying … facing death at every turn, every day … I never felt more alive.' Gabriel sits back down. 'But I owe Mako. I owe her my life.'

'Do you love her?'

Gabriel looks down and then back up.

'She'll be home soon.'

Trinity clamps her jaw and grinds her teeth madly. She nods.

'I don't suppose you have any weapons I can borrow?'

'I did have a shotgun, before you broke in and sliced the barrel in half.'

Bathed in an orange glow, both Trinity and Gabriel stand, their stares unbreakable, the heat from the fireplace as intense as the conflicting psychological force that pushes and pulls between them.

The last time I saw Gabriel, he made me blow a hole in his chest in an attempt to save me.

I didn't have to do it …

I let him do it …

And then I ran away …

Trinity looks to his chest.

'Can I see it?' she asks.

'See what … the shotgun?'

'No … the scar.'

Gabriel pauses before pulling down the front of his T-shirt.

Trinity bites her lip.

Stepping forward, she places her palm over his heart.

'Can I touch it?'

Gabriel remains silent.

Her finger circles the inch-wide depressed graft of tight, pale skin. She looks up at him and then back to his wounded heart, running her index finger along the lengthy incision scar.

Gabriel pulls his shirt back up.

Trinity slides her hand out from beneath it, her gaze locked onto his chest.

'I'm sorry your friends died in New York, Gabriel. Neither they, nor you, deserved any of the shit I dragged you into.'

Gabriel's lips close tightly.

Trinity puts her arms around him.

He pulls her head to his chest.

'Are you sure you have to do this, Trinity?'

'I have no other options. I'm tired of running. And I know you won't believe me when I say it … but I have changed.'

'I wish I could help …'

'Don't, Gabriel. Without knowing it, you've done enough … more than enough … more than I deserve.'

'For what's it worth,' Gabriel says, 'most houses in Switzerland have caches of weapons stored inside them. Not only is there a ton of shit left over from World War Two, but they have national service here …'

'…which means everyone brings home their guns and gear.'

'Exactly,' Gabriel nods. 'Therefore, a burglar might find more than they expected, should they rob certain houses.'

Trinity looks up, playfully squints her eyes.

'I don't suppose you happen to know of anyone in the neighborhood who wears an army uniform?'

Mako sits by the fire with her iPad, scrolling through the Swiss edition of The Local. An article grabs her attention.

'Have you read today's news?' she asks Gabriel, who sits in the chair alongside hers, watching television.

'No. Not yet, why do you ask?'

'It says there's been a spate of robberies in the area over the past week.'

Gabriel stirs.

'Oh really?'

'Yes. It says weapons and ammunition were stolen … the police seem to think the houses were targeted quite specifically.'

'Well, at least we know they won't break into our house,' Gabriel jokes. 'I'm sure my old shotgun is of no use to them.'

'Do you think it might have anything to do with … well, you know, all the trouble we had in Tokyo?'

Gabriel leans forward and takes hold of her hand.

'That was three years ago. No one knows we're here. There's nothing to worry about.'

'If you say so, though I am glad you fixed that broken window pane on the back door. I've warned you not to slam it closed all the time.'

'You're right. I don't know my own strength sometimes. While we're on the subject of security, later tonight I would like to go over some of the things I taught you … you know, about being vigilant when you go out, just in case somebody might … I dunno … decide to follow you one day.'

'Sure, honey.'

Gabriel smiles and returns to the international news on the television.

A curvaceous female reporter stands next to a gothic lamp post with the crystal clear waters of Corniche Beach behind her. Across the waterway, glazed skyscrapers puncture the perfect blue sky.

'… Thanks Steve. I'm Candy Faranda, reporting live from the United Arab Emirates. In the background is Abu Dhabi, the scene of what experts are calling the most recent terrorist attack on American interests in the Middle-East. We have confirmation that a CIA cooperative and Kuwaiti national, known only as Zubair, has been assassinated, his body found at the scene of a house fire in the suburbs just outside the UAE capital.

'Now, not much is actually known about Zubair's involvement with America's top secret agency, but what little information there is at the moment suggests that he was a key player—if not the global kingpin—in intelligence-gathering for the US government.

'However, unconfirmed rumours suggest that Zubair was also selling secret and sensitive information to the highest bidder …'

Gabriel picks up the remote control and increases the volume.

'… Some experts indicate that, given his violent death, the full extent of these allegations may never be revealed; Zubair may literally have taken his secrets with him to the grave.'

Gabriel moves to the edge of his chair.

'The hunt continues for the suspected terrorists responsible for his death, with US officials releasing very little information on their identities. What we do know is that there are two males involved and the government *is* aware of their identities. For security reasons, they are not prepared to release the men's names or countries of origin.

'Now, if all that isn't enough international intrigue for you, Steve, a recent gun battle three days ago at a busy train station in Mumbai resulted in the deaths of six men known to have Russian mafia connections. The incident has since been linked to another bloody shootout, this one unfolding in Hong Kong earlier today. Initial reports confirm that members from two rival Chinese Triads were gunned down by two unknown males in separate incidents: one in Kowloon and the other on Hong Kong Island.

'If indeed the two suspects are the same males alleged to have assassinated Zubair, they are both well trained and equipped, and appear hell-bent on distancing themselves from the scene of the original crime in Abu Dhabi. Nobody knows where they may be heading next.'

Gabriel murmurs, 'Tokyo.'

Mako raises her eyes.

'Did you say something?'

'Huh? Umm … no, I'm just talking to myself. It's all good.'

Mako smiles and returns to her iPad.

HONG KONG

Diversion

alo storms up to the shopfront door and rattles the handle. He assumes the Cantonese sign in the glass window says 'closed'; his boot says otherwise. He and Carlos rush though the doorway, slamming the glass panels behind them.

Carlos crouches below a window-sill and peers through the blinds.

'Weapons check!' Halo barks, his left hand drawing a fresh mag from his pocket, his right thumb pressing the magazine release button of the .40 caliber Glock. The partially depleted mag falls between his fingers and in one smooth motion he palms the new one in and tugs on it.

Carlos updates him: 'It's all clear outside.'

'Roger that.'

Halo removes his black 5.11 backpack and reaches into a side pouch and pulls out a handful of bullets to bomb up his mag. The reloaded magazine fits perfectly into the pocket of his leather jacket.

'It's still clear.'

Halo nods and breaks open a new box of hollow points. He tips them into the side pouch; the empty package goes back into the bag and a small handful of rounds into his other pocket. Unzipping the main compartment, he pushes aside several more boxes of ammunition, revealing protein bars, several bruised bananas, one red and one green apple.

'I'm out of water.'

'I'm pretty sure I have some,' Carlos says.

Halo checks his phone, his eyes flicking through a brief message.

'Switch,' he says, rising to one knee and turning to face the window.

Carlos turns and slides his back down the wall and sits on the floor.

'What's the plan?'

'There's a taxi stand across the road,' Halo says, making it up as he goes along. 'If one arrives in the next five minutes, we'll make a break for it.'

Carlos reloads his mags.

'Roger that.'

'We'll continue fighting our way to Shenzhen across the border and into China. Hopefully once there, we can push a little faster, heading north to Japan.'

'Any updates from your friend Yoshi in Tokyo?'

'He says Trinity is in Geneva, but she is moving on to her final destination today.'

'You put a lot of faith in this guy Yoshi.'

'Yoshimura helped to raise her when she was young, like a daughter. He would do anything for her. In fact, he's probably been the only constant source of goodness in Trinity's life. He's always been there for me as well; I trust him unreservedly.'

'Do you think she can do it?'

'Do what?'

'Kill this guy?'

Before Halo can answer, a taxi pulls up outside.

'We're up. Gather your shit.'

Carlos zips his bag and throws it onto his back.

'Good to go!'

'It's clear outside,' Halo says. 'But keep one eye on the alley, 20 meters left.'

Carlos sneaks a peek.

'Seen.'

Halo raises his pistol in front of his face and pulls the door open. Carlos peels left; Halo, half-a-second later, heads right.

'Clear.'

'Clear.'

After visually securing both ends of the sidewalk, the two fugitives make eye contact and nod. Without a word spoken, they hustle across the quiet road, shoulders hunched, arms extended, guns trained at the taxi.

The driver looks up and sees them approaching. He panics and fails to restart the engine.

Halo taps on the window with the muzzle of his gun and motions for him to exit the car.

Carlos scans the area behind them.

Gunshots break the early morning peace and the taxi's rear window. Halo and Carlos crouch down as bullets thump into the doors and roof of the Toyota sedan. More glass shatters; hundreds of shards sprinkle on the road and Halo's cap.

Carlos dumps an entire magazine toward the alley.

Halo does the same while Carlos reloads.

Back in the game, Carlos goes prone alongside the car, firing controlled bursts of two and three bullets.

Halo swings the butt of his gun upwards and smashes the driver's-side window. Reaching in, he unlatches the door and opens it.

The taxi driver slumps forward, the hair on the back of his head soaked with blood.

Halo yanks him from the car and then slams another mag into his Glock.

'Let's go!'

Carlos yells over the gunfire, 'Moving!'

Utilizing the car as cover, Halo crouches, the muscles in his thighs burning as he rises incrementally to send rounds safely downrange over the top of his partner.

Carlos stays low and crawls up into the taxi and over to the backseat, shoving his gun through the shot-up back window.

'Covering!'

Halo draws his gun back down.

'Moving!' he cries, sliding into the driver's seat.

Tink! Tink! Tink!

Bullets strike the car's trunk.

Carlos fires his gun in retaliation.

'Let's go! Punch it!' he cries.

Halo stomps in the clutch, starts the engine and shoves it into gear; the tires squeal.

Carlos keeps firing toward the alley until they turn a corner. Safely out of reach of the gunmen, he spins around and rests his head back.

Halo glances up at the rear-view mirror.

'Fuck! That was close,' he says, his throat parched, his gruff voice competing with the whining sound of the gear-box being thrashed as he speeds through the comforting silence of the backstreets.

Carlos nods and then reaches into his bag.

Halo feels a tap on his shoulder and turns to find Carlos's hand holding out a half-empty plastic bottle of water.

SOFIA

City of Secrets

Fuck, it's cold!

Trinity tugs at her coat collar and firms up the belt. Standing outside the Sofia Airport terminal, a light breeze bites at her face.

She looks to the right; the traffic control tower dominates a black sky. To the left is a lengthy line of small yellow Kia taxis. Trinity makes her way to the third cab waiting in line and enters the rear door. Sinking into the soft cloth material, she shuffles to the other side, Yamamoto's concealed sword across her lap.

Staring at the rear view mirror, she notes the surprised look on the driver's face is identical to those worn by the drivers emerging from the two taxis parked in front. It's not considered polite to avoid the first taxi.

'English?' Trinity enquires; the Bulgarian language and Cyrillic alphabet are anything but one of her strong suits.

The mirror reflects the driver's bleary eyes. Despite his unusually weedy Bulgarian frame, he confidently responds in a strong eastern-European accent, 'Yes. I speak English very good.'

Trinity monitors his approaching colleagues, waving their fists in the air.

'Drive,' she says.

The driver ignores their remonstrations and speeds off, then glances again at the mirror.

'Destination?'

Trinity looks past her reflection in the window at random stacks of prefabricated multilevel housing blocks—a legacy of Bulgaria's not-so-distant socialist past. Rising from unkempt grounds, no more than seven or eight storeys high and in desperate need of exterior paint and repairs, these flats comfortably house most of the city's locals, who commute daily into the capital, no more than ten minutes away.

Huge roadside lamps flash their light across Trinity's face. She answers softly, 'Sofia.'

'Sofia is big.'

She briefly gazes at the mirror before looking back into the darkness outside.

The driver raises his eyebrows and shrugs his shoulders. Reaching down, he increases the volume of his radio, tuned into a classic-rock station.

The driver glances up at the mirror.

'You are returning to Sofia?'

Trinity shakes her head.

'It is your first time?'

She doesn't acknowledge him.

He smiles regardless and lowers the volume on the radio.

'Sofia is one of the oldest cities in Europe,' he says. 'It exist four thousand years before the birth of the Christ. But the city ... the city is at odds with itself. It struggle to find new identity since the fall of the Berlin Wall, and the demise of communist Russia's grip on Eastern Europa.'

Trinity lowers her eyes and listens, her attention captured by the driver's passionate description of his beloved hometown.

'Sofia is capital of Bulgaria, which was a satellite state of the Soviet Union. There are 1.5-million residents, and all are divided over which direction the future should progress.

'And although we shook the Russian bear from our back in 1989, the powerful and crafty beast, he still lurks in the woods, prowling, ever sharpening his claws and flexing his muscles.

'Where once the Russian tanks and the Red Army soldiers kept the streets of Sofia beneath the heel of communism, now, our reluctant dependency on them for the gas and the nuclear energy simply replaces the ugly form of their heavy, black-leather jackboot.'

Trinity feels the car slowing down. She looks at her watch: 10:00 p.m.

'Demonstration,' the taxi driver announces.

Trinity looks at his ID badge displayed proudly on the dash.

Dimitri ... Somethingorother.

'What is it about?'

'The people, they are not happy with the government.'

'Why not?'

'The people are never happy,' he answers. 'Half the people, the older citizens — the ones who cannot let go of the old communist ways of living — wish to keep the government in business, but the younger generation, they want the western living, the rock and roll, the fashion … the money.'

Trinity leans her head back.

'I would have thought the older people would be happy to be free of communist rule after almost fifty years.'

'Da, you would think so. My grandparents, they had their land and business taken from them, like many others. My father, he remembers these types of things well. He tell me when he was a young child, living in the countryside not far from Sofia, Soviet soldiers enter his father's house late at night to occupy for several days, to eat and to sleep. He does not forget, but the others, they are scared, scared of change and maybe stubborn also.'

'Do you think you will ever be completely free of communism?'

Dimitri nods his head, 'Ne, we will never. Many Bulgarians, they approve of Russia. After all, they free our country of five hundred years of Turkish occupation and rule … we are forever in their gratitude.' He leans his hand against the horn and shouts angrily at the car cutting in front of him, 'Da ti eba maikata!'

Trinity smiles even though she doesn't understand what he is saying.

'And the Russia, they need our country,' adds the driver, returning his gaze to the mirror. 'Bulgaria, she is geographically strategic. They wish to run their energy pipes through our countryside. And Putin … he wish to use Bulgaria as … how you say … Trojan horse, inside the European Union. You know, to spy on everyone. I am not stupid.'

Trinity nods.

'I warn you,' he continues. 'Everywhere you go, in Sofia, people … they watch you.'

'What do you mean?'

'You will see. The spies, they are everywhere.'

'Who are they watching and how will I know where they are?'

'Everyone! They watch everyone. You open your eyes and you will see. I tell you … they are watching.'

Trinity smirks.

Dimitri lifts his head to gain a better look in the mirror.

'Enough talk of politics. Your mother, she is Bulgarian?'

'Why do you ask?'

'You don't speak like Bulgarian, but you are tall and beautiful, like most Bulgarian women. It is documented they are most beautiful in the world. Not many people know this … is big secret. You will see.'

'No, my mother is not from here.'

'Do you know why they are so beautiful?'

Trinity rolls her eyes.

'Tell me.'

'For many people, for thousands of years, Bulgaria is gateway from Europa into Asia and Asia into Europa. Here in Sofia, many many girls with the black hair and dark skin … like the Persians, but with the blue eyes and the green eyes and faces shaped like the Germans and the Swedes. Before long, is easy, you can nominate their ancestors. Also they are very tall and thin … very beautiful … like you. You will see.'

Trinity turns her head. Outside the window, slowly coming into view, are two cast-iron statues of eagles perched atop tall concrete bases, their weathered green ionised wings spread wide.

'Orlov Most,' Dimitri says. 'Eagle's Bridge ... there are two more the other side.'

Trinity rolls her head; sure enough, two more eagles.

'Da tragvame!' Dimitri vents, the traffic coming to a halt. 'Do not worry,' he says. 'I will make detour shortly into capital.'

Trinity closes her eyes to gather her thoughts.

I hate going to places I've never been before.

Too many things can go wrong.

You can get lost and disorientated real quick and end up in more shit than when you started.

No logistics support, no back-up, little-to-no intel ... No safe houses, or caches ... fuck, the list goes on.

I need to stay off the radar for a day or two ... no fancy hotels.

And hostels are too busy ... random people coming and going ...

Perhaps a church. I'm sure a place like this will be full of them, willing to take in a stray ... although I don't exactly look like one.

And if Dimitri's observations of women are correct, I might at least be able to wander around during the day as well as the night and check the city out, get a feel for it, without drawing too much attention to myself.

Fuck ... that will be a first.

Trinity opens her eyes at the sound of a familiar song.
'Turn it up,' she says.
'I see the pretty lady has good taste.'
Dimitri smiles and turns the dial. Holding a cigarette out of the partially opened window while his other

hand grasps a plastic cup containing alcohol, he steers the car with his knees and sings to Trinity, 'Ohhh ... oh ... living on a prayer ...'

Huh! ... Living on a prayer ...

It kind of sums up my life at the moment.

The traffic along Tsar Osvoboditel Boulevard is gridlocked. Exhausted from her flight and recent events, Trinity stares out the window, her mind barely engaged, placed safely in neutral. Directly across the road from her now stationary taxi towers an imposing 40-meter tall concrete monument. Erected in the middle of a well-lit, wide-open square, its base, surrounded by broken cement slabs is tarnished with signs of graffiti.

Standing atop its pedestal, a young, proud Soviet soldier, cast in bronze, hoists his Tommy gun high above his head. Shielded behind him, with the gratitude on their faces forever frozen in time, are a Bulgarian man, woman and child. The monument remains as a long-lasting symbol of the Soviet Army's historic liberation of Sofia from the Nazis ... or, as many locals like to call it, the Soviet Army *occupation*.

'The capital is beyond the next intersection,' Dimitri yells over the music. 'You have decided which direction?'

Trinity blinks, turns her head back towards him.

'Say again?'

Dimitri turns down the volume.

'I ask which direction. The capital is not far.'

'Are there any churches nearby?'

'Church! You wish to go to church?'

'Yes.'

'The city Sofia has many churches.'

'Then take me to one.'

Dimitri's eyes dart to the digital clock on the dashboard then straight back to the mirror.

'But at this time of night, they may not be open to the visitors.'

'Take me to the biggest one.'

'If you wish,' he says. 'I will take you to the grandest cathedral of them all. I know a shortcut. But you will have to walk a short way. The blockades for the protests prevent me from getting too close.'

Although it's late at night and bitterly cold outside, the cloudless sky allows the lustre of its large waning moon to reflect off an enormous gold-leafed dome and bell tower some two hundred meters ahead.

'Here is cathedral,' Dimitri announces. 'It is one of the most beautiful and biggest of its kind in the entire world.'

Trinity cranes her neck to catch a glimpse of more gilded domes rising above the dark shapes created by the nearby trees. The cobblestone road ahead glistens in the light of the taxi's headlamps; it's as though the streets of Sofia are paved in gold.

'I can drive no further,' Dimitri says, pulling over and cutting the engine. 'I will have to let you out here. Unfortunately this is the best I can do.'

'That's okay, you did a good job.'

'I will walk with you to the church. There is a danger-ous fakulteto close by. Many Krhyminali members live in-side its walls.'

She hands over a brown 50-Lev banknote.

'I'll be fine. Keep the change.'

Dimitri looks over his shoulder.

'Mersi my beautiful friend, but do not underestimate the gypsy Krhyminali! They are very cunning and very dangerous and very dirty. They not live by rules.'

'Thanks for your concern, but I will be fine. Chao!'

Trinity turns the handle and opens the door. The cold air slaps her face; a chill runs though her bones as she closes the door behind her and walks in the direction of the cathedral.

Trinity approaches a street blockade: small steel barri-ers with gaps big enough to walk through. A menacing dark-blue armored Gendarmerie van is parked off to one side, and nearby a seemingly unbreakable line of hulking riot police officers.

The special officers are dressed in uniforms the same color as their armored van and wearing soft-body armor, black general-duty boots, helmets and visors. Trinity can see their gas grenades and visually identifies they are also equipped with Russian Makarov pistols, chambered for the 9x18mm Makarov cartridge.

In an effort to circumvent them, she makes her way down a smaller side-street lined with tidy but bromidic brick townhouses and shopfronts. She passes by increasingly elaborate façades, each one adorned in soft pastel colors with ornate steel bars securing huge decorative windows.

The only light in the street comes from the bright three-quarter moon poised above the snow-capped summit of Mount Vitosha. The mighty mountain, as it has done for millennia, watches over the troubled but beautiful city below.

A mob of protesters rounds the corner—young men, fathers, mothers, children and the elderly, some carrying flags, other's whistles and small drums. They seem content and relatively quiet as they talk among themselves. Having made their point to the government, they are ready to go home.

Trinity steps aside on the narrow sidewalk and allows them to pass. As the last one brushes by, she continues along the cracked and at times uneven pavement.

Thank fuck I'm not wearing high heels!

She steps down onto the gray-cobblestone road, finding it a little easier to walk on. Negotiating parked cars, the occasional pothole in the road and a few stragglers left over from the protest, it's not long before Trinity notices a stark difference in the design and fabric of the buildings and houses.

Exterior walls are now a random collection of bricks, not only differing in size but in color and shape as well; some are half-rendered in white cement, while others are not rendered at all. Tiled roofing has given way to sheets of wrought iron, rusted and filled with holes. The tiny, ramshackle houses all have satellite dishes with illegal cables running wild, trailing from house to house and over the road to a nearby power pole.

Two small children, barefoot and grubby, stomp

through puddles of mud and dirty gray sand, carelessly soiling lines and lines of clothing hanging across the entire width of the fakulteto.

Trinity crosses the road to a small, shadowy park overgrown with trees. Goose bumps immediately sprout across her shoulders, up and around her neck and down both arms. She stops and listens.

The shadows in the background rustle.

Her head turns.

The shadows stop moving.

Trinity draws her sword and spins around at the sound of soft running footsteps.

The look of evil approaches fast: bared, rotting teeth, crazed-looking eyes. Trinity bends then stands and with a simple shrug of her shoulders hurtles the attacker through the air. She smells another's pungent odour as he charges from the shadows. Turning around, she plunges her sword into his chest.

He wheezes and looks down at the blade.

She kicks him to the ground.

Blood slides from the blade.

Trinity notices more shadows coming to life. Slowly she turns in a circle, her sword at arm's length, parallel to the ground.

Where's one of those fucking big cops when you need one?

A shriek pierces the air as a dozen gypsy Krhyminali rush forth. Trinity swings her sword 360 degrees, cutting limbs and slashing flesh, causing howls and cries of pain.

She's grabbed by the arm and attempts to shrug free; teeth latch onto her forearm. Fortunately, the jagged ivory stumps are unable to penetrate the bodysuit beneath her thick coat. She headbutts her attacker's eye socket, caving it in.

He screams and releases his bite.

Yamamoto's sword sends his dirty and unwashed head thumping along the ground.

A skinhead in desperate need of a shower grabs Trinity from behind; his body odour is foul, his already tanned face blotched brown with dirt and grime.

She repeatedly drives her elbow into his kidney, but his arm tightens around her neck; she struggles to breathe.

Others join in and grab at her.

She kicks at them with her designer combat boots, their thick solid heels cracking bones, but the mob has her arms pinned to her body.

A closed-fist—each finger adorned with a skull ring—slams into her temple.

Trinity's mind is overwhelmed by a sudden darkness filled with brilliant white stars, littered forever.

Her head slumps to one side.

There's No Place like Heaven

A young Trinity sits in the car alongside her father.
He stares through the front windshield.
She looks at him and wonders why he won't respond to her need for attention.

Her hand reaches out but he is too far away.

No matter how loud she yells, he continues looking forward, never blinking.

A sudden bright light illuminates his face.

His eyes widen, but still, he never blinks or looks away.

Trinity turns to the light.

She wants to scream, but she can't.

Trinity's eyes open wide; her hair is drenched in sweat. A bright light hanging above her face forces her to look away. A few seconds later, her pupils begin to focus on the whitewashed concrete ceiling. Sitting up on her makeshift bed — an old military canvas stretcher — Trinity rubs one side of her face, opening and closing her aching jaw.

Where in the fuck am I?

A cave?

She looks around her small subterranean chamber. A wall-mounted light beside a partially-opened arched wooden door flickers off and on. The high, curved ceiling and solid stone walls are all roughly finished in white cement. A small, timber desk and chair occupy one corner.

A chromed bar heater helps keep the room warm.

Trinity throws her patchwork blanket aside and swings her legs off the stretcher, placing her bare feet onto the concrete floor. She grabs at her ribs and grimaces. Fetching her boots from the corner, she slips them on and drapes the blanket over her shoulders.

Where the fuck is my sword?

Creeping toward the door, Trinity peers through the opening and into another chamber, only this one is much larger and brighter.

Religious icons and photographs hang from the white walls. In the center of the room is a small, round table made of oak; two fruit crates placed on their ends substitute for chairs. A large desk, overflowing with stacks of paperwork and documents, runs the entire length of the room, and there is a closet in one corner, beside a small sink and a bench with an urn on top.

Trinity shivers, the room temperature noticeably cooler, its stale air scented with a smokeless and flowery incense.

Sitting at the desk in an old rickety chair is an elderly man with long, white hair. He wears beaten-up leather shoes, baggy trousers and an oversized tattered brown coat. The strongly built man, hunched forward, appears engrossed in what he's reading.

Unsure of the situation she finds herself in, but eager to find out, Trinity takes hold of the bronze serpent-head handle and eases the solid door open.

The hinges creak loudly.

Fuck!

The old man at the desk doesn't move.

'Dobro utro,' he says.

Trinity stands sheepishly in the doorway.

'English?'

'Da,' he responds. 'Good morning to you.'

'Who are you?'

He answers with a strong, tired voice, his comprehension of the English language … good.

'My name is Anzhelo.' Standing from his chair, he turns to face Trinity. 'But you call me Angel.'

Trinity is taken aback by his appearance.

Although tall, his hunch appears permanent. His uncombed white beard matches his hair. His left eye is horribly scarred and it weeps uncontrollably.

'I am aware my face causes much discomfort. Do not be concerned … I am accustom to the reaction.'

Fuck! Stop staring at him.

Trinity's eyes dart around the room.

'Ummm … where am I? What is this place? How did I get here? Have you seen my sword?'

'Patience child, you are safe here.'

'Where is here?'

His arms extend both up and out.

'This is my home. You are inside the crypt beneath the cathedral.'

'You mean the church with the golden roof?'

'Yes.'

She screws up her face.

'So this is a burial ground?'

'No,' Anzhelo answers. 'Not all crypts are burial grounds. The rooms are kept hidden for many years. During the war, the priests hold secret meetings in here, and valuable religious icons are locked away within the walls for safekeeping.'

'How did I get in here?'

'I find you across the road in the park, not far from the eternal flame.'

Trinity looks all around and then at the ground, furrowing her brow.

'I remember being attacked ... there were many ... too many. I was being choked ... and then there were all these skulls and stars, and the next thing I know I'm staring up at the ceiling of a cave.'

'You are unconscious when I come to your aid. I check your breathing and is okay.'

'How did you find me?'

'Young gypsy boys chase the birds outside the cathedral. As I move them on, I hear screams and yells from inside the park. I immediately assume police are dealing roughly with protesters. I wander over to see and then I see them ... attack you. I want to help ... but I am old now and scared ... so I am sad and embarrassed to say I watch only.'

'How did I get in here?'

'I carry you. You were struck to the head and fall unconscious. As you lay on the ground, they kick and stomp …'

'That explains why my ribs are sore.'

'The police arrive at the same time,' continues the old man. 'They chase after the gypsy Kryhminali. It is only then I find my strength to sneak from the bushes and carry you from the park, before they return to ask many questions. I search for identification, but find nothing.

'The Krhyminali must take your documentation and possessions. I assume you are Bulgaria woman. You are thin, tall and beautiful … but your face, it has something of Asia.'

'So everyone keeps telling me.' Trinity looks at Anzhelo and moves toward him. 'Do not feel sorry. You saved my life … you are my very own guardian angel.'

A hint of a smile appears across his craggy face as Trinity kisses him on the cheek.

Trinity sips soup from her spoon.

'This is delicious.'

'I make it myself,' Anzhelo says. 'I am sorry the portion is small.'

'That's okay. What is in it?'

'Maybe you do not like to know.'

'I lived in Japan for most of my life … I have eaten many strange things.'

'It is the cow's stomach.'

Trinity looks up from her bowl.

'Tripe?'

'If that is what you call it, yes … tripe.'

Trinity pushes the bowl away.

'But do not worry, I clean it thoroughly and cook with milk and garlic and peppers and vinegar to disguise the smell and taste.'

Trinity looks at her bowl, pauses then drags it back.

'It does actually smell and taste nice. And I'm that hungry I could eat a horse.'

'That is tomorrow evening's meal.'

Trinity looks at him, unsure whether he is serious or not.

'After we finish the meal, I must attend to my duties.'

'What is it you do around here?'

'I tend to the cathedral. I help to keep it clean. I ask for donations and provide the money to the needy.'

'What about you? Do you get paid? Do you keep some money for yourself?'

'I have no need for such things. The cathedral is all I need. I am blessed. Many people have much less than I.'

'Where did you sleep last night?' she asks, only now realizing the stretcher in the other room is his bed.

'It matters not.'

'Please. Tell me.'

Reluctantly, he lowers his gaze toward the harsh concrete floor. A humbled silence overwhelms Trinity.

A complete stranger with few worldly possessions gave up his bed for me and took the cold, dirty floor.

He shares what measly food he has … and gives away all his money to others.

I don't deserve this … any of this.

'I want to thank you again for helping me,' she says.

'It is not necessary. But I would like to know your name.'

'My name is … my name is Trinity.'

Anzhelo nods with approval.

'Trinity is very strong religious name.'

'How so?'

'Perhaps another time, I will tell you.'

'I'd like that.'

The old man smiles, something it seems he hasn't done for decades, judging by its awkwardness.

'Can I come with you?' Trinity asks.

Unsure where it is she is going, Trinity walks behind Anzhelo, her fingers holding onto the string that holds up his pants.

He carries a bronze lantern; its feeble light shines on the smooth marble steps of the tight and cramped spiral staircase. The small steps work their way up from Anzhelo's subterranean chamber to a locked wooden door. He removes a key from around his neck and places it in the lock; it creaks as it opens inwards.

Pushing aside a large hanging tapestry that conceals the entrance to the doorway from within the cathedral, he ambles over to a darkened corner with Trinity in tow.

The interior of the cathedral is enormous. The side chapel's plaster walls, blackened by decades of smoke from thousands of candles, are entirely decorated with faded yet colorful religious frescoes and depictions of icons. Separating the side chapel from the central nave, ornate cast-iron stands support dozens of thin candles.

Anzhelo places his hand on Trinity's shoulder and leans in close.

'Look around. I will do my chores.'

Trinity nods as she slowly makes her way across the gray, white and caramel-colored marble tiles. Ornately shaped stained-glass windows, filtering a spectrum of light from outside, guide her into the otherwise dim and solemn cathedral.

A few solitary worshippers occupy wooden benches spread throughout the vast open spaces. Beneath the cavernous forty-meter-high central dome, connected to a single bronze rod and resembling the form of a king's crown, hangs a gigantic two-ton golden chandelier, perennially lit by more than a hundred electric candles.

Standing directly underneath the chandelier, with his shoes planted on either side of a marble slab embellished with an eight-point star, a middle-aged man performs a silent, self-exorcism, his face contorting, his hands held high in constant prayer.

Trinity moves past him and beyond several towering white alabaster columns. She looks up at the surrounding high walls. A huge fresco of an angel, his wings spread wide, appears to weep, but it is only water, leaking from a neglected window above and staining the wall.

An unusual noise redirects Trinity's attention and drags her to the other side of an alabaster lion statue.

Anzhelo runs a long-handled scraper along the marble floor, removing melted wax dripped from all the candles purchased cheaply at the gift store. It seems this is the decaying, ownerless church's only source of regular income.

Times must be tough if they have to reuse the wax.

Trinity gently taps his shoulder.
He stops scraping and looks up.

'I have some business to tend to,' she says softly. 'I will return as soon as I can.'

'Where will you go?'

'I had something from Geneva delivered to the capital. I need to collect it from the freight station.'

The old man leans on his scraper.

'I wait for your arrival. On my desk, hidden beneath the clutter, you will find a map for tourists. It will help you navigate the streets.'

'Thanks.'

'Earlier, you ask of your sword.'

Trinity's eyes glow.

'You will find your sword among the brooms in the closet alongside my desk.'

Fountains of Truth

T rinity closes the tall iron doors behind her and rubs both gloved-hands together for extra warmth. She makes her way down the steps and onto the gray cobblestones outside the cathedral; puffs of frost escape from her mouth. She adjusts her sword, wrapped in a rag and slung across her back.

She glances up at the gray misty sky beyond the expanse of the car park and encircling road. Above the distant tree tops are the concrete spires and golden cross of the Russian Church located in the heart of Sofia.

She waits for a car to pass before crossing the road. As she makes her way along the sidewalk, her ears fill with music and she turns to see a man playing his accordion in a park, beneath a mature chestnut tree.

A little further on, in complete contrast, a trendy café blasts electronic funk.

Trinity blends in with the morning crowds as they file into the city. The women walking past are all smartly dressed in designer black—raven hair, brown skin, blue eyes and green eyes, all tall and thin.

Dimitri was right ... the women here are all beautiful.

She glances up through the corner of her eye at an elevated police booth, noting she is the only one interested that someone behind the tinted glass is overseeing everybody's movements. In the silver reflective tint, she spots an armored van parked up across the road; four burly officers are bunched together outside its protective shell, smoking cigarettes.

Steel barriers from the previous night's protest continue to herd Trinity and the crowds from getting too close to parliament house, the center of the ongoing dispute.

Sofia: a city in perpetual lockdown.

She follows the yellow brick road, walking on the century-old cobblestones that she read somewhere were presented to Tsar Ferdinand I in celebration of his wedding.

Before long, the city comes to life with World-War-II-era trams and grubby buses clattering and rumbling through the streets, their electrical umbilical cords attached to ugly overhead cables that blot out the sky.

Motorbikes, stuck in traffic, rev their engines for no apparent reason, while annoying car horns perform an unwelcome concerto. Frustrated drivers lean from their vehicles, yelling and swearing.

Trinity steps up onto the pavement; uneven slabs tilt beneath her boots, as they sharply knock against each other. To escape the morning chaos, she cuts through a leafy refuge in the heart of the city: Gradskata Gradina. And, although it's mid-week, just as many people sit and enjoy the serenity of the park as do commute to their place of employment.

She moves past a crowd gathered to watch two old men sit and play chess. A small child brushes past her leg as he runs to a nearby marble water trough where he cups his tiny hands under the constant flowing water, spilling more than he drinks.

Steam rises from the water.

Trinity is curios and strolls toward the trough, passing by a green Art Nouveau kiosk selling local and foreign newspapers and various periodicals. Removing her glove she allows the warm water to run over her hand.

A tang of minerals permeates the air.

Trinity watches an elderly couple fill their empty, plastic bottles from the weathered spouts. She joins them and fills her hands, raising them to her mouth then sips.

The steam warms her face and although the water is tasteless, she feels a renewed energy flow through her cold, bruised body. Trinity steps aside as more people arrive wishing to drink from the fountain.

Sofia was built upon hot mineral springs, each one different from the other, and each capable of healing a different ailment ... or so the local legend goes.

This place is so beautiful ... people sit and relax ... read ... talk.

The trees are so green. Fresh healthy water flows from the ground. It reminds me of the Imperial Gardens back in Tokyo ... serene and safe.

Pulling Anzhelo's map from her pocket, she unfolds it and turns in a half-circle to orientate herself, glancing up and down as she finds her bearings.

But as much as I'd like to stay here and hang out, I need to remain focused and stick with the plan ... as loose as it is.

Trinity folds her map and arms as she passes through the chilly shadows of the majestic Ivan Vazov National

Theater, its neoclassical building and façade considered one of the finest in Europe. Leaving the park in her wake, she treks through the narrow backstreets, and in an effort to overtake a slow moving couple holding hands, she steps onto the road.

A speeding car appears from nowhere and blasts its horn, forcing Trinity to jump back over the curb and onto the cluttered sidewalk.

She slows her pace to keep time with those around her, and finds herself meandering through the urban obstacle course of street signs and poles, trees and vending machines.

With time on her side, she takes more notice of her surroundings. Small corridors lead from the sidewalks to lush, overgrown, intriguing courtyards. Behind every rusted, iron gate is more of the same and through every doorway stands another door, always colorful and creative, and always leading to somewhere else.

Here you cannot judge a book by its cover.

Nothing is as it seems.

People, young and old, watch from the safety of their doorways and tiny balconies. They stand silent, observing, always a cell phone in their hand or pressed to an ear. Others sit in cars, parked on the side of the road, jammed in like sardines. They too, sit and watch, waiting, waiting for something.

The more Trinity looks, the more she finds, as two strongly-built men walk around the corner.

Check out these guys ... they're fucking huge.

But I'm confused ... they're packing heat ... I can see the muzzle of their Glocks poking below the waistline of their jackets.

Is this intentional or are they sloppy amateurs?

And what is with these relics from the communist regime with their black mustaches and 1980s smoking jackets?

All of them parked up around the city in their little dark-blue Hyundai sedans ... watching.

Who in the fuck do they think they're kidding?

Seriously ... they have secret police written all across their foreheads.

What the fuck are they all looking for?

Elvis?

Trinity rounds a corner and walks past a green Defender four-wheel drive taking up two parking spaces. The two officers — one young and skinny, the other old and fat — lean against the police vehicle ogling and whistling at a group of girls.

She approaches them with caution and keeps her eyes looking straight ahead. The skinny cop whistles at her, but she ignores him. Through the corner of one eye, she spots the fat cop step away from the jeep.

He stands in her path, his dark-blue jacket barely covering his strained undersized shirt, half-tucked into his pants. A cap struggles to fit his massive bald head.

Changing course, she attempts to move around him.

He takes another step to the side and holds out his hand.

'Dokumenti!' he demands, his voice strong and authoritative.

Trinity looks into his deep-set eyes and shrugs her shoulders. This action serves only to piss him off, something he's not accustomed to.

'Identificatzia!'

'English?' Trinity asks, buying valuable seconds to try and work out what to do. She understands his request, but has no passport to produce.

His dark, angry eyes turn to his younger counterpart.

Standing up straight, both hands gripping the front of his leather gun belt with his thumbs tucked in behind, he swaggers toward Trinity.

'He wishes to view your documents,' he says, smirking. 'Your passport.'

'Why? What did I do wrong?'

With a hint of arrogance, he tilts his head slightly.

'Show him your passport.'

'I want to know what crime I have committed.'

'Do you have your passport?'

Trinity pauses.

'No.'

The skinny cop turns to his more senior partner and relays the information in Bulgarian. He, in turn, looks Trinity up and down, a sleazy smile across his fat face.

The two officers exchange more words.

The skinny cop says to Trinity, 'It seems we have a problem.'

'What do you mean?' she asks, hoping to resolve the situation without drawing her sword.

'In Bulgaria, it is illegal for a foreigner to not carry a passport and to not produce when demanded.'

Bullshit!

'Well, I don't have one.'

'Then this is problem. My boss wants to know, what are we going to do about it?'

Trinity turns up her hands.

'I don't have any money.'

'Money is not what he wants.'

Fuck this shit!

She smiles.

He grins.

Her right fist cracks skinny on the chin.

His body stiffens and topples against the jeep.

Pivoting her feet and swinging her hip, Trinity's left fist lands flush on the fat cop's cheek.

His teeth clatter and his eyes roll back into his head. Keeling over, he slams against the sidewalk.

Trinity slinks away and down into an underpass.

Trinity drags a small wooden crate behind her and across the barren concrete apron. She approaches the lone taxi waiting outside the railway station and taps on the trunk.

It makes a clunking noise, then opens.

Standing the crate on end, she slides it up and inside.

I wonder what Anzhelo is doing.

If he's still working when I get back, maybe I can help him with something.

'The big cathedral,' she says, sliding onto the back seat of the cab.

The driver looks confused.

Trinity explains with her hands.

'You know … the cathedral with the golden domes.'

'Da!' he says. 'Da. Katedrala.'

Trinity closes her, smiles and gently nods.

The driver smiles back at her.

Trinity's taxi pulls up outside the golden cathedral. She flings open her door, a look of horror on her face. Shoving her palm at the driver, she cries, 'Wait! Wait here!'

She sprints across the cobblestones to where a gang of teenage gypsies surrounds Anzhelo, laughing, pushing and shoving him back and forth. The old man appears distressed, unable to retaliate or escape.

Trinity drops in on the crowd and shoves the closest two boys away. The rest of them mutter indecipherable gibberish and close ranks on her. Trinity slaps each and every one of them as hard as she can. Combined with the cold air, the slaps are as effective as a fistful of knuckles.

Stunned by her actions and in pain, the young gang members disperse as quickly as Trinity's attack erupted.

She rushes to Anzhelo and supports him by the shoulders.

'Are you okay?'

He nods.

'Let's get you inside.'

The taxi driver, standing outside of the cab with his door wide open, comes over and helps to guide them up the steps and then down into the crypt.

'Sit here and relax,' Trinity says. 'I'll be back in a moment.'

She and the taxi driver disappear outside to retrieve her crate from the trunk.

Once back inside, she shakes the Good Samaritan's hand and thanks him.

He blushes before humbly heading up the stairs.

Trinity turns to Anzhelo.

'Are you okay?'

'I am a little shaken,' he responds, a slight tremor in his strong voice.

'A hot soup should remedy that. You sit and relax and I'll look after you.'

He forces a small smile.

From the sink, Trinity asks, 'Who were those kids?'

'They belong to local gypsies. They often loiter outside the cathedral and stir trouble … nothing of a serious nature, but one day they will sadly follow in the footpath of their elders and become members of the Krhyminali … such as those you encounter the other night.'

'Tell me more about them.'

'Not all gypsies are the same,' he explains. 'These are organized group who shape themselves more like western gypsies …'

'I remember seeing one with a Mohawk,' Trinity interjects. 'I thought it was weird at the time; he looked out of place.'

'Yes. Many call themselves skinheads. They are involved in crimes … stealing mostly, but becoming more frequent is also murder, and kidnapping.'

Sitting at the table across from Anzhelo, Trinity pushes a small bowl of chicken soup in front of him.

'Here you go.'

'Why are you here?' he asks.

Trinity is caught off-guard by her new friend's sudden boldness.

'What brings you to Sofia?'

She looks away and then back at him.

'I have something I need to do,' she says. 'Hopefully I won't stay long … everyone I come into contact with either dies or ends up hating me.'

'You are welcome to stay in the cathedral for as long as you need.'

She smiles and reaches across to take hold of his hand.

'Thanks Anzhelo. You are a good man, but I will only bring you trouble. You're better off without me around ... everyone is.'

His eyes look deep into Trinity's.

'Do not let my appearance fool you my child. I am not the man I once was.'

'What do you mean?'

'I have been to war ... an ugly war ... and committed things I am no longer proud of. At the time, I believe that I have no choice, but the more I reflect—and believe me I have much time on my hands to reflect—the more I am ashamed.'

Trinity squeezes his cold hand.

'After the war, I find it difficult to work, like many of my brothers also, so I find myself involved with criminal elements who take advantage of my fighting skills and military experience.'

'I know what it's like to do what you have to do to survive,' Trinity says.

'I no longer see it as survival, child ... I see it as self-ishness,' he says. 'That is why I now offer my life ... my possessions ... my soul ... to others and to the church.'

Trinity lowers her eyes; her cheeks heat up.

'If it is not too late for redemption,' Anzhelo continues, 'I hope to make up for my lost years—stolen from me by war and circumstances beyond my control—and by my own blind selfishness.'

Trinity lifts her eyes.

'You stay as long as you wish,' he says. 'My home is your home. I will do anything to help you.'

Trinity finds comfort with Anzhelo, even more so now that he has entrusted her with some of his past, his story. She feels comfortable enough to impart her own story to him, so that maybe he can help her.

'I'm in a lot of trouble,' she says. 'In fact, others are in serious trouble because of me. I can fix it though. Well, I think I can … No, I have no choice — I have to fix it. But I need help.'

'What is it you need?'

Trinity pauses for a moment.

'I need to find someone.'

'And then what?'

'And then I have to kill him.'

Anzhelo gently rocks back and forth, his eyes firmly fixed on the crate from the taxi.

'It's filled with guns,' Trinity says.

'Who is it you seek?'

Trinity steels her gaze.

'The Russian.'

He stops rocking.

'You wish to kill The Russian?'

'You know him?'

'I know of him,' Anzhelo replies. 'He is very dangerous man. But even more dangerous than The Russian … his girlfriend, Borisa.'

'Do you know where I can find him?' Trinity asks, excitedly.

'Ne, I do not.'

Trinity throws her hands up onto her head.

'But I know of those who do.'

The Three Fools

'Trimata glupaci,' Anzhelo says with confidence. 'You will have to travel to The Three Fools. It will be very dangerous to go alone. I must accompany you.'

'No,' Trinity says. 'I can cover ground more quickly on my own, and that way I won't have to worry about protecting you.'

Anzhelo hunches over the small table and peers up through his messy hair.

'There was a time I would have been the one protecting you.'

Trinity smiles at him.

'Who are these three fools anyway?' she asks. 'What are their names?'

'The Three Fools are not human ... buildings.'

Trinity appears confused.

'Buildings?' she asks.

He nods.

'Yes … apartment buildings in Mladost district. The man you seek, Levski, he lives within. He knows of The Russian's location.'

'Who is this Levski?'

'He is a local criminal. The authorities find it difficult to arrest him. He has family ties within the government. But he has connections with The Russian. He deals with his prostitutes and people smuggling. He will know his location.'

'Is he dangerous?'

'Physically, he is strong, but his heart and mind are weak. He calls himself Levski … lion ... but everyone else, they call him kotence … kitten. He thinks he is mafiot, but it is his connections that are truly strong and feared. He is mutra … a common criminal.'

'Mafiot?'

'Mafia.'

Trinity nods.

'As you know, the streets are dangerous at night,' Anzhelo adds. 'You must take with you one of your guns.'

'How far away is this district?'

'Not far. Twenty minutes travel by train and then perhaps another ten by foot.'

'Do you have the address?'

'You will need no such information. You will know The Three Fools when you see them. But unfortunately, Levski, he move from building to building, for security reasons.'

'How will I know which building to enter?'

'Is easy,' Anzhelo nods. 'Follow the pretty women.'

Directly opposite Sofia University, not far from the cathedral, Trinity enters a large, open pedestrian underpass and makes her way down to the St. Kliment Ohridski Metro Station.

A German shepherd and a black mongrel with a white flash across his chest rest peacefully on the station's wide concrete steps. Despite the surrounding noise, they are too content and too lazy to eat donated biscuits placed by their sides.

The underground thoroughfare is a hive of activity. Not only a popular meeting place for teenagers, it's a venue for impromptu live entertainment.

A fat, scruffy-looking man with long hair at the back but balding on top, wearing a blue checked-shirt, sits on the ground. His electric guitar, pitch-perfect, makes love to 'Smoke on the Water'.

Across the way, a young man and woman play classical music on their violin and cello. She has long brown hair and is pretty. He sits on a curved bench, his back against a copper column.

Trinity buys a ticket, passes through the turnstile and heads down the escalator to the Red Line. A lemon-colored train awaits her, its doors wide open.

She steps inside.

It's bright and half-full, with plenty of available seating, but Trinity prefers to stand near the purple doors. Within seconds, they slowly close and the train accelerates, the carriage squeaking as it floats from side to side. Wrapping her fingers through the overhead black leather hand grip, Trinity surveys the carriage.

A girl stands reading her Kindle while another girl, dressed in white, sits on the train's comfortable gray cushions, scrolling through her phone, her pink bag placed across her lap.

An old man with a birthmark covering one side of his face catches up with current affairs as he reads the local 24 Chasa newspaper.

A beautiful girl with long, crinkly blond hair and serious eyes stares into space. She sits alone, her petite hands gripping a purple rail.

Trinity studies the map attached to the curved ceiling and counts the number of stops to Mladost 3.

The train slows down and eventually comes to a halt. Trinity tilts her head forward to look across the carriage and out through the window. A large, red-tiled circle on the station wall confirms the second stop of six: Curie.

Catching her eye, three males, aged in their mid-twenties, board the carriage. Dressed in long black trench coats and with beanies on their heads, they lean forward and mutter to one another, paying no heed to those around them.

Trinity finds their behaviour strange and monitors them from the corner of her eye. She shuffles her foot to keep her balance as the train departs from the station.

The train eventually stops at Mladost. Trinity turns to face the door and prepares to step out onto the platform. The shady males barrel out past her and storm across the polished multicolored tiles toward the only escalator.

Trusting her instinct, Trinity follows them from a safe distance as they head toward the surface. Reaching the top, she steps out onto the sidewalk, folds her arms and shivers.

In the distance, well beyond the dull yellow street lights, four, enormous red and white smoke stacks struggle to keep Sofia warm at night.

Trinity takes in her surroundings, a mix of old and new apartment buildings occupying once productive and thriving cornfields. Illuminated by the moon, three drab, identical apartment blocks—situated side by side—rise above all others.

The Three Fools.

Trinity spots the men from the train heading in their direction.

Hmmm … I wonder?

Staying close to the street-side shadows, she ghosts their movements, passing by three large, brown air vents protruding from the open ground and the station below. Off to one side is a gaggle of eight similar but smaller vents.

The men soon disappear from her sight and into the darkness. Trinity's pace quickens as she steps from the sidewalk and onto a well-beaten, sandy path that leads her through a vacant lot overgrown with weeds.

Voices carry across the open area.

Squinting helps Trinity to make out the men's silhouettes against the three concrete monoliths looming in the background, twenty storeys high.

At the end of the vacant lot is a kindergarten, its playground lit by a single streetlamp. A pair of red sneakers hangs from a nearby telephone cable, high above the trees.

Trinity continues to shadow the three men who warm their hands in their jacket pockets, and with their heads lowered they walk down a deserted street lined on both sides with randomly parked cars. Suddenly they stop and mutter to one another. She also stops moving.

They split up, each heading toward a separate building. Placing herself between two parked cars beneath the branches of a tree, Trinity focuses on The Three Fools.

A corner room on the fifteenth floor of the middle building lights up.

Bingo!

Bounding from one shadow to another, Trinity zeroes in on the middle apartment block. She circumvents armed men, dressed in black, patrolling the grounds.

The lower-floor windows are barred with iron.

Two sentinels bearing arms stand on either side of a lone door, a small light above the entrance the only contrast to their cold, dark appearance.

A tall brunette approaches, seemingly from nowhere.

One of the guards raises his MP5.

She stops, smiles and turns in a circle.

The second guard motions for her to approach.

As she steps into the light, it becomes clear that her beautiful face is heavily covered with makeup.

The guard runs his hand across her shoulders and down her back.

He slaps her ass.

She giggles, prances toward the door and blows him a kiss.

The guard points his weapon at Trinity.

She raises her arms out to the side, causing her unbuttoned coat to fall open. Her breasts, bulging against the leather of her cat-suit, glimmer in the light, ensuring the guard's attention is diverted away from the sword strapped to her back and the Glock handgun tucked in behind her belt.

The ass-slapper steps forward.

Play it cool, dude ... grab some ass ... squeeze my tits if you have to ... anymore than that, you'll lose your fucking head.

The heavily rugged-up guard takes hold of Trinity's shoulder; his eyes stare at her breasts. Raising one hand, he slowly runs his finger across the uncovered flesh.

Her heart races in preparation for a fight.

Smile, Trinity ... smile.

He places the catsuit's zipper between his fingers, his wishful eyes looking at Trinity for approval.

Slowly moving away, she playfully shakes her head and waves her finger at him.

He grins and slaps her on the ass.

Once inside the building's small, deserted lobby, Trinity enters the narrow elevator and pushes the black button for the fifteenth floor. As the lift sluggishly ascends, she turns to the grimy mirror on the wall. Spreading open her coat, she draws the zipper further down.

The elevator jerks to a stop and the door opens wide on another goon standing across the hall.

Trinity winks at him.

His eyes light up.

With a spring in her step, she moves toward him.

His eyes move up and down as her breasts rise and fall, until she stops, standing right up in his face, hands on hips.

He struggles to make eye contact.

'Levski?' she asks.

The goon raises an arm to one side, the barrel of his AK pointing toward the door at the end of the hall.

Trinity runs her finger across his chest and struts toward the corner room. As she approaches, the door flies open and one of the young men from the train walks out. Trinity gasps and lowers her eyes hidden by her fringe, her deadly weapons concealed by her long flowing coat.

The young man sporting a fresh black eye passes Trinity in the hall, his mind somewhere else.

She twists the door handle, turns and smiles at the goon down the hall before entering the room. The lighting inside the tiny apartment is dim, the furniture and decor gaudy. Overflowing ashtrays pollute the air.

Trinity turns to the sound of sobbing coming from the couch facing away from the door. She can't see who it is. Drawing her sword, she treads softly, stepping over a spilt bottle of vodka and enters the living area.

The sobbing increases.

What the fuck?

She looks down to a naked woman curled up on the couch hugging a cushion, her wrists and ankles bruised.

Noticing Trinity, she lifts her mascara-stained face.

Trinity gently runs her finger over a small cut on the woman's cheek. Removing her coat, she places it over her and offers up a comforting smile. She turns to the sound of a vacuum cleaner starting up in the next room. Sitting her up, Trinity motions for her to stay put.

She nods.

Trinity creeps to the only other room in the apartment and presses her ear to the closed door. The whir of the vacuum is the only sound to be heard. She turns the handle and cracks open the door. The light is on but the curtains are drawn. The only furniture in the room is an unmade bed.

Trinity opens the door wider.

A naked, hairy man stands with his back to her. He appears big and strong, but carries a spare tyre around his waist. Trinity's eyes shift to the small domestic vacuum cleaner on the carpeted floor.

Seriously!

It's attached to an erotic vac bed: two sealed layers of red latex. Sandwiched between the layers and lying on her back is another naked woman, the entire outline of her form visible, every minute detail, from the wrinkles in her feet to the nipples on her buxom breasts. As the vacuum cleaner sucks air from the vac bed, the top layer of latex progressively clings tighter to her body.

The latex further tightens its hold.

Anxiety and panic set in as the woman attempts to move her legs, but they barely produce a wriggle. Her entire head is enclosed but for a small breathing tube inserted through a hole and into her mouth. Her compressed lungs cannot draw in enough air to scream; all but a low raspy noise escapes the tube.

 The only other gap in the sealed unit is a small penetration hole between her thighs.

Trinity scans the room filled with whips and chains, candles, leather masks, sex toys … racks and racks of leather and latex catsuits. In one corner, a VHS camcorder sits atop a tripod.

I hate this guy for what he did to that girl in the other room … but I have to admit he's got good taste in kinky shit.

And I've always wanted to try out one of those vac beds.

The noise from the vacuum cleaner helps conceal Trinity's movement as she sneaks up behind Levski. Reaching around him, she grabs his cock, the blade of her sword resting against its sensitive skin.

'You move … you speak … I cut it off,' she orders. 'Nod if you understand.'

Levski nods.

'Did you hurt the girl in the other room?'

Levski doesn't move.

Trinity stretches his cock and presses down with the blade.

'I won't ask again.'

His head suddenly jerks back and forth.

She leans in close to his ear.

'You only get one chance to answer my next question. Where does The Russian live?'

Sweat cascades down Levski's bald head, dripping from his nose and chin. He struggles to swallow.

'I do not know where he lives.'

Trinity increases the pressure.

'How do I find him?'

'I swear I do not know … please, don't … I'm begging you.'

'Tell me, how the fuck do I find him?'

'He will kill me if I tell you!'

'And I will cut off your cock if you don't!'

Levski hesitates before answering. He wants to look down but is too frightened to move.

'Sergei Vasilenko … The Russian … will be at The Imperial Hotel tomorrow.'

'Why? Why is he there?'

'He meets regularly … every week … with his comrades … to discuss business.'

'What time?'

'Noon, he arrives at noon.'

'How many guards does he have?'

'I do not know.'

Trinity yanks on his cock.

'I swear! I swear! Is not anyway the guards you must fear … is Borisa … his woman.'

'What about her?'

'She is evil … so very beautiful, but so very evil. She is more dangerous than The Russian!'

Trinity feels Levski's cock begin to stiffen.

Oh you sick fuck!

You're enjoying this.

In one swift movement, Trinity removes her hand and sword from his cock, striking the back of his skull with the hilt.

Levski the not-so-brave lion attempts to open his eyes, but the clinging latex holds them firmly closed.

Drawing in short, rapid breaths through the tube inside his mouth, his arms and legs barely twitch.

The two semi-clad women standing either side of him look at each other and nod. Kneeling beside him, they place their hands over the breathing tube.

Outside, Trinity stops, turns and looks back toward The Three Fools, pausing briefly before disappearing down and into the subway.

'So what do you plan to do?' Anzhelo asks, happy Trinity has returned safely.

'I need to stake out the hotel tomorrow. I have to confirm The Russian is there and see what his security detail consists of.'

'And Borisa …?'

'Fuck Borisa,' Trinity says. 'I'm sick of hearing her name.'

'Do not underestimate her.'

'Yeah, yeah,' Trinity says. 'I'll deal with her when the time is right.'

A Match Made in Hell

The Imperial Hotel, like most other buildings in Sofia, is a communist-era vestige of seventies' décor and eighties' ideals.

Sitting inside its modest-sized lobby, lounging deep into the comfortable pea-green sofa, Trinity holds a copy of Trud newspaper in front of her face. Her long black coat, glasses and white beanie help to disguise her appearance.

With her back to the wall, she has an uninterrupted view across the cream and brown marble floor to the large glass-front windows. Her only obstructions are a lone white column off to one side and an expansive floral decoration set on a glass table in the center of the lobby.

Through the window and across the way, on the other side of the wide golden road, is the grand National Assembly building. The white, red and green national flag flies above the brilliant-white Neo-Renaissance edifice.

Ahead of Trinity and to the left is the main entrance of the hotel: an inefficient, glass revolving door. Although large enough to handle several people and their luggage at once, it is slow and cumbersome for patrons to manipulate, even with the token assistance of a lazy doorman more intent on smoking and chatting on his cell phone than actually doing his job.

The only other public thoroughfare is the marble staircase to Trinity's right, sweeping up and around through a hole in the ceiling to the mezzanine level above. Fortunately for Trinity, the hotel is busy, which helps divert any interest from her lingering presence.

She glances at the clock on the wall above the reception counter: 11:59 a.m.

I've been sitting here for over an hour.

The longer I stay the more suspicious I look.

I hope he's punctual …

That fucking Levski had better not have lied to me.

Outside the hotel, three blacked-out SUV's—a Mercedes-Benz, Audi and Range Rover—arrive suddenly and with purpose. All three vehicles reverse up to the main entrance and park side by side ready for a quick departure if need be.

Trinity lowers the top of her newspaper.

Three large men wearing black earpieces climb out of the Range Rover. Dressed casually in blue jeans, black coats and dress shoes and shirts, they scan the surrounding environment.

People opt to walk around them and not cross their path, eager to give them their space; the citizens of Sofia have all seen this before and they do not wish to get involved.

The three men's facial expressions look serious.

One is of Middle-Eastern origin with dark, recessed eyes and a large hooked nose. His face is scarred and creased; he has fought and won many battles. The other two — thick-set, bald and paler-skinned — could pass for Bulgarian or Russian; hard to differentiate sometimes.

They all look like stereotypical Hollywood movie henchmen.

Is it a case of life imitating art or the other way around?

Which came first I wonder?

The man with the hooked nose signals with his hand to the other two. They move inside through the hotel entrance while he stays outside.

Walking to the center of the lobby, they survey the area, looking for anything unusual or out of place. One of them approaches a man standing in line and rips open his jacket; his eyes drawn to the hip holstered cell phone.

The other stares at a bystander watching the scene unfold; she quickly lowers her eyes and turns away. Luggage left unattended draws their attention and, as they storm toward it, a husband and wife scurry across the foyer, profusely apologising.

These guys mean business.

Trinity turns a page.

One of the men heads up the marble staircase.

The other stays behind.

Neither of them wears sunglasses. They want people to know they are looking at them. They want to induce fear. They want people to look away.

Trinity notices the doors to the Audi open up.

Three more men, just as intimidating as the others emerge and gather round the Mercedes, the rear door of which is flung open.

A black-gloved hand grasps the top of the door.

Trinity sits up, unable to look away. She watches a pair of black boots emerge and a woman wearing tight-fitting leather step onto the road and exit the car.

This must be Borisa … The Russian's girlfriend and primary protector.

Trinity lowers the newspaper.

Borisa's eerie black hair absorbs all surrounding light. Cut just beyond shoulder length and parted to one side, dangling strands partially mask her face.

She glances up and out.

Broken black pupils, contained within deep-brown shimmering circles, cast out an evil stare; the excessive whiteness surrounding them seems purer than snow. Cheekbones and a dimpled chin—sculpted by a godly artist, perfectly formed—frame the deadly siren's seductive and neon red-devil lips.

Trinity is awe-struck and helplessly stares, oblivious to those around her. She is in danger of forgetting her purpose.

Get your shit together Trinity …

Focus.

Self-correcting her amateurish actions, Trinity fumbles to turn another page.

Why am I so nervous?

Just relax.

The rumors of this woman's beauty are true …

I now have to assume she's as dangerous as everyone says.

Borisa steps onto the curb, her hand remaining in contact with the door. A sharp breeze ruffles her hair, revealing the empyreal beauty of her flawless golden-brown complexion.

Trinity becomes restless.

Borisa's eyes sweep the passing crowds, and with no immediate cause for concern, she leans down into the car.

The Russian, speaking on his cell phone, moves from the back seat and into view, his light frame struggling to fill his thick black coat.

Hook Nose, The Russian and then Borisa promptly enter the revolving door. The remaining guards stay outside.

Borisa stays close by The Russian's side.

All three make their way across the lobby and up the staircase. Halfway to the top, Borisa pauses and tugs at The Russian's arm.

He stops and looks at her but appears unfazed, contented to continue talking on the phone.

Trinity flutters her newspaper and folds it over pretending to read the front page headlines.

Borisa senses something is wrong; her nefarious eyes scan the lobby below.

Trinity hopes that to others she appears calm on the outside.

I could strike now ... kill The Russian ... his girlfriend too, if she gets in the way ... kill them all.

I'd like nothing more than to see his ugly head bounce down the staircase like a rubber ball ...

A well-groomed man in a pin-striped suit, carrying a briefcase, gestures with a smile for permission to sit beside Trinity.

She smiles back.

... and then I'd shove it on the top of that fucking flagpole across the road for all to see.

Fuck it!

I'm going to do it ... do it now.

Trinity sits up straight and hands the newspaper to the man beside her.

He seems somewhat bemused.

Standing tall, Trinity unbuckles her coat.

Borisa continues to act on her intuition, casting her scan even further.

Trinity takes half a step and stops.

Two young boys noisily chase each other across the foyer, then up and down the bottom steps of the staircase. They laugh out loud, teasing each other with childish names.

The Russian turns and scowls at them, the phone never leaving his ear.

Bending forward, Borisa throws out her arms and ushers the playful kids away, the corner of her eye catching something. She straightens and turns in Trinity's direction.

Trinity pivots and leans forward.

'Mersi,' she says with a smile, snatching back the newspaper.

'I just wanted to kill him ... right there in the hotel!'

'You did the right thing,' Anzhelo says. 'Innocent children are no part of your war.'

'But he was standing right there, Angel!' she exclaims, pacing back and forth, clenching her fist. 'I could smell him.'

'You would not have forgiven yourself if even one of those children had been hurt or killed in the crossfire ... not even you, Trinity.'

Trinity tenses her face in agreement.

'I know you're right,' she says. 'When I left the hotel, there were more cars and more of his men waiting in the side street. It would have gotten messy. I'm just frustrated. I want this to be all over with.'

'How long did you stay there?'

'I sat in a café across the road for another hour. I watched them exit and depart along the boulevard out the front of the hotel.'

'Tsar Osvoboditel?'

'The road paved in gold?'

'Yes,' he confirms. 'Osvoboditel Boulevard. What now?' Anzhelo asks.

Trinity shakes her head and stares at the ground.

'His goons are good,' she says. 'They're big and scary, a step up from his Kossacks I fought in Japan. But they're still sloppy … complacent ... perhaps arrogant … even The Russian. He walks around like he's invincible, untouchable, without a care in the world. Now, he's definitely arrogant … and that shit can get you killed.'

'And what of …'

'Borisa?'

Anzhelo pauses briefly. 'Yes.'

'She's not like the others. She's sharp.'

'Is she …'

'Is she beautiful?'

Anzhelo raises his eyebrows.

'She is. And that's what concerns me,' Trinity says. 'Everyone talks of her beauty and danger. You were right Angel … I cannot under-estimate her. She's the key to The Russian.'

235

One of twenty-four districts that make up greater Sofia, Vitosha is located on the southern outskirts of the capital. Occupying prime real estate within the district are the tree-filled slopes of Boyana, a neighborhood that was once a medieval fortress. It and thirty-four other garrisons once helped surround and protect the antecedent ancient capital, Sredets.

Fast forward to present day and Boyana is a popular residential paradise home to Sofia's rich and infamous.

Warrior, fighter ... murderer, Borisa has one purpose in life: kill or be killed protecting The Russian and his assets. In another life, another time ... another country – a different roll of the dice – Borisa might have been a successful model, actress, mother ... housewife.

But she isn't. Instead, she is a merciless reincarnation of the ancient Greek harpy Celaeno ... *The Dark One*.

Tucked into her camouflage pants, her loose-fitting white singlet is soaking wet, the thin cotton material now completely transparent. Her unbridled and enhanced breasts bulge out the sides and glisten with sweat.

Borisa drives her combat boot deep into the heavy punching bag. Regaining her footing, she spins around and slams her heel against the red canvas.

Sweat streams down her face.

Bouncing on the balls of her feet, throwing straight punches – jabs and hooks – Borisa finishes off her burst of energy with a deadly and spinning back fist.

With a flick of her head, wet hair swings from her face. Using her teeth, she removes the mitts from her taped-up hands and spits them to the floor. The Bulgarian female killing machine drops down and smashes out forty push-ups, just like a man.

Jumping to her feet, she struts to the large wall-length mirror to admire herself; her shapely arms hang by her sides. Turning away, she walks across the room to a sliding glass door and pulls it aside, stepping out onto a large balcony overlooking the capital's night lights.

Cool air chills her bones.

Off to one side, one of The Russian's men stands guard, an AK-47 slung over his shoulder.

Borisa approaches him.

He tugs at his collar, appearing uncomfortable in her presence.

She takes hold of his hand and places it against her breast. Neither speaks a word. He continues to stare straight ahead, his throat becoming increasingly dry.

A smirk appears across her face as she moves his hand across her chest and then down the front of her pants. Despite the cold temperature outside, sweat forms across his brow.

Borisa's eyes close; frost obscures her open and panting mouth. She forces his hand up and down and all around, moving his fingers in and out.

He doesn't dare move, nor blink.

Her other hand cups one of her breasts, her thumb caressing the erect pierced nipple's barbell. She begins to moan.

Another guard coughs aloud, making his sudden arrival known.

Borisa's eyes open.

'The Russian wishes to see you now.'

Ignoring his request she closes her eyes and continues to pleasure herself.

'Immediately,' he pushes, reluctantly.

Borisa's eyes pop open. Slowly removing the guard's hand from within her pants, she sucks on his fingers. Glancing upwards, and without warning, she slaps his face, his cheek stinging red from the impact.

Her eyes slowly shift direction. Her stare, colder than the Bulgarian night air, melts right through the messenger's soul.

A chill runs the length of his spine.

She moves toward him, watching him, her head slightly bowed and her hair falling in front of her face.

He nervously stirs.

Borisa slashes at his cheek with her razor-sharp, diamond-tipped fingernails, shredding his cold, pale skin.

The Russian sits alone in a darkened room.

'What is so urgent you interrupted my training? Borisa asks, noticing an IV drip attached to his arm. 'You are feeling weak?'

'I require further revitalizing,' he mumbles, slumped into a leather high-backed chair, appearing drawn and wan. He waves his hand, motioning for her to move closer.

She stands before him.

'Kneel.'

Borisa clenches her teeth and narrows her eyes.

The Russian raises an eyebrow as she remains unmoved. Raising his hand he crooks his finger and points to the floor.

Lifting her chin and flaring her nostrils, Borisa slowly falls to her knees.

The Russian relishes her reluctant obedience.

'The next time I send for you, come immediately. Do not make me wait.'

Borisa breathes heavily through her nose and nods.

'Good,' says her impatient keeper. 'Rise to your feet.'

Borisa stands, her eyes fixed on the ground in front of him.

'Take with you some of my men,' he says. 'And go to Mladost.'

'The Three Fools?'

'Yes. I have been informed that idiot Levski has been killed.'

'He was a fool ... but he was your fool,' Borisa says, lifting her eyes. 'Who would dare touch him?'

'You will find out for me. One of his whores was captured trying to escape the building. Get me an answer. I want their names and then I want their heads.'

'I will go immediately.'

'First you will again kneel.'

Borisa's eyes develop a vacant stare.

'Come closer ... much closer.'

Devoid of emotion, she kneels between his legs.

The Russian unzips his pants. Reaching around, he takes hold of the back of her head and forces it down into his lap.

Illumination

Beneath the cathedral, Trinity takes a seat at the kitchen table across from Anzhelo.

'I'm tired,' she says, resting on her elbows, 'but I need to send an urgent text message before I go to bed. Do you know where I might find a cell phone? Those gypsies stole all my shit the other night.'

'I have no need for such belongings,' he says. 'But visitors to the cathedral leave many items behind by accident.'

Trinity sits up.

'You mean you have a lost-and-found box?'

Anzhelo thinks before answering, 'Yes. Items that are lost and then found by me are placed into a box. Nobody ever reclaim anything.'

'Are there cell phones?'

'Yes.'

Dear Yoshi. I am in Sofia.
I have found The
Russian. :)
But I am concerned. I do not
believe that I can do this
alone. :(
Have u recently been in
contact with Halo? Has he
departed HK? If u
do speak to him tell him I
need his help. ASAFP!!!
I am OK and living in
a church with an Angel :) U
would like him. He
reminds me of u. It is the
golden domed cathedral.
I hope ur well.
Goodnight.
xoxoxoxoxoxo

Borisa approaches the two guards standing outside the ground-floor entrance. Her black mink coat keeps her warm. A silver fox-lined hood covers her head.

Neither guard recognizes her, until it's too late.

Whisking her hands from her pockets, Borisa's fingernails sparkle in the moonlight.

The guards grab their necks and drop to their knees.

She kicks them over with her slush-coated boots; saliva and blood gurgle inside their mouths. Flicking the blood from her fingernails, a wry grin on her face, Borisa moves into the building and enters the elevator.

The guard on the fifteenth floor watches the doors open wide and Borisa move toward him. Nervously, he points down the hall as she walks up to him and places her hand upon his chest.

She leans in close and places her red lips against his.

Unsure what to do he plays it safe - be silent and still.

Her tongue slowly works its way around his lips.

He flinches and pushes her away; his wide eyes lock with hers - she playfully blows him a kiss. Looking down, he sees a warm, dark patch spread across his shirt.

Borisa smiles and turns her attention to the door at the end of the hall, her bloodied hand clutching a small, sneaky knife with a crimson blade.

Sliding down the wall, the guard sits on the floor, his questioning eyes looking for answers.

His beautiful murderer walks away.

Borisa opens the door and walks inside the small apartment; light from the bedroom shines through the open doorway and into the living room.

A blond woman sits on the couch, her hands and feet tied, her teary eyes following Borisa's movements.

She enters the bedroom and looks down at the lifeless Levski, cut free from his latex coffin. Glancing toward the bondage collection, she turns around and makes her way from the bedroom and over to the couch.

The woman gasps for air. Black tears stream from her eyes; snot runs from her nose and into her mouth.

Borisa pulls back her hood and sits alongside her. Resting a reassuring hand on the frightened woman's bared and bruised knee, she quietly asks, 'What is your name?'

'Luminita,' she sobs.

'Pretty name,' Borisa says, stroking her messy blond hair. 'Romani?'

She nods.

'You must tell me what happened here tonight.'

Luminita notices blood on Borisa's hand, turns her sullen eyes away.

Borisa takes hold of her chin and turns her battered face toward her.

'Tell me who killed the *little kitten* in the other room and I will set you free. Refuse my questions and I will cut off your head and bounce it down Tsar Osvoboditel Boulevard through the center of the capital, for all to see.'

Luminita's wet eyes widen. Her bottom lip quivers.

'We did,' she says without blinking.

'We?'

'There was another girl ... with long, black hair ... she escaped.'

'A whore?'

Luminita lowers her eyes.

'Do not be ashamed,' Borisa says, wiping her face clean. 'Why did you kill him?'

Luminita's eyes shoot up, her expression changing from fear to indignation.

'Look at me,' she answers sharply, her eyes snapping to the ties that bind her limbs and then back to her interrogator. 'Look at me.'

Borisa sits silent.

'There was one more,' Luminita adds.

Borisa tilts her head.

'Another with black hair,' Luminita says. 'So beautiful and strong … like you.'

'Whore?'

'No,' Luminita says with conviction, shaking her head.

'What was her purpose? Why was she here?'

'She spoke with Levski. She was the one who place him inside the bed.'

Borisa looks puzzled.

'What did she want from him?'

'I do not know. I could not hear.'

'Is there anything else you must tell me?'

Luminita shakes her head violently.

'No! I tell you the truth.'

Borisa stares into her eyes.

'I believe you,' she says, gently pulling the distraught woman's head down and onto her shoulder. 'Close your eyes.'

No sooner do they close than a hot flash streaks across Luminita's neck. Blood gushes over Borisa's hand and oozes through her fingers.

Luminita squirms.

Borisa holds her tight.

Less than a minute later, her petite body is limp.

Borisa carefully lays her down on the couch. Wiping hair from her cold face, she kisses her cheek and cuts through the leather binds with her knife.

'You are finally free my little shining light. Now no one else can ever hurt you.'

Trinity senses something is wrong. She doesn't know what it is, why things feel different.

She feels alone … no other presence.

Where is he? Where are they? Why are they not here?

She knows what they all want. She will give it to them. They cannot resist what she has. They all want it.

They will come.

One button at a time, she unbuttons her blouse.

The surrounding shadows remain empty, lifeless.

She is confused. She can no longer wait for him — wait for them — to come to her; she can no longer stand to be alone.

Trinity moves from the safety of the light.

It is cold, deep inside the shadows.

She finds him; his back is turned.

Trinity has never seen his face.

She approaches carefully.

He doesn't move away.

Trinity is happy to see him standing there.

He looks down at the ground.

She senses they are no longer alone.

Someone else is here.

Something is not right.

Suddenly the temperature drops and the darkness becomes darker.

Trinity sits up in her make-do bed: some flattened-cardboard boxes, a rolled-up newspaper and an old crocheted shawl from the lost-and-found. She stares into darkness, her heart pounding madly. Jumping to her feet, she tentatively makes her way toward the half open door.

Standing in the doorway, she strains her eyes. The only light in the other room is an orange glow from the small bar heater in the corner. Anzhelo snores, enjoying a deep slumber on his stretcher. Trinity smiles to herself, comforted by the rise and fall of his chest.

These dreams I have ... I feel as though they're leading somewhere ... trying to tell me something.

Tonight felt eerie.

Somebody is going to die.

Someone I know ... someone close to me.

I can feel it.

Trinity retreats to her bed and picks up her cell phone to check her messages.

Nothing.

Fuck.

And the battery is almost dead.

She lies on her back, the shawl pulled tight around her neck, her eyes wide open.

Twisted Fate

Borisa stands before the closed door to The Russian's sanctum. She doesn't bother to knock. She knows he's inside; she can smell his pungent odor. The smell of the living dead is unlike anything else. She twists the knob and pushes open the door — The Russian stands naked in the middle of the room, his skinny hands on his bony hips.

A young and pretty blond, kidnapped from her home, stripped of her dignity ... robbed of any chance of a normal life ... squats in front of his skeletal frame. Her dry, pursed lips slide back and forth along his pencil-thin cock.

Borisa isn't shocked.

She's seen it all before, many times, with many different girls. If anything, she's glad; it's one less time she has to perform the insipid deed. She likes to suck cock, just not The Russian's pathetic excuse for a manhood.

He waves her over.

'What did you find?'

Borisa looks down at the girl. Her terrified eyes look upwards, tears welling, ready to spill.

'What did I find?' she asks smugly. 'That you need to recruit more men, and I use the term *men* lightly.'

'Stop talking in riddles. Who killed Levski?'

Borisa turns away, unable to watch the girl's misery, unable to look Sergei in the eye.

'Your brave *kotence* tortured two women,' she says with contempt. 'They were his executioners.'

'And what of them?' he asks.

'One had already escaped … the other I set free.'

The Russian shoves the blond away.

She falls onto her back.

Storming toward Borisa, he grabs her by the shoulders and spins her around. He draws back his arm before striking his hand across her cheek.

Knocked off balance, she steadies herself and looks him in the eye.

'How many times have I told you? Every time you *set free* one of my girls, you cost me money!'

Showing no sign of regret, Borisa raises her chin and looks down at him.

'Answer me!'

She remains silent.

'Answer me!' he again cries, inches from her face, spittle spewing from his mouth; the veins in his neck set to rupture. 'Answer me!'

Borisa wipes her face clean of his vile oral discharge.

'Many,' she mumbles.

'Many,' he repeats, calmly, taking a step back. 'Yes … many. Now go to your knees.'

Borisa pauses, kneels, closes her eyes and remembers how she ended up here.

Living and growing up close to the seaside resort of Varna on the Bulgarian Black Sea Coast should have been fun for Borisa and her younger sister Mila: beaches, gardens, mineral springs, mountains ... perfect weather.

But it wasn't. Living a mere twenty kilometers west of the resort, in the small industrial town of Beloslav, once an ancient Thracian village, they may as well have been twenty thousand light-years away. They were raised by their father alone, a hard-working manual laborer down at the nearby seaport, and money was scarce. Trips to the coast were even more so.

In Borisa's mind, joining the army at the age of eighteen seems like only yesterday, not the ten years since. Like so many of her fellow countrywomen, more than in any other NATO member state, she enlisted; it was the only constant source of employment available to her at the time. But leaving her sister behind meant leaving her one and only true friend. It was the hardest thing she'd ever had to do.

The army taught her many things: to fight, to shoot, to survive ... to kill. It also taught her discipline and loyalty, traits that would later cruelly define who she was and change her life forever.

Her time in the armed forces completed, she returned home to Beloslav, to her family, ready to make something more of her life. She was surprised and disturbed to find her sister had only recently moved from their father's house to the bright lights of Varna, looking for work.

Borisa promised her father she would find Mila and return her home. They both agreed that Varna, with its hotels, nightclubs, gambling and organized crime, was no place for someone like her. Mila was unlike Borisa. She was young and inno cent, neither battle-hardened nor exposed to tough training … to tough love.

Two weeks in the Bulgarian Las Vegas flew by with no sign of Mila. Borisa questioned herself many times as to whether or not her sister had even visited Varna. Wandering the tourist-riddled streets at night, visiting chalgothèques until all hours of the morning, exhausted of energy and money, she was ready to stop looking and to return home defeated.

Then one day, sitting by the side of the road, resting her weary feet, Borisa saw the worn-out figure of her once lively and beautiful little sister, Mila, riding in the back of a black sedan. She was not alone; she was with other young girls and – to Borisa's shock – local mutri.

Following the car led Borisa to a nearby warehouse and to what would soon be the origin of her new life. She watched from across the road as they ushered the spiritless girls through a side door. Borisa could have regrouped and returned better prepared another day, another time, but she wanted to end this now and take back her sister. Honor the promise made to her father.

Armed with a steel pipe from a trash pile and no more than two minutes of her time, Borisa killed six men; caved their shaved and bloodied heads in.

Protected within a circle of another ten gun-toting men, The Russian watched events unfold, amused and impressed by Borisa's heroics.

Borisa steeled herself, ready to take them on, her death a certainty.

Some say that for The Russian it was love at first sight; others say he saw in Borisa pure evil and a drive to win at any cost, even if that cost were her life.

A deal was struck that day.

Mila and the other girls walked free.

Borisa remained behind.

A decade on, she sees her life as not wasted.

That Mila is a stay-at-home mother of two young boys and loving wife to a hard-working, caring husband is all the light at the end of the tunnel she needs.

With military-drilled discipline and battle-born loyalty to a long-ago deal struck with the devil, Borisa soldiers on with her bright red lips.

Past, Present and Future

The leafy trees along the edges of Bulgaria Square add texture and color to the rows of straight-edged suburban apartment blocks hiding behind them. Their steep, orange-tinted tiled roofs host enormous advertising billboards, further evidence of the widening chasm between the socialist past of the Balkan States and their fast-growing acceptance of modern westernization.

Enjoying the brisk weather and blue skies, Anzhelo and Trinity stroll across the vast, open square, a mix of concrete slabs, trees and shrubbery. Once filled with free-flowing water, the popular meeting place's cement-lined waterways are now dry and dusty.

Many others enjoy the beautiful day.

At one end of the square looms a giant building, but much closer, attracting Trinity's attention, is a colossal eyesore.

'The pile of rusted steel and concrete you see reaching toward the sky was once a monument to our heritage,' Anzhelo says, noticing Trinity's interest. 'The rough hands of time, winds of all four seasons and sadly the neglect of the people it represents have all contributed to the state you now see it in. I remember it once covered in marble and free of the graffiti and fencing that now surrounds it.'

'It's ugly,' Trinity says. 'But powerful. What was ... what *is* it?'

'Almost a decade before the end of communism, it is erected to celebrate the anniversary of our country's creation in the year 681AD. Hence its name: *1300 Years of Bulgaria.*'

Trinity stares up at three massive concrete slabs, all tainted with rust stains from the many bolts within. A tall, steel structure, devoid of any former exterior, is now nothing more than a vehicle for anti-regime slogans. On one side, five forlorn male sculptures express an absorbing feeling of hope long passed.

'The three intertwining concrete structures symbolize the past, present and future,' Anzhelo says. 'They no longer attach, but each wall once presents profound words in large bronze letters. If my failing memory is correct, the left wall says: *Time is in us and we are in time* ... The middle wall: *He who falls in freedom's fight, he dies not* ...'

'And the right wall?'

'*March ahead, O revived people.*'

They continue walking along the square.

An elderly balding man with glasses sits on a weathered timber bench, reading the newspaper. Children run and play ball.

Young lovers walk hand in hand.

Trinity smiles and feels as though all her problems have temporarily disappeared. Placing her arm through Anzhelo's, together they make their way to the top of a small flight of steps. She cares not about her companion's looks and plight, or the occasional stares from passersby; she's living in the moment, enjoying every second.

'The large octagonal building you see,' Anzhelo says, 'is built by Soviets around the same time as *1300 Years* monument.'

'It has an overpowering effect,' Trinity says. 'It certainly makes a statement, with nothing else nearby to draw away your eye.'

'Yes. Even title is grand: The National Palace of Culture.'

Trinity chuckles, 'Sounds very Russian.'

'Most refer to it simply as NDK.'

'What is inside?'

'Many magnificent halls,' Anzhelo says. 'Concerts and film festivals, even exhibitions from around Bulgaria and the world, are all held within.'

'You love your country don't you?'

Anzhelo briefly lowers his eyes whilst continuing his slow pace. He raises them and says, 'I have almost died a thousand times over. Sometimes I wish I had died alongside my friends. This country, this city, is beautiful … but is not without scars. And its people … they need and deserve help. As long as I breathe, I will continue to do what I can for it. Yes. I do love my country.'

A lump sticks in Trinity's throat. She stops walking and draws the old man close.

'I need a hug.'

'We should return to the cathedral soon,' Anzhelo says, patting her back.

'You are tired?'

'Yes. We will take a short-cut across The Bridge of Lovers and make our way home through the smaller back-streets.'

'A lovers' bridge!' Trinity exclaims. She smiles, 'Now don't you get any crazy ideas.'

Anzhelo laughs, 'Sadly, my dear Trinity you are not my type.'

As they approach the entrance to the pedestrian bridge, they see a middle-aged man with messy gray hair and a beard, sitting on a small camping chair beneath a forest of flagpoles, busking for money. With his acoustic guitar held together by duct tape, he sings, '*I wanna go home …*'

Trinity stops and listens, the lyrics touching a nerve.

I wonder if I will ever be able to call a place home again?

'Give me a moment,' she says to Anzhelo.

Reaching into her pocket, she removes a handful of coins and drops them into the musician's hat at his feet.

Trinity and Anzhelo return home to the cathedral. They begin to relax following a long and pleasant day, but before long, the darkness of Trinity's reality sinks back in and their talk quickly returns to her unfinished business.

Anzhelo sits on a crate at the small table.

'What is your plan for dealing with Sergei?' he asks.

Trinity stands at the sink, making coffee.

'I have a few ideas bouncing around inside my head.' She turns to face him. 'But more importantly …'

Anzhelo raises his brow, concerned with what could possibly be more important than her private war with The Russian.

'… We're out of milk.'

He breathes a sigh of relief.

Trinity smiles.

'I'll walk to the store and buy some more, and when I return we can discuss my plans in detail.'

Anzhelo nods, 'I will take the opportunity to rest.'

'Good idea. I'll see you shortly.'

On her way to the store, Trinity passes a small, open-air market filled with dozens of stalls containing brightly colored silk and cotton linen. The sellers, old men and women, sit quietly in rickety foldout chairs.

The welcoming atmosphere draws Trinity in. Wandering around, she browses a wall covered in woodcarved icons, showing her keen interest in images of St George slaying the dragon and the Archangel Michael.

Nearby, a table overloaded with aged war medals catches her eye. She picks up a tarnished gold star attached to a small, frayed red ribbon.

'How much?' she asks the old man sitting behind the table.

'40 lev,' he responds in a deep voice.

She turns the medal over — someone has engraved a few Cyrillic letters on the back, followed by the instantly recognizable CCCP.

'Hero of the Soviet Union medal,' he says, rising from his chair and picking up another medal with his bear-like hands. He passes it to Trinity. 'This one is Bulgar-ian; is same price.'

'It is exactly the same,' she says.

'Ne.' The old man shows her the back of the medal. 'Is different,' he says. 'Hero of the Republic of Bulgaria.'

Trinity moves it around between her fingers.

'It is real?'

'Da,' he says, shaking his head.

Fuck, that's confusing.

Why can't these people move their head in the same direction as everyone else on the planet?

'How do I know it is real?'

'I know is real.'

'And how do you know it is real?'

The old man pauses, shifting his eyes down then back up again, his demeanour taking on a darker shade, his voice filled with grit.

'The medal is mine.'

Trinity is quiet.

'If I buy the Russian medal for 100 lev,' she asks, 'will you take your medal off the table and keep it for yourself?'

'You have a kind soul,' the old man says, looking be-yond her eyes. 'I have no need for them. Sadly, my memo-ries remain clear.'

Trinity notices his eyes turn glassy. Placing the Soviet medal back down, she keeps the Bulgarian Gold Star and hands him 100 lev before walking away.

She meanders through the markets, sifting through ta-ble after table of military antiques, homemade jewelry and second-hand clothing. Attracted to a black leather motor-bike jacket, she tries it on. It's a little large but she instantly falls in love with it. The shoulders, elbows and forearms all have Kevlar inserts for added protection, and there are scuff marks all over it, evidence the jacket has been down the road once or twice.

Having parted with more money, Trinity decides to complete her errand, excited to share her purchases with Anzhelo.

'Angel!' Trinity shouts, entering the crypt wearing her new jacket, milk in one hand, medal in the other. 'Wake up. I bought you a present.'

Trinity stops, feels the carton slip from her hand and hears it hit the ground, splitting open, spilling milk.

Anzhelo, already awake, sits at the table facing her. Standing behind him are two weary travellers: Halo and Carlos.

'When did you get here?' she asks.

'They arrive shortly after you leave to buy milk,' Anzhelo says.

Trinity rushes Halo, pressing her cheek deep into his chest.

'What are you wearing?' he asks.

'It's my new jacket. I love it. Shut up and hug me.'

Halo embraces her.

'I got your message from Yoshi. He said you needed help. We came as soon as we could.'

'I'm so glad you're here,' she says, gently pushing him back, turning her head to face Carlos. 'Thank you. I can never repay you.'

'I told you I would look after him,' he says.

'Tell me what happened after you left Dubai? No

wait. Have you met Angel? He saved ...'

'Slow down,' Halo interrupts with a grin. 'Take a breath. There's someone else here to say hello.'

Trinity steps back, somewhat confused.

Valentina moves from the bedroom's darkness and into the light. By her side is a pure-white Doberman, his eyes as black as night.

Trinity is speechless.

'We've been communicating with each other ever since you left BA,' Halo says. 'When Valentina made enquiries as to my whereabouts in the Middle East, I kept in touch with her. I invited her to join us in Istanbul before crossing into Bulgaria. After Carlos and I left you in Abu Dhabi, we only got as far as Hong Kong where we got into a few skirmishes.

'On the way to Tokyo, we decided to divert to come and help you by crossing overland through Russia and Turkey. It wasn't easy, but we were determined to make it.'

'I hope you don't mind?' Valentina asks, beaming. 'Say something.'

'I ... I ... I don't know what to say. I wasn't expecting you. What about Jorge?'

'He insisted that I come. I left him behind. He is a lover not a fighter. I don't think I'll kill this one; he's loyal ... a keeper.'

Trinity and Valentina throw their arms around one another.

'I never wanted for you to get caught up in any of this,' Trinity says.

'I'm a big girl,' she smiles. 'What do you think of my new friend?'

'Where did you find him? I have never seen a white Doberman. Is he an albino?'

'No albino. See, his eyes? Too dark ... It seems Hector was busy with the lady dogs in my neighborhood. The old woman two streets from my house raised him from a pup, but she could no longer afford to feed him. I know how much you connected with Hector, so I thought you would welcome him.'

'How did you get him through quarantine?'

Valentina winks.

'I have my ways.'

'What is his name?'

'He does not have one.'

'What do you mean?'

'It is strange. He would never respond to anything.'

'What have you been calling him?'

'Nothing. He simply follows me around,' she laughs. 'When I whistle, he comes to my side. Dobermans are very loyal and instinctively know when to fight and when not to.'

Trinity turns to Anzhelo and raises an eyebrow.

He ponders for a moment.

'Viktor,' he whispers.

All eyes in the room focus on Trinity.

She drops to one knee and holds out her hand.

'Viktor, come here.'

The white Doberman pulls back his cropped ears and lowers his head. Wagging his docked tail, he walks gingerly toward her, sniffs then licks her hand.

Trinity rubs behind his ears and he presses his muzzle against her leg.

'So,' Halo says. 'What's for dinner?'

Spread throughout the crypt, sitting on the crates, the floor — wherever they can — Trinity and her friends enjoy a meal of Anzhelo's teleshko vareno: a soup made of large cuts of tenderized beef shin simmered with carrots, potato and onion, all topped with sprinkles of fresh parsley.

'This is good,' Carlos says, spooning the soup into his mouth as fast as he can, eyeing off a large, colorful bowl of Shopska salad: diced and salted tomatoes, cucumbers, onions, peppers and grated cheese.

Trinity sits on the ground with her legs bent and her back against the wall.

'I still cannot believe you are all here.'

Viktor rests peacefully by her side.

'You have many friends, Trinity,' Anzhelo points out, sitting up at the table across from Halo. 'Many more than you realize.'

'How did you find this place?' Valentina asks, as she places an empty bowl in the sink. 'How did you find Anzhelo?'

Trinity looks across the room and smiles.

'He found me.'

Anzhelo returns her smile and nods.

Halo addresses everyone.

'As pleasant as all of this is, we need to focus on why we're here.'

The sound of Viktor yawning is the only noise to be heard in the acoustically enhanced cavern.

Valentina breaks the awkward silence.

'He is right. There will be plenty of time for rejoicing once the head of The Russian sits upon a stick.'

'Let's clear the table,' Halo says, taking control. 'And then we'll get down to business.'

While the others finish their meals and tidy up, Halo pulls Trinity to one side.

'How did you go when you traveled home?'

She lowers her eyes.

'You know,' she sighs, raising them again. 'All these years I hated my mom, wondering what I did wrong, believing that she hated me. I'm not so sure now. I doubt I'll ever find or know the truth, but I do think I understand things better … which seems to help.'

Halo runs his hand through her hair.

'Geneva? Did you find what you were looking for?'

Trinity's heart flutters. Staring into Halo's eyes, she opens her mouth, but nothing comes out. No words; not a sound.

He looks down and nods, removing his hand from her hair.

'I'll go help the others clean up.'

Trinity reaches out her hand, nothing more than a token gesture.

Killing Machine

Anzhelo sits at the table, both hands holding flat a tourist map of Sofia, Trinity's team bunched up behind him, looking over his shoulder.

She faces them from across the table.

'There's not a lot I know about The Russian and his movements,' she says, 'but what I do know is he visits The Imperial Hotel in the city every Tuesday around noon.'

'Where does he live?' Halo asks.

'I'm not certain,' Trinity answers, her eyes shifting to Anzhelo.

'Most likely he will live in a guarded mansion,' he responds, his finger touching the map. 'Here in Boyana, a district 20 minutes from the capital.'

'Can we get his address?'

'Perhaps,' Anzhelo says. 'It will take time.'

'I think the hotel is our best option,' Trinity continues. 'It's a more level playing field.'

'A lot more variables out of our control as well though,' Carlos says.

'True,' Trinity nods. 'But hopefully those variables may work in our favor, not his.'

'Have you laid eyes on him?' Halo asks.

'Yes. I watched his movements at the hotel.'

'What did you see?' Valentina asks.

'He's cocky.'

Trinity stands erect, stretching her back.

'And this makes him vulnerable. He and his team move in luxury SUVs ...'

'Are they armored?' Carlos asks.

'Again, I'm not certain. You would have to assume they are. His primary CPOs—I call them goons—number around six, with who knows how many more in the vehicles or parked off in the distance. These guys are hard ... they've played major league ball elsewhere. But they appear a little sloppy ... complacent. Most likely they haven't had a game in a while.'

'Weapons?' Carlos asks.

'I know they carry concealed small arms on the street ... pistols of some sort. That's all I could see.'

'We'll have to assume there's bigger hardware in the vehicles,' Halo jumps in.

Carlos raises his eyebrows.

'There are a lot of assumptions at this stage of the game. Not ideal.'

'I've seen some of his other men bearing AKs and MP5s,' Trinity says.

'Tell them about Borisa,' Anzhelo mumbles, staring down at the table.

'Who's Borisa?' Valentina asks.

Trinity pauses.

All eyes are on her.

'She's The Russian's 2IC and girlfriend. She controls all his movements and sticks to him like glue.'

'What's her story?' Halo asks.

'I can't confirm anything, but rumours abound of her skills. It seems most are more frightened of her than they are of The Russian.'

'Is she some sort of female Russian weightlifter?' Carlos jokes.

Trinity shakes her head.

'This chick is lean and mean ... and fucking hot.'

'I like the sound of her already,' Carlos smiles.

Anzhelo looks up through the corner of one eye.

'Do not let her looks deceive you, my friend.'

'Okay,' Halo says, glancing at Trinity. 'So she's hot. We got our own hot-as-fuck killing machine.'

Trinity looks at the ground.

'What about our weapons?' Halo continues. 'Carlos and I only have a couple of pistols and some boxes of bullets between us. I suspect we're gonna need a lot more than that and your katana.'

'I picked up a few souvenirs when I was in Geneva,' Trinity says. 'Wanna give me a hand, Carlos?'

The two of them drag a wooden crate into the middle of the room.

Trinity lifts the lid.

It's filled to the top with munitions.

'Cool,' Carlos says, his eyes sparkling.

'I grabbed what I could,' she says. 'Then I freighted it on by rail with the help of an old contact.'

Halo nods.

'You've done well. Hey Carlos,' he says. 'You wanna go through the crate and see what we got in there?'

'Sure thing, I'll lay it all out.'

'I'll assist,' Valentina says.

Anzhelo tends to Viktor, feeding him scraps from their meal.

Halo looks at Trinity.

'We're gonna get you through all this.'

'I hope so. I'm so fucking over it. Earlier today, walking through the park with Angel, I felt weird ... I actually felt normal for the first time since I was a kid.'

'It's hard to imagine you being normal. But hey, if that's what you want.'

'You seem different, Halo,' Trinity says. 'I noticed it a little in Dubai, but didn't mention it.'

'Yeah I've noticed it too,' he says. 'I've had to grow up ... adapt to the shitty hand life sometimes gives you. I also did some serious soul-searching since the last time we met in Tokyo. I thought after our little talk that night at Yoshi's that maybe ... maybe we could honestly try again ... start all over. But when I awoke the next morning and you'd gone, the realization that I might not have you forever ... might not even see you again ... hit hard.'

Trinity places her hand on his shoulder.

Halo sighs.

'I wanted to tell you all this in Dubai,' he continues, 'but for some reason I didn't. It's hard to explain.'

'I'll always love you, Halo ... never forget that. But my life is in turmoil. I'm not a nice person. I'm not the young girl you once knew.'

'But you keep telling me you want to change.'

'And I do. But until that day, I am still a monster.' Trinity takes hold of his arms. 'No matter the outcome of our battle with The Russian, promise me you'll do everything you can to protect and look after Angel for me.'

'I'll do my best.'

'That's not enough,' she says. 'Look after him as though he were me. Okay?'

'Okay. I promise.'

'I hope I'm not interrupting,' says a shadowy figure standing at the entrance to the crypt.

Halo instinctively shoves Trinity behind his large frame and, in the same swift motion, removes a hidden Glock from the small of his back.

Reacting to Halo's movements, Carlos lifts his shirt, draws his pistol and drops to one knee.

'Nooo!' Trinity screams, forcing her way past Halo and rushing toward the entrance. 'Don't shoot! Don't shoot!'

'Step aside!' Halo yells.

'No, Halo!' she cries, using her body as a shield. 'No! He's with me ... I know him ... he's one of us.'

Halo's left eye narrows and he breathes heavily through his nostrils. The semi-auto pistol's front sight rises and falls alongside Trinity's head, the slack on the trigger taken up, the sear set to trip, the striker poised to plunge forward.

'Please, Halo,' Trinity begs. 'Lower your weapon.'

Halo continues breathing heavily, his heart trying its best to escape from within the confines of his muscular chest.

'Please,' she pleads, softly, motioning with her hand for him to lower his gun.

Halo reluctantly complies, glancing sideways at Carlos. Carlos stands, keeping his gun down by his side.

'What the fuck, Trinity!' Halo yells, his heart pounding. 'Who in the fuck is he?'

Trinity closes her eyes and catches her breath. She opens them and turns around.

'What are you doing here, Gabriel?'

'I've come to help you kill The Russian.'

Trinity pushes him back through the entrance and all the way up the stairs, through the front door and down onto the sidewalk.

'What are you fucking doing here?' she asks angrily, shoving him in the chest. 'How in the fuck did you find me?'

'I told you. I came to help.'

'You could've got killed in there.'

'Your boyfriend, he's pretty quick on the draw.'

'He's not my boyfriend.'

'Could've fooled me,' he says. 'The way he protected you … I'd say he has strong feelings for you.'

'Of course he fucking does,' Trinity barks in a controlled tone, looking from side to side to ensure no one is listening. 'We used to be together.'

'Have you told him about me … about us?'

Trinity clams up, but quickly becomes agitated.

'No,' she says quietly through clenched teeth. 'I haven't told him anything … about us. And I'm not going to.'

'Is that a smart thing to do? Perhaps you should be honest with him.'

She shakes her head.

'No. He's not to know.'

'How will you explain me then?'

Her mind turns in circles.

'I'll tell him and them I met you in New York … that you worked for Yamada … we did some jobs together … I asked you to come here.'

'And you think they'll buy it?'

'Why wouldn't they? You know enough about me and my past for it to be credible … it will also explain how you know so much about killing and guns and all that shit.'

'I think you're making a big mistake.'

'I don't give a fuck what you think. Before I forget, Valentina knows a little about you, but she's cool … I trust her to stay quiet.'

'You told her?'

'Apparently I talk in my sleep.'

'So you dream of me?'

Trinity shoves her face into her hands.

'What are you doing here? What about Mako? Does she know you're here?'

'She told me to come.'

Trinity drops her hands and looks up at Gabriel, her mouth open in disbelief.

'I felt guilty,' he says.

'You didn't have to come here, Gabriel. I understood your situation with …'

'No,' Gabriel says. 'I felt guilty about not telling Mako that we had met.'

Trinity looks away, her cheeks flushed, despite the cold air.

'I told her what happened. I owed it to her to be truthful. I didn't know how she would handle it, but I had to be up front.'

'What did she say? How did she take it?'

'At first she was upset … She cried, fearful I would leave her for you.'

Trinity turns toward Gabriel.

'I not only explained your predicament,' he continues. 'I told her how I felt … empty … and that I missed the excitement of near-death. I told her there would never be any closure or future for us until The Russian was dead, and although upset, she agreed … she agreed.

'She stood by my side when I pulled the trigger on Tanaka. She doesn't like any of this, but she gets it … she understands that she and I can never have a normal life while he breathes.'

'So you're not doing this for me?'

Gabriel pauses, clenches his jaw.

'I'm doing this for all of us.'

Trinity nods.

'How did you find me?'

'It's not important.'

'Like hell, it isn't. Tell me … how you found me.'

'I attached a tracking chip to your sword.'

'You did what?'

'Back in my house in Geneva, while you were getting changed, I removed the handle from your sword and installed a small tracking chip.'

'Are you fucking serious?' Trinity's breathing becomes rapid. 'Why? Why would you do that?'

'Why would you make me watch you suck some guy's cock back in New York?'

Trinity is speechless, her stare blank.

'I'm here now,' Gabriel says. 'Let's finish this shit off and reset our lives.'

Valentina appears at the top of the cathedral's steps.

'Is everything alright?'

Trinity blinks, turns her head to her friend's voice.

'Yeah … yeah, everything's fine. We're about to come back down.'

Valentina disappears back inside the cathedral.

Trinity faces Gabriel, pauses and then launches herself around him.

Show and Tell

Back inside their cavernous headquarters, Trinity has the task of introducing her guest to the rest of the team. A little nervous, she glances across the room at Valentina, who responds with a knowing and comforting wink.

The others stop what they're doing and turn to face the two standing at the entrance.

'Guys, listen up,' Trinity says. 'This is my ... friend, Gabriel. Like every one of you, he's here to help. We've worked together before and have a good understanding of each other's needs. He's skilled and I want you all to embrace him.'

Trinity directs her attention at Halo, who stands motionless, watching her, his mind brooding over the unexpected arrival of Gabriel.

'I trust Gabriel with my life,' Trinity says, turning to face him. 'In fact, I owe him my life.'

Gabriel gently nods.

'Anyway, Gabriel,' she continues, turning to face everyone. 'I'd like you to meet my friends. This is Valentina, from Argentina … speaks good English and is just like me.'

Valentina smiles.

'Anzhelo, my guardian angel whose cave we are all in …'

Anzhelo also smiles.

'… Carlos, former SEAL …'

Carlos nods.

'… And last but not least, Halo … a merc, and my oldest, dearest friend.'

Halo remains staunch, neither flinching nor blinking.

'You forgot Viktor!' Valentina exclaims.

'Oh yes … and Viktor, of course.'

'Thanks for the introduction,' Gabriel says. 'I'm here for the same reason you all are … to kill The Russian, nothing more.'

Trinity lowers her eyes.

Halo notices.

'After his death, you will never have to see me again. I'm not here to step on toes. Just tell me what to do and I'll get it done.'

Valentina breaks the tension in the room.

'Come meet Viktor.'

Halo approaches Trinity.

'Can I speak to you in private?'

'Sure.'

The two of them wander outside the entrance, out of earshot of the others.

'What's going on?' he demands.

'What do you mean?'

'Don't play games, Trinity. Why didn't you tell me about him?'

'There are a lot of things I haven't told you about.'

Halo shakes his head.

'I told you he's here to help,' she says.

'I see the way you look at him. I'm not fucking blind.'

Trinity doesn't know what to say.

Halo buries his eyes deep inside Trinity's.

'Have you fucked him?'

She pauses, her stare unwavering. 'No.'

'I don't trust him,' Halo says, turning away.

'You've only just met him.'

'I don't care. Something isn't right. One or both of you isn't telling the entire truth.'

'You trust me, don't you?' she asks.

Halo continues to look away and doesn't respond.

'Look, Halo,' Trinity says. 'I get it and I understand you're jealous he's here.'

Halo turns to face her.

'I need him … we need him,' she argues. 'Work together and help get the job done. Please. Do it for me.'

Halo's chest rises and falls.

'For you, Trinity,' he says. 'But make no mistake. I'm doing this for you and no one else.'

'For me,' she smiles, somewhat nervously.

'Okay,' Carlos announces, placing the last of the weapons down. 'Here's what we got. Three assault rifles, one shotgun, one sniper rifle, two pistols, a couple of hand grenades, an assortment of freaky shotgun rounds and close to a thousand bullets of one sort or another.'

'Cool,' Halo says. 'You've done well Trinity.'

'Yes, you have been busy,' Valentina nods.

Trinity smiles.

'Steyr AUG,' Carlos says, picking up the Austrian-made rifle. 'This one is an early model, comes with the original fixed Swarovski telescopic sight and standard 20-inch chrome-lined barrel. It has five 30-round double-stacked magazines loaded with 5.56 NATO ball ammo. The bullpup configuration has the ejection port situated behind the trigger. Is anyone here left-handed?'

Valentina raises her hand.

'Then you can't shoot this gun. The ejected shells will hit you in the face.'

She acknowledges with a nod.

'Compared to the other weapons, it's lightweight and easy to throw around,' Carlos adds. 'Maybe you should take this one, Trinity.'

She playfully rolls her eyes.

'Great!'

Carlos swaps the Steyr for the SG550.

'Swiss assault rifle and one of the finest ever made. Same NATO ammo as the Steyr, traveling at three thousand feet per second; capable of firing seven hundred rounds per minute: single-shot, tri-burst or full-auto. Four 30-round magazines, translucent like the Steyr's, but with one advantage: they can be snap-locked together for quicker reloads.'

'Jungle style,' Halo quips.

'Right on,' Carlos agrees, shouldering the sturdy rifle. 'Twenty-inch barrel, skeletonised folding stock, iron battle sights, rear drum aperture and shrouded front sight with flip-up tritium post for night shooting.'

'Is that a bipod under the fore-end?' Gabriel asks.

Carlos demonstrates that the spring-loaded accessory is exactly that.

'The other one,' he says, pointing to the floor, 'is a carbine version of the SG550 with a much smaller 9-inch barrel; it's lightweight, easy to conceal … four 20-round mags.'

'Perfect for me,' Valentina says with a smile.

Picking up a shotgun, Carlos extends his arms in front of his chest.

'Remington 870 with ghost ring sights,' he says, showing it to all in the room. 'It has a four-round side-saddle carrier and a two-point sling carrying another fifteen rounds of 00-Buck. This beast will get anyone from Point A to Point B with very few questions asked. I fucking love it.'

Placing it back on the ground, he picks up two boxes.

'There's some crazy-ass, red-neck ammo to go with it: Bolos and Dragon's Breath. Bolos are nasty. Two lead balls connected by six inches of braided steel. Guaranteed to cut you up and leave behind some serious wounds.'

'Accuracy?' Gabriel asks.

'Close range for optimum effect.'

'And the Dragon's Breath?'

'They're more of a gimmick,' Carlos says. 'But in certain circumstances they could be effective.'

'What do they do?'

'Simply put, each round fired will project a three-second burst of flames out to one hundred feet, depending on wind conditions.'

Valentina's eyes light up.

'I like fireworks.'

'It's a fucking homemade flame thrower,' Carlos says with a grin, taking a knee. 'And now for the Sako TRG. As you can see, this sniper rifle has a fold-out bipod. Made in Finland …'

'Those Finnish are mad-keen hunters and amazingly accurate shooters,' Halo interjects.

All eyes in the room turn to Halo for more riveting information.

'That's it,' he says. 'Just saying ...'

'Anyway,' Carlos continues with a wry smile, his index finger pointing to the various parts of the weapon. 'Again, another twenty-inch barrel with a screw-on three-chambered flash eliminator, adjustable cheek-piece, bolt action, light-as-fuck trigger and Schmidt-and-Bender 5-25 x 56 scope.'

'That's a good scope,' Trinity says. 'I had the same one on my Blaser rifle back home in New York.'

Gabriel shifts his eyes to Trinity and looks at her for a moment before returning his gaze to Carlos.

Trinity notices his lingering glance.

Fuck!

I just reminded Gabriel of the day his best friend and colleagues were murdered because of me.

Fuck!

'Unfortunately, there is only one staggered ten-round box magazine.'

'What caliber?' Gabriel asks.

'It's chambered for .308, bombed-up with 180-grain Super Hammerheads. Not the perfect round for sniping, but their boat-tail design does allow for a flat trajectory and they have relatively good penetration. It'll stop a moose in its tracks.'

'Against armor?' Trinity asks.

'I'm not sure.'

'What distance is it effective to?' Gabriel asks.

'In this urban environment, with the bullet traveling anywhere from six to seven hundred meters a second, I'd say from the top of the cathedral's bell tower … if you can see anything within the city through the scope … you can destroy it.'

Valentina raises her chin.

'What is in the bag?'

Carlos reaches in and removes two round white hand grenades, lobbing one at Gabriel.

'HG-85 frags.'

Gabriel catches it softly with two hands, cradling the deadly bomb like an egg. Everyone's eyes, including his own, are wide open.

Carlos grins.

'Safest grenade ever made. Swiss, so you would expect that. Pass it around and let everyone have a play with it … just don't pull the pin out.'

'It's heavy,' Gabriel says.

'That's because of the steel liner.' Carlos holds his grenade high. 'You'll notice the dimpled surface. Inside the grenade is a small amount of explosives. Once that shit ignites, it explodes, shattering the steel liner, sending thousands of sharp steel fragments in all directions.

'The good thing with this grenade, it has a small lethal radius, therefore it has a small safety radius as well. So you can be close to your target if you have to be.'

'What distances are you talking of?' Valentina asks.

'It will annihilate anything, living or man-made, within ten meters. With decent cover, you should be safe as close as twenty. However, I have read reports of non-lethal frag wounds out to a hundred meters.'

'It has a time fuse?' Halo asks.

'Yep. Grasp it in your master hand with your palm pressed against the handle; pull the pin with your other hand and launch it. The moment it leaves your hand, the countdown commences.'

'How long do you have until it explodes?'

'A few seconds ... throw it high in the air and throw it hard.'

After it has been passed around for all to see, Valentina hands the grenade back to Carlos.

'That's it, ladies. That concludes your lesson today. Oh ... and before I forget ... we have two Glocks with a few mags and approximately one hundred rounds, and a couple of basic cleaning kits.'

'Thanks, Carlos,' Trinity says. 'Hopefully we won't need to utilize everything.'

'Hopefully we have enough,' Gabriel says.

'What do you mean?' Halo asks.

'We're on The Russian's home turf now. We really know very little of his true infrastructure. For all we know, half of Sofia is on his payroll, ready at a moment's notice to down tools and pick up a weapon.'

Halo squares up to Gabriel.

'You know you don't have to be here,' he growls. 'We can handle this.'

'Just saying,' Gabriel mumbles.

Trinity steps between the two.

'Play nice boys, we have much to do and little time to waste.'

Gabriel turns his attention from Halo to Trinity.

'When do you plan on initiating the attack?'

'We go to war at noon on Tuesday.'

'Tuesday!' he exclaims. 'Today is Sunday.'

'I know ... so all the more reason to stop wasting time on how big everyone's dicks are.'

Carlos helps to get things back on track.

'We need to clean and test fire all these guns.'

'How do you propose to do this?' Valentina asks. 'The guns will make much noise.'

'The bells,' Anzhelo whispers. 'There is a service tomorrow morning at eight o'clock. To announce its commencement, I strike the largest bell once.'

'Is it loud?' Carlos asks.

'There are twelve bells. The largest weighs almost twelve thousand kilograms ...'

'That's twelve tonnes!'

'Yes, it is very impressive. On a clear day, it can be heard in certain villages nearly thirty kilometers away ... but sometimes as little as only fifteen.'

Halo nods.

'That's fucking loud.'

'We can synchronize our watches with Anzhelo and fire the weapons at the same time as he rings the bell,' Carlos says.

'But where we can we do this without taking a trip into the countryside?' Valentina asks.

The room fills with silence.

Eyes dart in all directions.

'Here,' Trinity says. 'We have to do it here. It's the only place we have control over.'

'And the noise from the bell will be at its loudest,' Gabriel adds.

'A hole,' Carlos says. 'We'll dig a hole through the ground and fill it with cloth, soft rags and shit, so the bullets don't ricochet back out and bounce off the walls and ceilings, killing us all.'

Valentina looks concerned.

'The noise from the guns will damage our ears. We need something to protect them.'

'We'll shove wax in them,' Trinity says.

'Wax?'

'Candle wax,' Anzhelo smiles looking at Trinity.

She smiles back.

'This is crazy,' Halo says. 'But I agree … it just might work.'

Trinity takes charge.

'Okay. Here's the deal. Angel and I will go over the map so I can get my head around the streets to orientate myself better and help plan our attack. Halo and Carlos start digging. Use my sword if you have to … Scratch it and I'll cut off your heads while you're asleep.'

Carlos doesn't blink.

'I'm joking, Carlos, it's indestructible.'

Carlos blinks; a nervous smile flickers across his face.

'Gabriel, you and Valentina rummage through the lost-and-found box for shit to stuff into the hole and then start servicing some of the guns. We'll all gather in an hour and hopefully formulate a plan. Tomorrow is going to be a big day as we prepare for Tuesday. And before you all go … thanks once again.'

With the cathedral closed for the night, Gabriel and Valentina move about with liberty, a large candle their sole source of light.

'Trinity is glad to have you here,' Valentina says softly, fearful someone from their group might hear.

'I'm not so sure,' Gabriel responds. 'She didn't look too happy when I arrived.'

'You surprised her. She wasn't expecting you.'

'I guess so. How much do you know?'

'Know about what? About you and her?'

Gabriel stops walking and holds up the candle close to their faces.

'Yes. What do you know about the two of us?'

'Not a lot,' she answers. 'She mentioned your name briefly in Buenos Aires and in the end I put two and two together. She was not very willing to share much information. I pressed but she always backed off. She can be very frustrating at times, so guarded … even with me. Fortunately, she talks in her sleep. Have you noticed?'

Gabriel is lost for words at first, then responds, 'No. I never had the opportunity to find out.'

'She likes you a lot. I see an aura surround her when you are nearby. You care for her also, don't you?'

Gabriel's mouth closes and his eyes look down.

'She's very special, Gabriel … complicated, mixed-up, broken … selfish … but oh so beautiful. She's hard to resist.'

Gabriel's eyes stare at the ground.

'Everything about her is wrong, yet everything about her is what draws me nearer.' He looks at Valentina. 'I have tried so hard to forget her, but I can't. Yet I know I have to.'

'Once this is all over … once The Russian is killed … revisit your feelings for her.'

'It's not that simple,' Gabriel says.

'Nothing with Trinity ever is.'

'No, I have a new life now. I'm with someone else. I told her all of this.'

'Do you have the same feelings for this other woman as you do for Trinity?'

'No,' Gabriel answers without hesitation, with absolute certainty. 'They are two different people, not even remotely the same.'

'Let me ask you one thing, Gabriel, and answer honestly. Who do you think of when you go to bed at night and when you first awake in the morning?'

Gabriel stands silent.

Valentina smiles, 'I know who she dreams of.'

'He doesn't seem so bad,' Carlos says, chipping away at the concrete floor with Trinity's sword.

'I just don't trust him, mate,' Halo says, sweeping rubble aside. 'He's not like Trinity and Val ... like contract killers. He's different, more refined. If Zubair were alive, I'd pay good money to have him checked out.'

'Give him a chance. He's a big fucker ... could come in handy.'

'I'll try. But if he fucks up or I find he's been lying to us ...'

'Chill, brother,' Carlos says, placing his dusty hand on Halo's shoulder. 'It'll all be cool. Anyway, this hole is plenty deep, let's go service some of the guns.'

'Have you done this shit before?'

'Done what?' Carlos asks. 'Service guns?'

'Nooo ... shot into a fucking hole in the ground before?'

'Fuck no!'

Trinity glances at the clock on the wall: 11:00 p.m.

'I know it's getting late and the next two days are going to be big ... life-changing ... but we need to nut this shit out now ... tonight.'

'Show us what you got,' Halo says.

'I want to start off by saying my war … our war ... is with The Russian and his goons … no one else, police included.'

Carlos stirs.

'That's going to make things a little awkward.'

'Both Angel and I are firm on this. We do this with the least amount of collateral damage possible or we don't do it at all.'

'By collateral you mean civilian?' Halo asks.

'Yes,' Trinity says. 'Are we all on the same page?'

Eventually they all nod.

'Good.'

Trinity and Anzhelo reposition the map on the table for all to see.

'The obvious place to hit them,' Trinity says, pointing to the map, 'is at the entrance to the Imperial Hotel, but at noon it will be crawling with people. So we need to strike before they arrive or once they've departed.'

Trinity places her hand upon Anzhelo's shoulder.

'Taking advantage of Angel's local knowledge, and having walked the streets myself, I personally think we should strike prior to arrival, in the smaller side street, rather than when they depart along the bigger, busier boulevard out the front.'

'We don't know if their vehicles are armored do we?' Gabriel asks, looking around the room, having missed Trinity's earlier brief.

'No, we don't,' she says. 'They will most likely travel down Shishman.' She runs her finger along the route. 'It's a busy street, but it's not very wide, with cars permanently parked on the right-hand side.'

'It is only one direction,' Anzhelo adds.

'That's right, one-way traffic heading toward the hotel and to us here, in the cathedral.'

'Okay,' Halo says. 'So we have a potential route. Any ideas on how you want to attack the convoy?'

'I want this ambush to be swift and final,' Trinity says. 'This whole ordeal has dragged on long enough. I want to hit him and hit him hard. But after the hit, we stay in the city, lay low for a few days, even longer if we have to. The authorities will cover all the main avenues of escape: major highways, rail and air. And as well as the police searching for us, immigration and customs will be on the lookout too ...'

'Not to mention any criminal elements,' Gabriel interjects.

Trinity nods.

'All of you are probably unaware,' she says, 'but the city is currently in lockdown anyway.'

'What the fuck does that mean?' Gabriel asks.

'There are city-wide protests. They've been going on for months. So far they've been peaceful, but I'm sure by now the cops are tired and frustrated, so their nerves are probably a little frayed.'

'So the city is full of cops?' Valentina asks.

'Yes. The good thing is that the protests usually start at the other end of the city around 13:00 and take several hours before they reach anywhere near us. Most of the police will already be in place long before that time, therefore leaving our area relatively unattended to begin with.'

'How much time do we have?' Carlos asks. 'How long will it take the cops to cross the city?'

All eyes shift to Anzhelo. He pauses.

'Ten minutes ... maybe more with the protests.'

Gabriel stirs.

'How do you intend to hit him *hard*?'

'The Gendarmerie have armored vans,' Trinity says. 'Solid-looking bits of hardware. I say we commandeer one and use it to ram The Russian's car.'

Halo folds his arms and frowns.

'Let me get this straight. You want us to sneak into a city full of wound-up, twitchy cops in broad daylight and steal one of their armored trucks?'

'Yes.'

'How?'

'The other day when I walked through the city, I noticed the vans' crews like to smoke. We distract them while they are all outside, take them hostage and steal their van.'

'And how do we distract them?'

'You leave that to me,' she says with a smile.

Carlos thinks out loud, 'Then we need to stop the convoy or at least slow them down so they can be rammed.' He leans over the map. 'How high is the bell tower?'

'The ladder to the platform is exactly two hundred and twenty steps,' Anzhelo answers. 'I climb it daily. The top of the tower is approximately fifty meters from the ground.'

'With that sort of height,' says an animated Carlos, 'assuming there's a clear line of sight as you look down Shishman Street, the Sako rifle could probably take out the lead car, effectively leaving The Russian a sitting duck.' He points to the map. 'Here, at the intersection of Shishman and Parensov!'

'Do you think you can make that shot?' Gabriel asks.

Carlos straightens.

'It's hard to tell at this stage. I'll need to know the distance. Also depends on the lighting and weather conditions.'

'Is the bullet up to the task?'

'Again, I'm not sure. Once I know the distance, I'll have a better idea if it will be effective. And at some point I will need to zero the scope ... God knows where it's di-alled-in at the moment.'

'How do you plan on doing that?' Gabriel asks.

'I'm not sure. Let's see if it works first.'

'It's starting to take shape,' Trinity says. 'Everybody get ready to synchronize your watches by the clock on the wall.'

'I need no watch,' Anzhelo says. 'I will toll the bell at exactly 08:00 a.m.'

'Okay,' Trinity smiles. 'Our first order of the day for tomorrow is to fire those weapons into the hole and make sure they function. Valentina, you have the carbine and I'll take the Steyr. Carlos you got the Sako ...'

'I'm all over the shotgun,' Gabriel grins.

'That means you have the 550, Halo.'

'Cool.'

'Are there any questions regarding the weapons?' Trinity asks. 'No? Good. Following the testing, Carlos, you need to head up to the belfry and get some eyes on Shish-man Street and see what you can see.'

'Roger that.'

'Valentina can assist you with working out distances and anything else you require. Just get that shit sorted.'

'Too easy.'

'Myself, Gabriel and Halo will do some recon on the armored vans and work out which route to take to get to the intersection. We'll have a final brief tomorrow evening.'

Carlos picks up the cleaning kit.

'The Steyr and shotgun still need to be cleaned.'

'Let's do it then,' Trinity says. 'The sooner we get them done, the sooner we get to curl up on the cold, concrete floor and get some sleep.'

Located within a vast, open valley, surrounded by timeless, tree-lined mountains and a clear blue sky, the city of Sofia begins to wake. And like it has done for centuries a sharp breeze swirls its way down the steep, rocky slopes of Mount Vitosha, slicing its way through the city's continuous and cramped cobblestone streets.

Finding its way up to the cathedral's belfry, the cool, wintery wind, whistles in and around its small open arches.

Feeling like the king of the world, Anzhelo stands alone on top of the majestic basilica, the place he has happily called home for more than half his life. The seemingly unending view of the capital and the nearby countryside ordinarily brings him much joy, but today it is diminished by anxiety over the impending battle.

From across the other side of the city, its dazzle catching Anzhelo's eye, early morning sunlight strikes the golden crown belonging to the seductive Saint Sofia.

The statue holds a position of prominence once occupied by an iconic monument to Vladimir Lenin and his Communist Party's oppressive ideals. Since that was toppled from its marble base and replaced with the capital's beautiful patron saint, her fresh, lustrous visage has breathed new life and hope into an old and tired city.

Standing with his eyes closed and his mouth open, Anzhelo enjoys the wind sweeping back his hair and ruffling his unkempt beard.

He finds the cold air refreshing.

In his mind he is young again.

Anzhelo is eighteen years old. In some countries, he would be considered old, in others ... still a child.

She is two years younger, and pretty. All the boys from the village like her and chase after her.

But she is interested in only one person ... a tall, shy and athletic boy, the son of a farmer ... Anzhelo.

Together they wander the fields of his father's property, hand in hand. The summer is hot; they swim in the dam and lie beneath shady trees, listening to the rustling leaves.

Life is good ... life is simple for the two young lovers. But Anzhelo knows it will all change, and quickly.

He has joined the army and will soon have to leave.

Delaying his boarding of the train, standing silent, he looks back at her.

Her long ebony hair falls alongside her innocent face; her puffy eyes well with tears, poised to overflow again.

Never did Anzhelo imagine that this moment – now his most treasured – would be the last time his strained eyes would gaze upon her beautiful face.

Opening his wet eyes, burning red with anger, not sadness, Anzhelo stares across the city's rooftops, his heartfelt pain stinging his face. He turns around and walks to the middle of the platform.

Suspended above and below him and all around, are twelve decorative bells, big and small, cast and donated by Moscow a little more than a century ago.

To Anzhelo, the bells are like children, his very own. They sing and dance for him, making the old man happy, making his lonely existence bearable. They give him purpose, another reason — no matter how trivial — to live. Stepping up to the wooden rail he lifts a thick, worn rope. Holding it tightly with both hands, he takes up the slack and once again closes his eyes.

'What the fuck!' Halo exclaims, looking down at the hole in the floor. 'A Teddy Bear?'

Gabriel appears nonplussed.

'You wanted as much soft material as we could find to stuff into the hole. We figured the bear would give us all something to aim at.'

Halo shakes his head.

Everyone else in the room laughs.

Carlos looks at his watch.

'Okay. It's almost shooting time. Start plugging up your ears.'

Trinity walks around carrying a bowl filled with soft candle wax.

'Lick your fingers and moisten the inside of your ears first,' she instructs. 'It'll make them easier to clean afterwards.'

Compressing the wax between their fingers, they proceed to soundproof their ears.

Valentina winces.

'This feels weird.'

'What did you say?' Gabriel says, motioning toward his own wax-filled ear.

'I said ...'

Gabriel smirks.

'Never mind, you prick.'

'Okay, take up your positions,' Carlos commands as

self-appointed range master. 'Remember, we get one shot at this. Make sure you load two rounds so you can check your weapon chambers a new one after it fires.'

The unlikely gang stand shoulder to shoulder around the homemade bullet trap, sharing concerned glances with one another.

Carlos runs a final visual safety check.

'Where is Viktor?'

'I locked him inside the other room,' Trinity answers.

'And you are certain this will work?' Valentina asks, looking at Carlos.

He grins with a sparkle in his eyes.

'Ladies, lock and load!'

Gabriel feeds two bullets into the shotgun and works the fore-end to the rear and then back again. The others insert a magazine each before actioning rounds into their chambers.

Carlos glances at his watch.

'For those about to die, we shoot you. Ready ... ready!'

Anzhelo opens his eyes. He knows the time has come. Bending at the knees he yanks on the rope with all the strength he can muster. The huge, cast-iron clapper swings to one side, striking the inside of the twelve-tonne monster. The bell barely moves, but due to the sudden impact, a shock wave reverberates back and forth through the metal surface, creating a soundwave within the bell's voluminous air space. The resulting ringing noise is almost deafening.

Carlos struggles to see through the gun smoke.

'Is everyone alright?' he yells.

Halo wafts one hand about.

'I'm good.'

'Me also,' Valentina coughs.

'Where's Gabriel?' Trinity asks, looking around the room.

The door to the makeshift gun range opens wide allowing smoke to freely flow from the room.

'I'm over here,' he says, still holding the doorknob.

With a surprised look on his face, Carlos confesses, 'I can't believe that shit actually worked.'

Valentina reaches into the hole and removes a headless Teddy Bear.

'Did everyone's weapon function?' Halo asks.

A collective nod is all the response he needs.

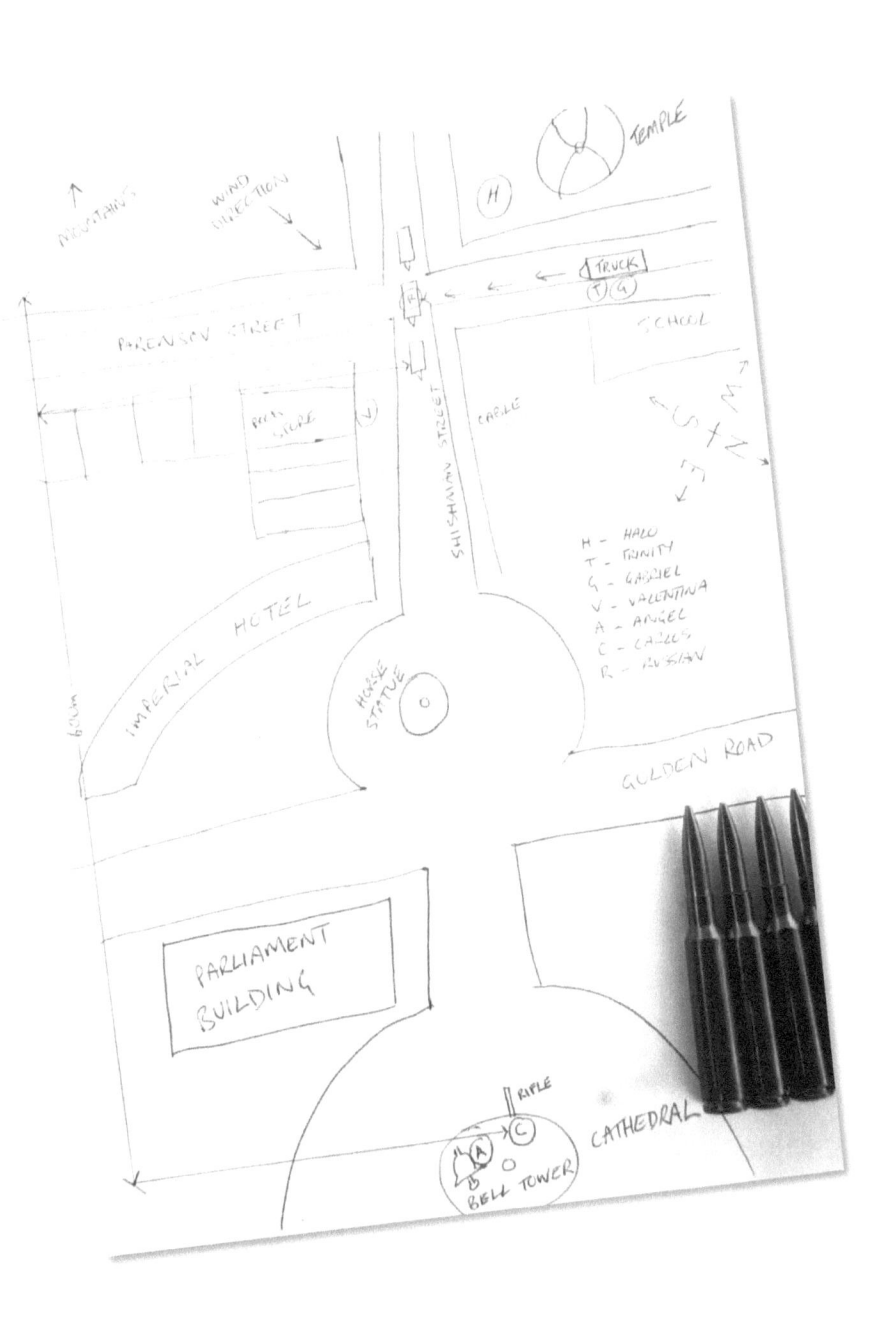

One Bullet at a Time

From his vantage point above the cathedral, hidden deep within the belfry's shadows, Carlos looks through the Sako's scope. Its enhanced magnification allows him to see clearly all the way along Shishman Street.

He sketches the area of interest onto a small sheet of paper, making note of the overhead cables at all of the crossroads and mapping the locations of those trees whose branches reach over the street.

Valentina looks over his shoulder.

'So what do you think?' she says. 'It is possible?'

Carlos stands and straightens his back.

'I can see the intersection.' He scrawls an 'X' on his makeshift map, indicating its location. 'There are some cables and branches that may be in the way. I'm gonna need you to take a walk down there.'

'Is a nice day for a stroll.'

'When you're standing in the sweet spot, I'll flash this mirror. When you see it, I need you to count how many paces it is back to the base of the cathedral, directly below the belfry.'

Valentina rubs her hands.

'This sounds like fun.'

'And make sure your hair is down,' he adds. 'So I can see the wind direction.'

Halo turns to Trinity.

'You want us to steal that piece of junk?'

'That piece of junk is built to smash its way through hardened barricades and to survive an ambush,' Trinity says, sipping on her espresso inside the corner café. 'I'm certain it will do the job nicely.'

'I think it's perfect,' Gabriel says.

'You would,' Halo mumbles under his breath.

The three of them sit comfortably at a booth, warming their insides with a long-needed shot of caffeine and looking out across the boulevard through the plate-glass window. There, discreetly parked in a side street, shaped like a house brick, is a menacing armored police van, its chassis sitting high above the road on four large, knobbly tyres. Steel mesh protects the windshield from attack.

'From what I've seen,' Trinity says. 'The van has two compartments: a front cab, accessed by doors on both sides, and a cavernous rear cab, accessed only through a back door and a small hatch that leads into the front cab.'

Three gendarmes stand near the back of the van, talking and puffing on cigarettes.

'They're big boys,' Gabriel says.

Trinity nods.

'Yes, but at least they are out of the van, making our job so much easier.'

'What makes you think they will surrender the van so easily?' Halo asks.

'We will give them no choice,' Trinity responds with a shrug of her shoulders.

'And then what do we do with them once we hijack their vehicle?'

'We take them with us.'

'What do you mean?'

'We tie them up using their handcuffs and leave them in the cabin.'

'Back up a little,' Gabriel says. 'How do you intend on jacking the van in the first place?'

'Simple,' she smiles. 'I'll provide the distraction while you and Halo sneak up and remove their weapons, along with their freedom of choice.'

'And how are you going to distract them?' he asks with a cheeky grin, confident he already knows the answer.

'I'll walk right past them.'

'No offence,' Gabriel says. 'But since we've been sitting here, I've noticed about a hundred of the most gorgeous women I've ever seen in my life pass by the window. What makes you think the gendarmes will even notice you?'

'How many of those gorgeous women were taking their *white* Doberman for a walk?'

Carlos runs the rifle's scope over the row of cars parked down one side of the street. Several of the vehicles appear occupied, the silhouettes of unknown faces just visible through unclean and shaded windshields.

Heavily cloaked and gloved commuters bustle their way along the gray hexagonal paving stones of the narrow sidewalks. Many stoop or kneel to buy cigarettes and snacks from colorful basement-level shop windows; the subterranean convenience store owners smile, grateful for their patronage.

Further along, Carlos sees Valentina position herself just short of the street corner at the intersection of Shishman and Parensov. She stands alongside one of the street's many waist-high, pedestrian poles.

The intersection is a relatively small crossroad compared to those found in downtown Sofia. Sans stop signs and traffic lights, it's reliant on the flow of traffic for its effectiveness.

Of its four corners, three of them house multilevel cream-colored apartments with ground-floor shopfronts. Most of these are cafés, but there is also a lingerie outlet — one of many located throughout the city — and a quirky English-language bookstore.

On the remaining corner filling an entire city block is the Temple Sveti Sedmochislenitsi, once the Ottoman-era Black Mosque now a Bulgarian Orthodox Church.

Val steps from the curb and glances at the cathedral.

Carlos notes the direction of her hair blowing in the light breeze as she makes her way into the middle of the street; her blurry face fills the eyepiece of the Schmidt and Bender scope. Within seconds, the scars on her cheek are crystal clear, although the vague outline of an electrical cable spoils the view.

She patiently waits for the signal, constantly checking over her shoulder for oncoming traffic.

'Keep moving, Val,' Carlos mutters. 'Keep moving, just a little bit more.'

After waiting several seconds, she moves backwards, closer to the middle of the intersection, although an approaching car is of some concern.

With no sign of the cable, Carlos refocuses the scope on her face. Her anxious look is replaced by one of relief as Carlos holds up the mirror and a small flash of light sweeps across her eyes.

'This is it,' Trinity says to Gabriel and Halo, the three of them standing beneath a sprawling, barren tree on General Parensov Street, no more than a hundred meters away from the intersection. 'This is where we will park up and wait for The Russian's car.'

The spot Trinity has chosen is secluded, hidden away by many other similar trees. On one side of the street, in the public grounds of the Temple, hundreds of birds feast on stale bread crumbs left behind by dozens of playful children, while the open-air café basking in the sunlight, satiates the hunger of those who live and work nearby. Park benches beneath weeping willows seem a popular place for watching the world slowly pass by.

Opposite the Temple, at one end of Parensov Street, are two gated schools. The sounds of children's laughter escape their tall protective walls and iron gates.

'By this time tomorrow,' Halo says, 'we'll all be free of The Russian's influence.'

'I can't believe we're actually going to do this,' Trinity smiles.

'Are you sure you want to go ahead with it?' Gabriel asks. 'It's not too late to walk away.'

Halo encroaches on his space.

'What is your fucking problem? You rock up late to the party and then tell us all what to do. How about you do everyone a favor and *you* walk away?'

Gabriel keeps his shit together for Trinity's sake.

'This plan is so last-minute. Sure, it might work, but it might not. Something of this nature needs months of careful planning, not to mention the right equipment and manpower.'

Trinity places a hand on each of their puffed-out chests.

'Guys, relax. Please. I know where you're coming from, Gabriel. I really do. I know you're not used to flying by the seat of your pants. But lately, I am. It happens tomorrow … with or without you.'

'Tonight is possibly the last time we will all meet together under cloak and dagger,' Trinity says to her team gathered back at the cavern. 'Tomorrow is the start of our new lives. Tomorrow, we stop looking over our shoulders.'

'Tomorrow, we get drunk,' Valentina says with a big smile.

Laughter fills the room.

'On a serious note,' Trinity says, 'we need to finalize our plan so we can all get our shit squared away and get a good night's rest. Carlos, you need to sight in that rifle … tonight.'

'All under control,' he says. 'As the protesters march past the cathedral, I'll head upstairs and see where it's at.'

'How many rounds do you think it might take?'

'It's hard to say. At least I now know the distance, thanks to Val's calculations. I'm hoping no more than three.'

'Make every shot count; you don't have any to waste.' Trinity looks at Anzhelo. 'We need you to teach us some key words in Bulgarian to help facilitate the process when we take possession of the Gendarmerie's armored truck.'

'I'm sure everybody understands the international language of *shotgun*,' Carlos jokes.

'I am sure you are correct,' Anzhelo says. 'But please do not underestimate how tough some of the older police may be. They have seen and done a lot in their lifetimes. But I will teach you some words to use, just in case.'

Trinity smiles.

For what should be the final time, Anzhelo spreads the map across the small table.

'Here it is,' Trinity says. 'We all know The Russian will arrive at the hotel at noon. His convoy will travel down Shishman.' She traces the route with her finger and then taps the map. 'It's here at the intersection with Parensov that we ram his vehicle with the stolen armored truck.

'Now, for this to happen, Valentina needs to step in front of the lead vehicle.'

'How will I know when they are coming?' she asks.

'Carlos is our eye in the sky. When he sees the convoy enter onto Shishman, he'll notify Anzhelo, who will then strike the bell.'

'Roger that,' Carlos says.

'Once they enter the intersection, Carlos will again notify Anzhelo, who will strike the bell a second time.'

'That will be my cue to step onto the road.'

'Exactly,' Trinity says. 'The tricky part comes next though. We want to keep the element of surprise for as long as we can; even seconds may make a difference to the overall outcome.'

Carlos stirs.

'This is where I really come into play.'

Halo looks at him and says, 'You need to make sure that lead car doesn't go any further.'

'How you do it,' Trinity says, 'is up to you to decide. You're the best skilled by far to use that rifle.'

He nods.

'I'll brainstorm some ideas with Val and Angel after this.'

'Cool. At this point, Gabriel and I will drive the truck toward The Russian's car …'

'What about the rear vehicle?' Valentina interjects.

Trinity points to the map.

'Halo will be stationed here, somewhere near the temple.' She looks at him. 'You need to force that car to stay where it is and use it to help box in The Russian's vehicle.'

'Piece of piss,' he boasts, raising his chin.

'What's the plan after we ram his car?' Gabriel asks.

Trinity leans over the table and lowers her head, sighing loudly.

Her team look at each other in the silence that ensues.

Halo breaks the ice.

'I'm pretty sure we've all been in a tricky situation before more than once or twice in our lives. Judging by the shaking of heads in the room, the consensus would be in the affirmative.

'All things considered, Trinity has covered most of the bases here. Once that truck ploughs into the side of The Russian's car, who knows how it's all gonna play out? We improvise, role with the punches. We all have a job to do … after that … well …'

'Shoot fast … shoot straight,' Carlos says with a smirk.

Halo adds, 'When the guns start shaking … the bones start breaking!'

'Okay,' Gabriel says out loud. 'I'll play the dumb guy in the room.'

Halo glances sideways and winks at Carlos.

'I get it that when we slam into his car, it's impossible to predict the outcome, other than *we* kill The Russian. But what about our contingency plans? What if it all goes to shit? Where do we fall back, rendezvous, regroup … escape …?'

'It's all or nothing, Gabriel. I told you, I want to hit hard.'

'You can't be serious, Trinity … really, a last stand?'

'The Russian has to die; there's nothing more I need to say.'

Gabriel shakes his head and looks around the room for support.

'Think about it, mate,' Halo says. 'How much harder will you fight if you know it's your last?'

'That's ridiculous! I've fought many battles where I've almost died.'

'But did you know in advance it might be your last?'

'What the fuck? You're all fucking mad.'

'Trust me, mate, you'll see shit just that little bit quicker and clearer tomorrow; a crisp front sight … maybe even the flight of the bullet spinning through the air. You won't fumble a reload, or stumble, make a bad decision.'

'Fuck me,' Gabriel moans, shaking his head at Trinity. 'I'm not beyond the fight … I'll sit behind that wheel, I'll crash that armored truck into The Russian, I'll do all I can … but seriously, to have no back-up plan? Well, helter-fucking-skelter.'

'If you must,' Anzhelo weighs in. 'That is, if things do not go to plan, you can move toward the golden road and disappear into the crowds of protesters. I will show you on the map the best way to get there through the back streets.'

'Sounds like a plan.' Halo turns to Gabriel. 'You said it yourself, mate, it takes months of planning to make this shit happen. We don't have a couple of months. We have tonight.'

With nothing more to say, Halo walks over to the map. The rest of them, resigned to their fate, huddle around the table.

Gabriel makes his way over to Trinity.

She stares right through him.

Gabriel places his hand on her shoulder.

'Are you okay? Trinity, are you okay?'

She blinks.

'Huh? Yeah, sure … I'm fine.'

'You seem …'

'Lost?'

'Yeah … somewhere else, that's for sure.'

'You're right you know, Gabriel.'

'About what?'

'This plan of mine, it's …'

'Shit.'

'Well, I wouldn't go that far. No, actually I would. It is shit.'

'You know my thoughts, Trinity. But I guess having half a plan is better than no plan at all. We'll just have to make it work ... even if it means killing The Russian and his men one bullet at a time, or dying trying.'

Trinity moves closer to him.

'If I lose myself tomorrow, promise me you won't get in my way and try to stop me.'

'I'm not sure I even know what that means.'

'Trust me, you'll know. Promise me?'

Gabriel pauses then says, 'I promise.'

'I'm so glad you're here,' Trinity confides. 'There are some things I want to say to you that I never had the chance or balls to say before.'

Gabriel takes her hand.

'It's okay. You don't have to say anything.'

'No but I do,' she whispers.

'Seriously ...'

'Shut the fuck up, Gabriel, and listen to me.'

'Okay, okay, okay ... what then?'

'If it does go well tomorrow ... after this is all over ... I was wondering if we ...'

Valentina grabs Trinity by the shoulder, spinning her around.

'Come watch the sunset over the city from the bell tower,' she says. 'It's amazing!'

'I can't ...'

'Yes, you can! Come, come.'

Trinity's hand slips from Gabriel's grasp.

From the entrance to the crypt, hidden from Gabriel's view, Halo stands alone, silent, his gaze buried deep into the ground.

The sounds of democracy ring loud, ring true, on the streets of Sofia: whistles, trumpets, horns ... cheers and chants ... all in time to the slow and rhythmic beating of drums.

TOM, TOM, TOM ... TOM, TOM, TOM ... TOM, TOM, TOM ...

Perched atop the roof of a deserted storeroom on the corner of Shishman and Parensov, a lone dove tucks in its wings and settles down for the night.

Six hundred meters away, Carlos adjusts the brightness of the red crosshair, positioned steadily in the center of the dove's white chest. Commencing his breathing cycle, he places his finger against the trigger and slips his mind into the groove.

TOM, TOM, TOM ... TOM, TOM, TOM ... TOM, TOM ...

... BOOM!

The sound of the gunshot is swallowed up by the third beat of the drum, a puff of smoke appearing on the wall six inches below his point of aim; small chunks of brick and plaster explode outwards into the air.

The unsuspecting bird raises its rotating head.

Carlos manipulates the bolt, first rearward then forward, his point of aim remaining true. Reaching up, he adjusts the scope half a turn.

TOM, TOM, TOM ... TOM, TOM ...

... BOOM!

No puff of smoke is to be seen anywhere through the

scope of his rifle; instead, just a handful of white feathers floating back and forth.

Carlos grins.

Trinity senses both of them.

She no longer seeks them out.

She has decided if they want her, they must come to her.

She knows they will … they always do.

The darkness shifts.

She is restless; her heart pounds.

He moves from the shadows, slowly but surely.

She cannot blink; her bare skin is flushed.

He stands there, his face hidden no more.

Trinity looks not at his face, but at the mangled, shattered remnants of what was once a strong and pure heart, just barely beating within his chest.

Seeking her attention, another steps from the dark.

Trinity turns, her chest tight, her eyes drawn to the cavernous hole in the side of his head.

His melted brain oozes down his cheek.

She turns away, knowing she must choose.

But to choose one will disappoint the other.

She is confused, but knows what to do. She smiles and turns.

But both are gone.

Trinity sits up, her rapid heartbeat pounding inside her head. She looks around the room. Everyone appears to be asleep.

If any of them were awake, they might see the orange glow from the heater reflecting off the tear forming in the corner of her eye.

Hell's Bells

Three large, unfit gendarmes gather toward the rear of their armored truck to enjoy a cigarette in the semi-privacy of a shaded laneway. And although the city they swore to protect is in the middle of civil unrest, they find the time to share a laugh as they warm their hands inside their thick coat pockets.

One of them gives his colleague a short, sharp jab with an elbow, accompanied by a nod and a raised brow.

The other officer's eyes follow his gaze, tracking a dark-haired beauty walking her dog through the crowd.

Nearing the entrance to the laneway, Trinity squats to pat her four-legged companion's steady, white head.

The men look at each other and smile.

Trinity looks up at them through dangling strands of hair, the remainder, pulled back tight in a high ponytail, falls over the shoulder inserts of her motorbike jacket.

She smiles, not at them but at their plight, as her accomplices stealthily approach from behind.

'Hey, kuki!' Gabriel yells.

All three officers spin around at the same time, angry at having been insulted. Confronted with a shotgun and an assault rifle, the youngest officer instinctively goes for his holstered pistol, but the more senior of the group reaches a tree-trunk-sized arm across his chest to stop him getting them all killed.

Aggressively, Halo leans forward, the rifle tucked into his shoulder, his finger on the trigger, eyes wide as saucer plates.

'Otkliuchi kamiona i vlizai!' Gabriel orders.

The gendarmes all look at each other.

Halo's eyes remain fixed on the younger officer though he addresses Gabriel.

'You're not talking like them.'

'What the fuck do you mean?'

'You're not rolling the letters with your tongue. You sound like an American tourist. And say it with a deeper tone ... say it like you fucking mean it.'

'Well, seeing how you're a linguist expert, how about you say it?'

Halo's eyes shift to Gabriel for a heartbeat and then return to the young cop at the end of his rifle.

'I thought as much,' Gabriel says. Clearing his throat, he repeats the order, 'Otkliuchi kamiona i vlizai!'

The gendarmes continue to ignore him.

Trinity storms up behind them and, one at a time, removes their pistols and radios. Standing behind the more senior officer, she shoves the barrel of his service weapon up and under his chin. Baring her teeth, she whispers in his ear.

'Vednaga!'

The officer orders his men to comply, promptly unlocking the truck and ushering them into the back.

Dressed in black, wearing an oversized coat to conceal her weapon, Valentina makes her way down Shishman toward its intersection with Parensov, her flowing hair pushed back by a sharp breeze. Despite the many scars marking her face, she smiles to herself as she manages to steal a few admiring looks from the men walking by.

Carlos rests the Sako's bipod on the flat rough wooden surface, chocking one of the table's legs with folded cardboard to help steady the shooting platform. Nailed to the top of the table is his sketch of the scene in front of him, distances and landmarks highlighted in red for easy referencing.

His eyes dart back and forth as he lines up the gun with the street ahead.

A minor twist of the rifle's butt and its barrel points across the cathedral's vast, surrounding square. Some further tweaking and it's aimed alongside the nearby white walls of the national parliament building and all the way up Shishman Street.

Vitosha Mountain forms an impressive backdrop.

Lifting his head to take in a windswept aroma of roasted red peppers, garlic and onion, he removes the remaining eight rounds of .308 from his pocket and places them on the table.

Anzhelo passes him a crate to sit on.

He kicks it into place.

'Are you ready?'

Anzhelo sucks in a mouthful of air and expels it with vigor.

Carlos takes him by the shoulder.

'You'll be fine. All you have to do is ring that bell when I tell you to.'

'How will I know?'

Carlos positions himself behind the table.

'It's easy. I'll yell out ... GO!'

'So, when I hear the word GO, I will pull the rope?'

'Yes.'

'It will take a moment for the bell to strike,' he adds.

'Okay,' Carlos says, carefully wiping down each bullet with a soft cloth, holding them up in front of his eye. 'I'll have to factor that in when I signal for Val to move. Stopping the car in the exact spot is crucial.' His eyes shift to Anzhelo. 'Thanks for that, buddy!'

Anzhelo's lips twitch as he attempts to smile.

Halo and Viktor sit in the back of the armored truck, facing the gendarmes, all of whom are blindfolded, bound and gagged, held in place by the bench-seat's restraining harnesses.

Two of them are naked but for their underwear.

Halo cocks his head as he feels the truck slow down.

The brakes squeak as they slowly come to a stop.

Gabriel kills the engine; the rear of the truck rumbles before going quiet.

Trinity hunches over at the bulkhead door separating the front cabin from the rear.

'Is everything alright?' she asks.

Halo replies, 'All good. Have we arrived?'

Trinity nods.

'Confirm the time is 11:15?'

She looks at her watch.

'Roger that. I hope everyone else is in place by now.'

'I'm sure everything is going to plan.'

Carlos doesn't blink as his finger takes up the slack of the trigger.

'Get ready to ring that fucking bell, Angel.'

'But it is not noon.'

'We may have a situation,' he says, positioning the crosshair over a gendarme's forehead. 'Stay calm, Val,' he whispers. 'Stay calm. I got ya back.'

The world around Carlos—the real world, not the snapshot of reality confronting him—could be on fire and he wouldn't even know, such is the focus he now channels through the scope and onto the street below.

He catches Valentina's gaze switch from the gendarme to the cathedral and then back again with the blink of her eye.

'I see ya, Val; I'm right here.'

'What is happening?' Anzhelo asks.

'She's being questioned by the cops. She's slowly reaching into her coat … she's handing over her passport

... he's reading it ... now he's showing it to his partner to look at ...'

'Is she going to be okay?'

'Just chill, Angel ... everything will be fine. The female cop is giving it back to Val ... Val's smiling ... the cops are walking away ... Val just gave us a wink. I told you it would be all good.'

Anzhelo breathes a long sigh.

With a smile from ear to ear, Carlos follows the gendarmes' movements until they disappear from sight and down another street.

The Russian's convoy of three vehicles has little regard for any other traffic on the road; the powerful V8 Range Rover bullies its way from lane to lane, clearing a path for the Mercedes SUV, which is closely followed by an Audi Q7.

Motorists brake hard and swerve to avoid contact.

Borisa sits on the back seat behind the driver, her thick black coat scarcely covering her bare thighs. She tugs on her form-fitting leather boots, laced all the way up past her knees.

Sergei sits alongside her, talking business on his cell phone.

'I want you to arrange another shipment of young girls to Varna ...'

Borisa tunes out. She doesn't care to listen to the conversation; it only reveals old wounds.

'Turn up the radio,' she instructs the driver.

He looks at her in the rear view mirror.

'Do it now!'

Reluctantly, he increases the volume.

'Louder!'

Turning it up some more, he glances in the mirror at The Russian.

The back of Sergei's bony hand strikes Borisa's cheek, causing her to bang her head against the thick, laminated glass; blood spills from her split lip.

The driver turns down the radio.

The Russian continues his conversation.

'What's it like outside?' Halo asks.

Gabriel looks through the mesh cage.

'It appears similar to yesterday. The café is filling up with the lunchtime crowd and there are a dozen or so random visitors walking about the temple grounds.'

'The school kids will be out soon,' Trinity says.

Gabriel checks the mirrors and down both sides of the armored truck.

'Now is a good time for you to get out and take up your position, H,' he says, careful not to mention their real names in front of the prisoners.

'Roger that,' Halo says. Getting to his feet, he tugs at the harnesses on the gendarmes one final time. 'These guys are good to go.'

Trinity swivels in her seat.

Halo moves up front, leans forward and kisses her cheek. Caught by surprise, she doesn't move away.

'Look after yourself, and I'll see you back at the cathedral,' he says.

Dressed in one of their captive's police uniform and with his rifle concealed beneath the overcoat, Halo opens the rear door of the truck. Tugging on Viktor's lead, they both quietly slip away.

Trinity turns to Gabriel.

'I had nothing to do with that!'

'You don't have to explain anything to me.'

'It's just that …'

'Seriously, I don't care.'

'Then why won't you even look at me while I'm talking to you?'

Gabriel doesn't answer.

Trinity shakes her head.

'You wanna know why I sucked that guy's cock in New York?'

Gabriel stirs in his seat.

'I did it for you,' she says.

Gabriel's head snaps around.

'For me? You did it for me?'

'Keep it together.'

Gabriel's face burns red.

'When you and I … were together,' Trinity says, 'you brought out feelings in me I had never experienced before.'

'Don't do this.'

'I loved the way you looked at me.'

'I don't want to hear anymore.'

'I'm not normal,' she says, talking over the top of Gabriel's voice. 'I'm fucked up. I have a lot of issues.'

'And no one else does?' Gabriel barks.

Trinity weathers his retort, determined to keep her cool.

'At the time, I didn't know you all that well,' she continues. 'I wasn't used to your level of affection. You frightened me. I thought it best for you to never think of me again. That's why I did it … sucked his cock.'

Gabriel appears flustered.

'And for what it's worth,' she adds, 'until recently, I'd not been with another man since you and I were together … that's almost three years!'

'Why are you telling me all this shit?'

'Let me finish,' she says. 'For three years I never wanted to sleep with another man. Do you have any idea how out of character that was for me? I wanted nothing more than to savour our experience.'

'And then?'

She pauses.

The grimace on Gabriel's face is painful, even for Trinity to bear. She knows she's digging her own grave. Leaning forward, both elbows on her knees, she lowers her eyes.

'I didn't even want to do it … but I did … it just kind of happened. But the entire time … all I kept thinking of was you, Gabriel … no one else but you.'

'Are you listening to what you're fucking saying? Stop it! Stop it now!'

'Maybe I'm not explaining myself properly,' she says, becoming agitated. 'See, this is why I don't talk to people … interact with them … I can't … I don't know how to.'

Gabriel shakes his head and shuts his eyes.

'I never asked for any of this,' Trinity says. 'Whatever this *is* we have.'

Looking up through the corners of her eyes, she attempts one more time to express herself.

'Believe it or not, before you and your train wreck of a life crashed into *my* world, as much as I hated my shitty life, it was *my* shitty life. I had order … routine … I had a fucking purpose.'

To his surprise, a pang of remorse forces Gabriel to open his eyes.

'Train wreck?'

Trinity goes out on a limb and smiles.

'You've got to admit,' she says, 'in your own way you're a little fucking cuckoo!'

Gabriel chortles.

Trinity laughs.

But the mood changes quickly; an awkward silence fills the cab. Gabriel and Trinity stare at each other.

Something or someone is about to give way, when the single toll of a bell shatters the air.

Situated in the grounds of Temple Sveti Sedmo-schislenitsi, close to the intersection, Halo loiters alongside an open-air fruit market; Viktor sits by his side.

He lifts his head to the roar of the Range Rover's five-liter engine making its way along the thin, cluttered street. Taking one final bite, Halo throws his half-eaten apple into the trash.

Valentina steps away from the bookstore window and moves closer to the road. Looking back across the tops of parked cars, she spots the bright flashing headlamps of the four-wheel-drive heading her way.

In the background, Halo can be seen dashing across the pavement with Viktor in tow, the pair of them passing in front of the temple. Removing her gloved hands from her pockets, Valentina loosens her coat and prepares for battle.

Gabriel revs the truck's engine; smoke billows from the rear stack. He looks across at Trinity.

She tugs on her seat belt.

'Are you ready for this?' he asks.

'Yeah … yeah, I'm ready.'

Placing one hand on top of the steering wheel and the other on the shifter, Gabriel leans forward and narrows his eyes, again revving the engine before grinding the gears into place.

Anzhelo stands within the cool shadows of the belfry, holding onto the thick rope with both hands. With one foot in front of the other, bending at the knees, he looks sideways through his dishevelled gray hair and awaits another signal.

With the aid of the rifle's scope, Carlos tracks the movements of The Russian's convoy.

The three all-terrain luxury vehicles travel unnecessarily fast down the one-way street. A little further on, up ahead at the intersection, light traffic comes and goes. Hemmed in by a row of parked cars and small roadside bollards, the Range Rover is forced to slow down. Aware of the sudden drop in speed, Borisa looks out her window as the temple comes into view through a smattering of trees.

'Shit's about to get real,' Carlos mutters. 'Get ready, Angel!'

The old man braces himself, determined to do his part, stand tall and not let the team ... not let Trinity ... down.

'Ready,' Carlos prompts with a firm, steady voice, his cheek resting against the butt, his eye glued to the scope, finger on the trigger. 'Ready ... ready ...'

Borisa notices Viktor's unique white coat as he runs through an otherwise sedentary crowd of elderly temple worshippers. Her gaze intuitively shifts further ahead, to Halo, in a dark-blue overcoat, running in the same direction, his right arm pinned by his side. Sensing something is not right Borisa sits up straight in her seat.

Carlos's tone is solid as a rock, 'Ready … ready …'

Anzhelo adjusts his grip, his cold fingers aching, his old legs quivering.

The Range Rover enters the intersection.

Carlos' voice quickens, 'Ready, ready, GO!'

Anzhelo stands and squats back down, yanking on the rope with the strength of a young man.

Helter Skelter

Valentina steps from the curb, her heart pounding.

The Range Rover comes to a sudden halt.

The Argentine beauty owns the middle of the road, wisps of hair flicking to one side, explosive eyes set to burst beneath the dark tint of her sunglasses.

The driver stares at her through the windshield and throws his hands in the air.

She doesn't move.

From the passenger seat, Hook Nose leans over and beeps the horn.

In the car behind them, Borisa swivels her head and curtly asks, 'Why are we not moving?'

The two men up front argue amongst themselves.

The Russian holds his phone away from his ear and speaks to Borisa, 'What is the problem?'

'I do not know,' she responds.

'Then find out!'

The bell tolls loudly.

Up ahead, a substantial chip appears in the Range Rover's laminated, armored windshield, directly in front of the driver's face.

He turns to Hook Nose.

'Kakvo po diavolite?'

Within seconds, the familiar sound of the cathedral's largest bell again resonates through the city streets. Only this time, the driver's head explodes, showering the inside of the car and its occupants with blood, bone, hair and brain. What was only a chip in the windshield is now an inch-wide hole.

Hook Nose, with one side of his face covered in blood and his mouth wide open, stares at his headless partner, the dead man's twitching hands still gripping the steering wheel.

The three men in the back seat are speechless, looking at one another in disbelief, hoping that one of them miraculously has an explanation for whatever-the-fuck just happened.

Hook Nose reaches for his vibrating cell phone from inside his sullied jacket.

Anzhelo again yanks on the rope.

Another chip appears in the windshield, this time in front of Hook Nose's face. A man of many talents, few of them legal or morally sound, Hook Nose is anything but stupid. He didn't survive a thousand fights and a hundred wars in a dozen different countries by being slow off the mark. Scrambling to remove his seatbelt, the big man twists in his seat and reaches for the door handle.

'Ne, nedei!' a colleague yells from the rear of the vehicle, reaching forward to grab a hold of his arm.

'Answer your fucking phone,' Borisa demands, staring angrily at her own cell phone, as though it will somehow force Hook Nose to pick up.

The chatter from the front of the Mercedes increases in volume. Borisa looks up to see Hook Nose emerge from the vehicle in front, a look of concern and blood across his twisted face.

Suddenly and violently, the sound of gunfire bursts forth.

Hook Nose ducks behind the car, bullets ricocheting off the Rover's reinforced roof and spiraling through the air, smashing shopfront windows and decimating decorative cement façades.

The secret is out; the gloves are off. No amount of bell ringing can conceal the fight for survival playing out on the backstreets of Sofia.

'Karai!' Borisa shrieks, shifting in her seat. 'Karai!'

The driver puts the car into reverse and rams the Audi parked behind, sending colored glass in all directions. Spinning its wheels, the car now slams forward into the Range Rover.

Anzhelo passes the rifle down to Carlos.

'Stay up there, Angel! Your work is done.'

'But I want to help some more!'

'You've done enough. It's too dangerous. I'll come back for you after it's all over.'

'But …'

Carlos scampers down the ladder and into the darkness.

Gabriel guns the truck toward the intersection, his foot flat to the floor.

A young boy on his lunch break from school, confused and frightened by the nearby shoot-out, foolishly tries to cross the road.

Trinity rises from her seat and screams, 'Look out!'

Gabriel swerves the truck; the thick rubber tyres groan. Metal-on-metal, the heavy truck glances off nearby parked cars. Side mirrors and glass explode. On the verge of losing control, Gabriel fights to steer the truck back on course.

'Do something!' The Russian spits, directing his desperation at Borisa. 'Earn your keep or I'll send you and your sister back to Varna!'

She turns toward him, and reacts to the look of terror on his face. Twisting back around, she gulps at the sight of the indomitable purpose-built armored truck bearing down on them. Her heart racing, Borisa leans away from the window, her bug eyes fixed to the glowing, light-blue orbs behind the truck's mesh and its two-inch thick bullet-resistant windshield.

'Do something!' The Russian shrieks, his pitch elevated, like that of a girl.

Knowing there is nothing she can do, even if she wanted to, Borisa closes her eyes and prepares for impact as the ten-tonne truck snakes its way through the intersection toward them.

With the power of a German tank and the force of a nineteenth-century steam locomotive, the armored truck ploughs into the side of the Mercedes sending invisible shockwaves through the smaller vehicle and its four occupants; their bodies, although restrained, flail uncontrollably.

Both Valentina and her adversary Hook Nose stop shooting at each other, their heads turning in unison to a sickening sound.

Metal bends and twists; creaks and creases under the enormous strain. The driver absorbs the full measure of the truck's momentum, his neck snapping sideways, breaking like a stick, his internal organs turning to mush.

Borisa and The Russian's heads collide, rendering them unconscious.

Blood runs down the front passenger's temple and his nearby window, his bald head slumped forward, both eyes shut.

Trinity is groggy, her eyes slow to open. She grabs at her shoulder and winces, sore from the seatbelt digging in. Her ears ring. Responding to her immediate thoughts, she turns to Gabriel.

Supported by the heavy-duty harness, he leans forward, blood dripping from his forehead.

'Wake up, G!' she yells. Getting no response, she reaches across and shakes his shoulder. 'Wake up! We have to keep moving.'

Outside of the truck, ageing Russian technology and Swiss innovation renew their battle for control; swarms of bullets criss-cross the road.

Trinity watches on through the mesh as Valentina bobs up and down from behind a car, firing her carbine toward the Range Rover. In retaliation, Hook Nose hangs his AK around the corner of the bumper and empties an entire magazine. Releasing her seatbelt, Trinity leans over to Gabriel and pushes him back into his seat, his head flopping backwards, his airway opening.

'G!' she cries. 'Open your fucking eyes!'

Edging into her field of view, three men exit the Audi; she flinches as their bullets smash into the windows and sides of the truck. Desperate to revive Gabriel, she violently shakes his shoulders, all the while her eyes remaining focused on the three men, firing.

From the cover of a thick tree, Halo releases four controlled shots toward the Audi, forcing the confused men to redirect their bullets. Chunks of wood and bark explode all around him.

Trinity pinches Gabriel's ear, the innocuous pain more than enough to stimulate his senses. Regaining his faculties, he groans and raises his hand to his head.

'It's about time!' Trinity cries. 'Get your shit together. We have to get out of the truck.'

Gabriel's bleary eyes look through the windshield and beyond the swirling smoke. The Mercedes, shaped like a boomerang, has been shunted from one side of the intersection to the other, the force of the impact crashing it against a parked car and, like a domino effect, damaging a further two vehicles.

Carlos grits his teeth and sprints up the middle of the street toward the crash site, his heavy rifle held in place by both hands as it shifts side to side in front of his heaving chest. Determination fires his eyes as the frightening sound of a skirmish up ahead competes with the screams of innocent people fleeing in the opposite direction.

Bullets slamming into brick and mortar—cold and hardened steel—echo down the street, funnelled along by the two and three-story high buildings on either side; their small balconies overflow with cell-phone-wielding *concerned* citizens. Ironically, in the city of secrets, nobody seems to know how to keep one.

And although the crash up ahead has stemmed the flow of traffic, with most choosing to abandon their cars and run for their lives, the occasional speeding car forces Carlos to the sidewalk.

It's here he bullocks his way through the congestion, contesting with the crowds for what precious little room is available on the pavement. Bogged down with the on-slaught of people, determined to bust back onto the street, he knocks them out of the way.

In less than a minute, Valentina's carbine has gone through two full magazines, the bullets serving only to subdue Hook Nose and the occupants of the Range Rover. In an effort to overcome the deadlock, she breaks from the protection of her cover and sweeps out wide.

Crouching behind the front wheel, Hook Nose catches sight of her reflection in a shopfront window. Swinging his AK in her direction, he raises the muzzle, but Valentina fires first: two rounds, the first striking his forearm, tear-ing flesh and shattering bone, the second, his chest, punc-turing a lung.

Hook Nose coughs blood from his dry mouth.

Valentina winces at a burning sensation in her thigh. She wants to scream, to hide … to be somewhere else.

One of Hook Nose's men steps from the rear of the Range Rover and again has her in his sights.

With a swivel of the hips and a peek through the carbine's rear drum aperture, she releases two rounds in quick succession. Through watery eyes, Valentina witnesses both bullets punch through his chest, turning his white shirt to red.

Pinned down behind the tree, Halo realises he must shoot and move. Spraying several bullets toward the incoming fire, he lowers his head and bolts no more than a few meters in the direction of a parked car before diving onto the pavement. Once there, he leopard crawls the rest of the way to safety, his elbows and knees banging against the unforgiving surface.

Gabriel and Trinity make their way into the rear of the truck.

'Are they dead?' she asks.

Leaning in close, Gabriel listens for signs of breathing.

'They'll be fine,' he says. 'Probably have one helluva headache when they come to.'

Trinity squats beside him.

'What now?'

'Once outside,' he says, bending over, hands on knees, too tall to stand up without hitting his head on the roof, 'you take the left corner of the truck and give V some covering fire and I'll go to the right, doing the same for H.'

'And then what?'

'Fuck knows,' he replies. 'Make more shit up I guess. Isn't that how you do it?'

Trinity leans forward and grabs Gabriel by the coat, kissing him on the lips.

'What was that for?'

Shrugging her shoulders, she looks him up and down.

'You look good in a uniform,' she says 'even if it belongs to a fat Bulgarian cop.'

Spinning around on the balls of her feet, she kicks open the back door.

Borisa's eyelids flutter; blood streams down both sides of her face. Rolling her head to one side, she looks at The Russian slumped beside her.

His eyes are shut; moist blood sticks to his temple.

Borisa opens her mouth, a little, but she doesn't speak. Without success, she tries to move her leg stuck between the caved-in door and the seat in front.

Turning her attention to the scene outside where two of her men exit the Range Rover and aim their weapons across the street — opening fire at the same time, same target — she spots Hook Nose slouched against the front tyre, bloodied arms by his sides, AK on the ground.

The ghost-ring sight of Gabriel's shotgun hovers over the Russian goon's chest and face. At the relatively close range of ten meters, he knows the buckshot will destroy everything in its path.

KA-BOOM!

One down, two to go.

Halo turns and nods approvingly at Gabriel, who slides the shotgun's action back and forth two more times, blowing out both of the Audi's front tyres.

'I'm moving forward!' Trinity yells. 'I can't see a fucking thing!'

'Roger that!' Gabriel responds, firing another round at the two remaining men in the Audi.

Before she moves off, Trinity feels something brush her leg; Viktor jumps up with excitement.

'Get down!' she yells. 'Get down!'

Viktor sits, looking up, panting.

'Let's go,' she says, skulking alongside the truck, Viktor excitedly following.

Valentina retreats to the doorway of the nearby bookstore, trailing blood behind her. From there, she leans out and engages the two goons positioned at the rear of the Range Rover. Barely a second later, yellow cement dust and rubble, explode in her face. She pulls back her head, gulps in some air and again leans out.

Her weapon jams.

'Fuck!'

Recoiling back around, she slides down the wall. A quick visual inspection of the breach reveals two bullets attempting to feed into the chamber at the same time. She rips out the magazine and shakes the gun.

A bullet falls free.

Repeatedly racking the charging handle, she manages to eject the other bullet. A glance inside ensures the breach is no longer jammed. Taking short, sharp breaths, she reinserts the magazine and chambers a new round.

Carlos, closing in on the action, his powerful legs serving him well, watches with horror as one of The Russian's goons from the Range Rover scampers toward Valentina. With a one-foot take-off, Carlos leaps through the air, his heavy boots crumpling the randomly parked car's bonnet beneath them. Gaining his balance, he slams the bipod onto the roof and sprawls across the windshield, leaning in behind the rifle's scope.

From his steady platform, Carlos takes in a deep breath through his nostrils and holds it.

The crosshair rises and levels off in mid-air, just above the top of the goon's head. Making allowances for the Sako being sighted in at six hundred meters, he tracks the red illuminated cross from right to left, overtaking his target's face, in line with the leading edge of his nose. Breathing out through his mouth, Carlos follows through with the shot, continuing to track the rifle sideways.

The running goon's scalp peels back, flapping to one side like a cheap hairpiece in a storm, exposing what little is left of his glistening brain. His blood-fuelled legs continue to cover ground before he falls flat on his face in the street, well short of his intended goal.

Carlos closes his eyes and groans.

Reacting to the hot flash searing inside his abdomen, he instinctively rolls to one side just as another bullet exits the windshield beneath him. In an effort to fight back, he heaves himself forward and spins around on the bonnet, actioning another hammerhead in the process. Wielding the rifle like a toy, he shoves the barrel through the bullet hole in the windshield and pulls the trigger.

Regaining consciousness, the goon in the front seat of the Mercedes looks over his shoulder.

'Get outside,' Borisa yells at him. 'Get out and find me … find The Russian an escape route!'

Pulling up behind the Audi, another car-load of goons arrives at the scene. Halo lets them know this game is for real, peppering their car with bullets to keep them in check.

His see-through, snap-locked magazine runs dry.

In the blink of an eye, he detaches it from the rifle and shifts it across, just enough to insert a fresh mag up and into place.

He spies Gabriel's signal for him to retreat to the

armored truck and, under the protection of the shotgun's covering fire, he does so, rushing toward him and slamming his back against the truck.

'Where's Trinity?' he puffs, removing his bulky overcoat and throwing it to the ground.

Gabriel takes his off as well.

'She moved forward,' he says. 'She couldn't see anything.'

Trinity takes aim at the goon dragging himself from the Mercedes. She rushes off a few rounds, several skipping off the bonnet and windshield, hurtling indeterminately down Parensov Street.

Ducking behind the wheel arch, he shoots back in her general direction, sight unseen.

Trinity crouches, holding the Steyr on its side; it moves about as she lets rip in return.

WHACK! WHACK! WHACK!

Rounds from another direction slap the side of the truck not far from her head. Copper shards of shrapnel detach from the projectiles and tear into her neck; beads of blood immediately surface. Swinging her rifle around, she fires round after round until the action locks back. Caught in a cross-fire and without cover, Trinity goes prone and hastily reloads.

Stepping from the protection of the Rover, another goon seizes the opportunity to get a better shot at her.

Viktor pins back his ears.

Stream-lined and powerful, from a standing start he quickly closes the gap on the goon and attacks.

'I'm running low on ammo,' Gabriel cries. 'Switch out!'

Halo taps his shoulder.

Gabriel steps aside.

Halo's focus rides the shrouded front sight of the SG550 and nails two goons with two shots.

Carlos kicks open the door to the bookstore. Dragging Valentina inside, he removes her coat.

'Where are you hit?'

She points to her leg and holds her arm.

He rolls her to one side.

She moans.

'The bullet hasn't gone through your leg,' he says. Reaching down, he slides out a three-inch dagger from the inside of his boot. He runs the blade's edge along the length of her leather pants, exposing the wound and scooping out the blood with his fingers. Then, cutting strips from her coat, he packs them into the cavity.

Valentina grits her teeth and moans some more.

He takes hold of her hand and places it over the top.

'Push down hard,' he says.

Within seconds, Carlos applies makeshift bandages to both her wounds, applying pressure, stemming the bleeding.

'You're hurt too,' she says.

Carlos looks down at his stomach.

'Fucking secret police shot me.'
Valentina is puzzled by his response.
'Let me look at it.'
He sits alongside her and grimaces.
'It's okay, I got it,' he says. Removing his shirt, he stuffs a rolled up ball of fur cut from Valentina's coat into the hole. The warrior's teeth draw together; blood spills across his fingers.

Borisa tugs at her knee, her hands eventually pulling the trapped leg free. For a brief moment, she leans her head back. Ignoring the pain and discomfort, she slides across the seat and straddles her keeper.

His sharp chin rests upon his chest.

She slowly leans in, her dangerous eyes never once blinking or looking away, despite the war raging outside the confines of the metal coffin.

Stray 556 bullets strike the side of the Mercedes; empty seven-six-two shells roll across the roof, down the windshield and onto the bonnet.

Pushing The Russian's head back with her palm, Borisa places her deadly fingernail to one side of his skinny neck, pressing the keen edge of the industrial white diamond against his pale skin.

Halo looks over his shoulder.
'I need some help here mate.'

Gabriel stokes his shotgun with bolos.

'I'm coming, I'm coming!'

Goons advance toward them, bounding from one parked car to another.

Gabriel's Remington 870 shotgun barks like a hungry junkyard dog poked with a stick. Sending a bolo whistling through the air, hurtling end over end, the six-inch braided steel strikes a goon on the hand and slices off three of his fingers.

He lets go of his MP5, stops and props, his eyes staring at his bloody fingers on the ground.

The dog barks again.

This time a six-inch red line appears across his cheek.

'How much ammo is left in the carbine?' Carlos asks.

'It's the last mag,' Valentina replies, 'half full.'

'Your fight is over,' he says. 'I'll take the carbine and leave you the Sako. It only has two rounds left. I can be more effective with the smaller rifle.'

She makes a token effort to get to her feet.

'But I can still fight!'

Carlos places his hand on her shoulder.

'No. You're done. Stay here and I'll come back for you as soon as I can.'

'What about you? You're also hurting.'

'I've had a lot worse. Anyway, it was only a nine-mill.' Hiding his pain, he wraps her hands around the Sako. 'If anyone comes through that door and doesn't look like me … blow them straight back out again.'

'What of the others? Are they okay?'

'I guess I'm about to find out.'

Bullets slam into the armored truck, keeping Halo and Gabriel at bay.

'This is fucked,' Halo says.

'I'll tell you what's fucked,' Gabriel counters, pointing across the street.

Anzhelo hugs a small tree, out in the open in the Temple grounds.

'What the fuck is he doing here?'

'I dunno,' Gabriel says. 'But we can't leave him there. I think it's time we use one of the grenades. We're going to run out of ammo soon anyway. We may as well try and even the odds a little. Anzhelo can take advantage of the explosion to run over here.'

'Roger that,' Halo says, pulling the HG-85 from his pocket. 'On the count of three …'

He pulls the pin.

'One …'

He draws back his arm.

'Two …'

He holds.

'Three!'

Swinging his arm forward in a sweeping underhand motion, he releases the spherical steel grenade from his grasp. It rolls and bounces its way toward the Audi, being used by a group of The Russian's men for cover. The grenade holds its line, rolls over the curb and inches out from underneath the car, coming to a stop on its side.

Following a brief orange flash is a dull thud.

Birds flutter their wings and abandon the Temple grounds. The armored Audi lifts an inch off the ground and six more to one side. Countless tiny shards of shrapnel search for something to destroy.

Shopfront windows explode, glass shattering in a million different directions.

Car alarms sound.

Six men die.

A ball of smoke engulfs the Audi and surrounding area.

Anzhelo's ears ring.

'Angel! ... Angel! ... Angel!' Gabriel cries, waving his arm. 'Run!'

Turning his attention from the explosion to Gabriel's voice, Anzhelo scurries across open ground to the relative safety of the armored truck.

Gabriel hauls him in.

'You were told to stay at the cathedral.'

'I want to help.'

'There's nothing you can do. It's too dangerous.'

The old man lowers his eyes.

'You did a great job with the bells,' Halo jumps in.

Anzhelo lifts his eyes, a child-like smile appearing across his face.

'But we need you to stay put,' he says. 'Don't move. There's so much shit going on it's hard to keep track of everyone.'

He shakes his head.

'Da, I will stay out of your way.'

Now standing outside of the Mercedes, Borisa pushes the dead goon aside. The entire left side of his body and face have been ripped apart with the grenade's shrapnel. She takes up his weapon and signals for her men to fall back and surround her.

Trinity enjoys the lull in the fight, enjoys not being shot at. She takes stock of her situation: two rounds of ball ammo in the Steyr's magazine, one in the breach ... and a mystical sword slung across her back.

Carlos turns his head to another shadow passing the window.

Valentina adjusts her grip on the Sako and looks up.

'Be careful.'

Gritting his teeth and hunched forward, holding the carbine with one hand in front of his face, Carlos moves up to the door.

Footsteps and strange voices can be heard.

He bursts onto the pavement and watches a gang of Gypsies advance along the street, scattered from one side to the other, moving with haste, through the middle, along the sidewalk — up and over parked cars — gibbering and shrieking.

Carlos stands face to face with a group of four; the largest of them bares his broken teeth. Unimpressed, the wounded ex-soldier stands firm.

The toothless gypsy raises an iron bar.

Taking a step back, Carlos grins, shooting him all the way to the ground.

With her ranks filled by the arrival of Khryminali and the inevitable sound of sirens alerting her of the Gendarmerie's impending arrival, Borisa restarts the battle and keeps Trinity pinned down by a constant stream of bullets.

Fuck!

She survived the collision.

Then there's also a chance The Russian's still alive.

Trinity shouts to Gabriel, 'Throw me a grenade!' She shouts again. 'Gabriel! Grenade! Give me a grenade!'

Anzhelo tugs at Gabriel's shirt.

'Trinity is calling for you.'

Gabriel moves to the corner of the truck and yells over the top of ferocious gunfire, 'Are you okay?'

'Grenade! Throw me a grenade!'

Halo leans in.

'What's the situation?'

'She wants the last grenade.'

'Throw me the fucking grenade!' Trinity cries.

'Give it to her,' Halo says.

'I can't just throw it!'

'Yes you can, or roll it to her.'

Gabriel shakes his head.

'What if it fucking goes off or doesn't reach her?'

'Give it to me then ... I'll fucking do it.' Halo reaches into Gabriel's pocket and pulls out the grenade.

Gabriel's hand grasps his wrist.

The two lock eyes.

Anzhelo fidgets, his eyes moving up and down and side to side. He snatches the grenade from Halo.

'Angel!' Halo cries, instinctively reaching out to him.

'Don't do it!' Gabriel yells.

Anzhelo runs toward Trinity.

She holds up her hand.

'No!'

The brisk wind pushes through Anzhelo's long hair and tousles his beard. His tired legs straighten and stretch. He finds it easy to move, to run … fast … faster than he's ever run before.

Trinity is within his reach.

Borisa raises her rifle.

Trinity's head swings around to look at Borisa standing behind the Mercedes, then back again, her mouth stretched wide, her eyes swollen.

Borisa tracks Anzhelo's movements. Dialling back her focus … front sight, rear sight … front sight, she releases a hailstorm of bullets.

Anzhelo stumbles yet maintains grace.

'Run faster!' Trinity shrieks. 'Faster!'

He digs deep; his gut burns and his legs weaken as Trinity pulls him down. He melts into her arms.

She hugs him tightly.

'What were you thinking?'

Breathing heavily, his chest rises and falls; air whistles through his nose.

'What are you doing here?' she asks.

'I want to help you … I want to show you …'

Trinity gently places her hand over his mouth.

'You have nothing to show me, Angel … you have nothing to prove.'

She gently sweeps hair from his face.

'I have something for you,' he says, his voice raspy. Reaching for her hand, he places the grenade against her palm.

She wraps her fingers around the cold steel surface.

He coughs, blood tainting the gray whiskers surrounding his mouth.

Trinity draws away her blood-soaked hand and raises it in front of her face. She lowers her head.

'Trinity! ... Trinity!' Gabriel yells in the background. 'Throw the grenade! Throw the fucking grenade!'

It feels to Trinity as though an invisible bubble encases her and Anzhelo, shielding them both from the world outside. Everything important to her, at this single point in time, is inside it.

'Trinity ... listen to me! Throw the fucking grenade!'

There is so much she wants to say to him, so many words, but none of them will make any difference. Death is more powerful than the sharpest sword, purest heart ... strongest mind. Death is what all men and warriors secretly fear ... it cannot be avoided ... it cannot be defeated. Her broken heart pounds; slow, but loud.

A glow surrounds Anzhelo, still nurtured within her arms.

'Halo! Watch out behind you!'

'BOOM! BOOM! KA-BOOM!'

'Ammo ... ammo ... I need more ammo!'

Trinity pulls a medal from her pocket and folds her dead hero's fingers around the gold star. Leaning forward she kisses his forehead.

'Trinity! Switch ... the fuck ... on!'

Her heart expands, palpitating wildly, and she narrows her bloodshot eyes. She blinks.

'For fuck's sake, Trinity, do something!'

Rising to her feet, breathing heavily through her nose, Trinity strips off her coat. She stands tall, her shoulders pinned back. Her height, her curves — her hair in the wind — she is magnificent.

With the katana's curved single-edged blade she cuts through the leather jacket and into her skin; her arm weeps tears of blood. A frightening, shrill cry pierces the air along with the spines and minds of her enemies. Full of anger, filled with pain, she launches herself toward the Mercedes.

Halo lurches forward.

Gabriel takes hold of his arm.

'What are you doing?' Halo cries. 'Let me go!'

'No. I've seen this before,' Gabriel says, calmly. 'Leave her be. There is nothing you can do. She needs to do this.'

'I can't just stand here and do nothing!'

'This one is not our fight … there are plenty of others.' Gabriel swings the shotgun into action and fires a lethal bolo, decapitating a rampaging gypsy's head.

Viktor joins in on the hunt as Trinity charges full tilt at two goons, both stupid enough to break ranks and attack. As smooth as silk and without missing stride, her sword flashes back and forth, her beloved katana no longer shiny but colored in red.

Viktor mauls at their shredded flesh.

Halo snipes a goon in the head; blood flicks into the air, catching rays from the midday sun.

Trinity swipes and slashes at anyone within reach. They are no match for her skill and anger.

Carlos runs to the fight, his stomach in dire need of repair. Throwing himself against a wall, he superimposes the carbine's battle-sights over the backs of several gypsies. One by one, they drop to the ground.

Borisa marshals her troops around her.

Gabriel is down to his last two rounds. Shoving them into the shotgun, he racks the slide. Moving from the shelter of the truck, he goes wide and outflanks the Mercedes.

One of The Russian's goons spots his approach and turns to shoot, but he's engulfed with a breath of fire.

Gabriel ejects the empty shotgun shell.

Rolling along the ground, whispers of smoke filter from the red plastic case.

Trinity kicks and punches her assailants as they swarm toward her. Too close to swing her sword, she is just as happy to bite and scratch, head-butt and stomp. Not since the invasion of the Turks and the installation of communism has the battle for supremacy on the streets of Sofia been so intense.

His rifle empty, Halo rushes forward, firing his pistol with one hand.

Carlos crushes a gypsy's head with the rifle's butt.

After setting alight another gypsy with his last dragon's breath, Gabriel trades blows with a Russian goon, also apparently out of ammo. Swinging their weapons at each other, the steel barrel of Gabriel's shotgun cracks the wooden fore-grip of the AK-47.

Taking a step back, he thrusts the barrel forward into the goon's face, opening up his cheek, revealing moist flesh underneath. Using his signature move, Gabriel plunges his boot into the tall, bald goon's soft stomach.

Doubled over, he allows Gabriel to bring his shotgun down onto his head, bringing the fight to a brutal end.

Borisa evaluates the carnage wreaked by Trinity and her team. Lowering her rifle, she fires a magazine of bullets into the Mercedes' grill. A veil of steam surges from the radiator and conceals her movements.

In a life-or-death struggle, Carlos rolls into the gutter, his body entwined with a Khryminali gypsy.

The former navy SEAL grinds his teeth as he employs what's left of his strength, somewhat depleted from the bullet lodged within his gut. The loss of fluid and drop in blood pressure are taking their toll.

High on drugs and fuelled by adrenalin, the gypsy head-butts Carlos, the sudden impact causing him to loosen his grip. The momentary lapse is all that is needed for the filthy criminal to come out on top and press his elbow down hard against Carlos's neck, making it difficult for him to breathe. Then using his fist, each bloodied finger ringed with a silver skull, he pounds the side of Carlos's face.

Memories, pleasant ones — his ex-wife on their wedding day, long before he joined the military — play out in his mind.

The gypsy sits up, his reinforced fists flailing at his opponent's sorry and crimson face.

Then, to Carlos's surprise, red globules rain down.

The gypsy, now headless, topples forward and lands on his chest, blood oozing and spurting from the neck.

Carlos rolls him off and then sits up. Through blurry eyes he sees Valentina lying on her stomach, stretched out across the bookstore's doorstep and onto the pavement, her head rising from behind the scope, a wicked smile across her face.

Trinity's dry mouth stretches wide; her eyes look crazed. Spinning, lunging, rolling and twisting side to side, she kills at will with her sword.

Gabriel smashes a goon's face into the roadside curb and looks up at the silhouette of Halo standing tall, his arm outstretched, his gun pointing down at the goon by his feet. The Glock's sharp report causes Gabriel to blink.

Surrounded by a pile of dead bodies, Trinity turns in circles, her sword at arm's length, thirsty for more blood; her devilish eyes survey the carnage.

Death is everywhere.

The whereabouts of her team is not her primary concern as her mind refocuses and her out-of-control heartbeat settles. Looking up through red tinged hair, she screams, 'Where is she?'

Smoke from the Mercedes' radiator is all but blown away; Borisa is nowhere to be seen.

Bloodied and dishevelled, Trinity swaggers over her many victims. Clenching her fists, she stops, bends at the knees and rises back up, generating maximum anger through her core.

'Where the fuck is Borisa?'

Gabriel wanders over, his battered hands gloved with blood.

'She's gone, Trinity. Forget her. We came for The Russian. Let's finish it and go.'

Violently, she twists toward Gabriel. Her laser gaze cuts through his; her tone is deep and chilling.

'Forget her? Forget her? I will never forget that bitch.'

Her eyes switch to Anzhelo's lifeless body.

'Gabriel's right,' Halo says, the Glock pistol hanging by his side, his finger curled around the trigger. 'Kill the red cunt and let's move on.'

Police sirens pierce the tension.

Gabriel looks at his watch: 12:12p.m.

Trinity breathes in, breathes out, her chest heavy, her bloodless eyes never once blinking. Slowly she turns around and stomps over a mountain of dead bodies, dragging her sword behind her, Viktor trotting alongside his snout red with blood.

Shot up and injured, with both eyes swollen, Carlos summons the remainder of his strength to carry Valentina over to Gabriel and Halo.

'What is Angel doing here?' he croaks, shocked to see him. 'Is he okay?'

'He didn't make it,' Gabriel answers softly, his own eyes feeling heavy.

Carlos lowers his head.

'Put me next to him,' Valentina says.

Carlos lays her down.

She strokes his hair.

Gabriel turns to the others.

'We gotta get out of here ... now!'

'You need help right away,' Halo says, probing into Carlos' gunshot wound.

Carlos grits his teeth.

'Where's Trinity?' he asks.

Gabriel motions toward the Mercedes.

'And The Russian ... is he ...?'

MICHAEL JOHN BARNES

Gabriel smirks.

'I bet he wishes he already was.'

Standing in front of the Mercedes' shot at and dam-aged bullet-resistant window, Trinity notices the incision crossing over The Russian's throat from ear-to-ear.

His lifeless eyes stare at the roof.

The only signs of movement are the gentle waves of warm blood easing down his neck.

In a fit of rage, Trinity unleashes a volley of full-auto gunfire at the car, the fierce sound breaking the fragile calm settling over the urban battlefield.

Her rifle empty of bullets, the barrel too hot to touch, she casts it aside.

Trinity's protective walls close in tight, the pressure deep inside of her increasing. Within seconds, an invisible force shoots through her body, pressing hard against the back of her eyeballs, looking for somewhere to vent.

Her skin heats up and a sharp pain intensifies within her head; her raspy breathe increases in volume and speed. She tightens her jaw, grinds her teeth and narrows her eyes. Denied true love, denied any sense of belonging, she has now been denied the sweet taste of revenge.

Temporarily devoid of the will to care for anyone else or anything at all, weary from her tortured, transient life-style, she begins to tremble.

'Hurry up!' Gabriel yells. 'We're running out of time.'

Trinity remains motionless.

'Hurry the fuck up, Trinity! We have to go.'

Her vacant eyes blink, not once, but twice.

'Trinity! We have to go ... now ... right now!'

She glances at Gabriel and looks at him for what seems like a lifetime. Pulling the pin from the grenade, she drops it by her feet.

The small explosive device rocks back and forth.

Swinging around, her long locks whip to one side and with hell's fire raging deep within her, Trinity does what she has always done.

She runs away.

Where Angels go to Die

A simple wooden cross bearing no markings sticks out of the ground. Surrounded by tangled, knee-high grass, it is nothing like the Cyrillic-engraved crumbling masonry tombstones on either side of it.

There are very few fresh flowers in this ageing cemetery, separated from neglected toiled fields by nothing more than a handful of messy, shapeless green bushes. It contains the remains of an entire village, its children and their children, lured to Sofia in search of work, leaving behind yet another ghost town.

Four figures, dressed in black, holding roses, stand around the fresh mound of sand.

The sky is light blue, but the mood is dark.

Halo takes Valentina's hand, her silken glove soft and delicate to the touch.

She lowers herself to one knee and places her red rose upon the dark sand. With some assistance, she rises and hobbles back.

One by one, the others move forward to pay their respects. Gabriel is the last to step up and spends considerable more time by the side of the grave than the others do. Leaning down, he leaves behind two red roses.

Liberation Day

The shiny, diamond-black Ducati Monster motorbike slices its way through midday traffic, the 800cc lightweight Desmodue power plant more suited to the sweeping curves of Mount Vitosha than to Sofia's congested city streets.

Drifting from one lane to another, its front and rear Pirelli tyres grip and mould to the golden bricks of Tsar Osvoboditel Boulevard.

The fearless black-leather-clad rider leans over the fuel tank, knees pressed against the red chassis, gloves gripping the handlebars; black helmet, black visor, black slung shotgun.

His shapely passenger, also dressed in black, wears thigh-high boots and carries a backpack. Sitting up straight, she holds on tight to the grab handles at the rear of the bike, her brunette hair sneaking from the bottom of the helmet.

With perfect timing, the Ducati cuts across the flow of traffic and on through Narodno Sabranie Square, its single round headlight beaming brightly. Riding beneath the shadow of the Tsar Liberator's equestrian statue and beyond the entrance to The Imperial Hotel, the motorbike mounts the curb and comes to a sudden stop.

Within seconds, two identical Ducati Monsters arrive on the scene from different directions, all of them parking outside the Bulgarian Capital and Commercial Bank; a gray cement, six-story corner building with a ground level glass front.

The three riders dismount, but the brunette stays seated and hands one of them the backpack. Together they brazenly stride toward the bank's entrance, scared of nothing and no one. If the sight of the shotgun were not confronting enough, the Glock pistol and SG 550 terrify the crowds walking past.

The intimidating figures all look at their watches. The one wielding the shotgun stops at the glass door. He glances at the NO HELMET and NO GUNS sign on the window before kicking the door open.

All three rush through.

The roar of the shotgun quickly gains everyone's attention. Unfortunately for the Bulgarian Capital and Commercial Bank—a relic from the country's communist past and recently subjected to tough economic times, as with most of the Balkan Peninsula—they have not upgraded their security for more than half a century.

This makes Halo's job easier as he jumps over the counter, Gabriel tossing him the backpack.

'Forty-five seconds,' Carlos says.

Halo first empties the drawers of cash and then grabs the manager by the scruff of the neck, pushing him toward the safe.

The skinny man with a pencil-thin mustache looks away as Halo waves the Glock in front of his face. Reluctantly he turns and unlocks the door.

'Thirty seconds!'

Halo pushes him inside the vault, where he drops and cowers in the corner, his arms pressed tight across his chest.

Stacks of cash fill the shelves.

Halo shoves as much as he can into the bag.

'Twenty seconds!'

Grabbing a wad of cash, Halo throws it at the frightened manager, who catches it, looks at it, pauses then smiles.

'Ten seconds!'

Halo exits the vault, scooping up an armful of money on his way out. Jumping up onto the counter, he dishes out wads of cash to the bemused staff and customers.

Carlos looks through his visor at his watch.

'Time's up!'

The three men storm out of the bank.

Halo launches the bag at Valentina, who straps it across her back. And then, as quickly as they appeared, all three motorbikes ride off in opposite directions.

A Day of Reckoning

Several weeks after the bank heist and two months since the ambush on The Russian, news of the 'audacious assassination of Sergei Vasilenko' has been relegated to the back pages, pushed there by Ukraine's ongoing borders dispute with Russia

Dressed to the nines, though still walking with a limp, Valentina, with Viktor by her side, approaches the cathedral. She stops momentarily to gather herself, then lifts her chin and carries on. Down by her side, a large bag swings to and fro in her gloved hand.

Awkwardly making her way up the steps to the grand entrance, she ambles over to the modest donation box. Resembling a child's woodwork project, more often than not the simple box contains very little of value and doesn't warrant a lock.

Her eyes move side to side.

No one is watching.

She opens the lid and tips rolls of cash inside.

Schoolchildren surge from the cathedral's entrance.

Valentina closes the lid and moves slowly outside. Taking in a deep breath of crisp air, she looks up at the blue sky. Sunglasses may hide the tears of joy in her eyes, but nothing can hide the smile across her beautiful, marred face.

Full Circle

Several hours into the long-haul flight, sitting in the darkness beside the window, Trinity stares at the seat in front of her. Her eyes appear cold, her focus deep and sharp. All that separates her from a young man in his late twenties is an empty seat, but it might as well be a brick wall between them.

The aircraft jolts as it enters a jet stream.

Trinity blinks.

From two seats away, her interested neighbor takes his shot.

'Penny for your thoughts?' he asks.

She blinks again before turning to face him.

'A Penny,' he smiles, '… for your thoughts?'

For a brief moment she stares, then turns and faces the window.

The young man, unsure what he has done wrong, unbuckles his seatbelt and stands up.

Trinity watches his reflection in the window as he walks away. Shuffling across the seats, she leans into the aisle, her eyes glued to his movements, her face lit by the stream of color emitted by his entertainment screen, the only source of ambient light in the night-time cabin.

He makes his way to the front of the plane and enters the toilet.

Trinity follows and stands with her back to the door.

A female Japanese passenger squeezes past on her way back to her seat.

The toilet door opens.

Trinity places her hand on the young man's chest.

He opens his mouth to speak.

She holds a finger to his lips and steps inside, pushing him backwards, locking the door behind her.

КРАЙ

GLOSSARY

2IC – second in command
3-D – three dimensional
4WD – four wheel drive vehicle
9-mill – 9-millimeter caliber
Abaya – black long-sleeved robe
A/C – air conditioner
Action – place a round into the chamber of a firearm
AK-47 – Kalashnikov Automatic Rifle, 1947 Model
ASAP – as soon as possible
BA – Buenos Aires
Barrios – neighbourhood
Belle époque – beautiful epoch (a period of comfortable well-established life in Europe prior to World War I)
Bomb – load a firearm's magazine to the maximum
Bullpup – a firearm with the action and magazine located behind the trigger allowing for a more compact design
Burqa – a loose garment covering the entire body worn by Muslim women
Cache – a hidden store of weapons, provisions etc
Carro – cart

Cartonero – a person who collects paper, plastic and cardboard for profit

Catena Zapata – family owned Argentine winery

CCCP – Union of Soviet Socialist Republics (USSR)

Chalgothèque – nightclub featuring Bulgarian Pop-folk music

CIA – Central Intelligence Agency

CITGO – gas station

CPO – close protection officer

Criollo – a person born in Latin America with European (Spanish) ancestry

Dirham – standard monetary unit of the United Arab Emirates

Emirati – citizen of the United Arab Emirates

Europa – Europe

Fakulteto – slum, shantytown, favela

FBI – Federal Bureau of Investigation

FMJ – full metal jacket (bullet)

Gendarmerie – Police agency

Gendarme – Police officer

G-SHOCK – wrist watch

HQ – head quarters

ID – identification

Kandura – long white cloak worn by male Emirati

Kossack – fictional Russian gangster

Krhyminali – fictional Bulgarian Gypsy gang

LED – light-emitting diode commonly used in flashlights

Lev – standard monetary unit of Bulgaria

Luigi Bosca – oldest family-owned winery in Argentina

M4 – shorter and lighter version of the M-16 assault rifle

M-16 – United States military designation for the AR-15 assault rifle

M-70 – Yugoslavian assault rifle based on AK-47

Mag – magazine

Malbec – type of wine
M&P – Military and Police (Smith & Wesson semi-auto pistol)
Mélange – mixture
Merc - mercenary
ML63 AMG – Mercedes-Benz model
MP5 – machine pistol model number 5
NATO – North Atlantic Treaty Organization
Niqab – a cloth garment covering the face of Muslim women
NY – New York
Oya-kata - master
Romani – Gypsies
SEALs –Sea, Air, Land (Navy SEALs)
SF – military special forces
SPAS-12 –special purpose automatic shotgun
SUV – sports utility vehicle
Tomodachi – friend
UAE – United Arab Emirates
UN – United Nations
Yabusame – Traditional Japanese mounted archery

www.ingramcontent.com/pod-product-compliance
Lightning Source LLC
Chambersburg PA
CBHW031054260626
47172CB00001B/64